Resurrection

DAEMONS & LUMENS SERIES
S. D. PAINE

Resurrection by S. D. Paine —Copyright © 2024
All rights reserved.

No part of this publication may be reproduced, stored or transmitted in any form or by any electronic, mechanical, photocopying, recording, scanning means, including the information storage and retrieval systems, without written permission from the author. It is illegal to copy this book, post it to a website, or distribute it by any other means without permission, except for the use of brief quotations in a book review.

This novel is entirely a work of fiction. The names, characters, and incidents portrayed in it are the work of the author's imagination. Any similarity to real persons, living or dead, events, or localities is entirely coincidental.

ISBN ebook: 979-8-9901373-5-6
ISBN Paperback: 979-8-9901373-7-0
Cover Design: Miblart
Editor: Andrea Halland, Editing by Andrea

DAEMONS & LUMENS SERIES

Retaliation

A Daemon's Alliance

Resurrection

Alis volat propriis
She flies with her own wings.

I dream of gods and monsters, and of the man who knew I was both. - Anon

Dear readers, this book will tease your minds, choke your dreams, and fill your pretty little…hearts.
And you'll like it, my sweet sadists.

AUTHOR NOTE

This book contains dark themes and the characters make questionable decisions. Tropes and triggers include graphic violence, torture, physical and mental assault, bdsm-related scenes, and explicit intimate scenes.

For more information about this book and future books in the series, visit my website and sign-up for my newsletter! www.sdpaineauthor.com

BOOK TWO PLAYLIST

Find me on [Spotify](#) to listen to this Daemons & Lumens Playlist!

The Beginning of the end by Klergy and Valerie Broussard
Killer by Valerie Broussard
Song Seven by Deathpact
FACTS by Tom MacDonald and Ben Shapiro
Beautiful Things by Benson Boone
Hear Me Now by Bad Wolves
You Broke Me First by Tate McRae
Broken Bones by KALEO
I Choose Me by Amanati and Roniit
Wildfire by Bad Wolves
Circus Psycho by Diggy Graves
Red Lips by Sky Ferreira
Drop Dead by Grandson, Kesha, and Travis Barker
Don't Fear the Reaper by Denmark + Winter
Duality by Slipknot
Make Me Feel by Elvis Drew
I'd Rather See Your Star Explode by SLAVES
Misery Business by Paramore
Let the Flames Begin by Paramore
Empire Now by Hozier
This Is Who We Are by Gary Clark Jr. and Naala
How The End Begins by Sum 41
Waiting On A Twist Of Fate by Sum 41
Hell Together by David Archuleta

Resurrection

Formaldehyde Footsteps by Houndrel
You've Created a Monster by Bohnes
Vicious by Bohnes
Lonely Day by System Of A Down
Lethal Woman by Dove Cameron
Madness by Muse
Man or a Monster by Sam Tinnesz and Zayde Wølf
Teeth by 5 Seconds of Summer
Miss Murder by AFI

THE V.I.P. LIST

Seraphina Valdis Bronwen - Daughter of Aurora Valdis, known alias - Sara Braun
Tabitha "Tibby" Marsden - Tech wizard and friend of Sara, mind controlled by The Obscuritas

Andras Blackbyrn - Prince of The Obscuritas, son of Laszlo
Typhon "Ty" Radnor - Prince of The Obscuritas, son of Darren
Leviathan "Levi" Delano - Prince of The Obscuritas, son of Samuel
Devon "Dev" Parrish - Prince of The Obscuritas, son of Ezekiel

Laszlo Blackbyrn - King of The Obscuritas, Leader
Darren Radnor - King of The Obscuritas, Enforcer, Deceased
Samuel Delano - King of The Obscuritas, Seducer
Ezekiel Parrish - King of The Obscuritas, Technician, Deceased

Aurora Valdis Bronwen - Mother of Lailah, Seraphina, and Michaela, Murdered by The Obscuritas
Joseph Bronwen - Husband of Aurora, Father of Lailah, Seraphina, and Michaela
Lailah Valdis Bronwen - oldest daughter of Aurora and Joseph, murdered by The Obscuritas
Michaela Valdis Bronwen - youngest daughter of Aurora and Joseph

King Corson Ormaenus - King of Caligo and all daemons
Prince Belial Ormaenus - Oldest son, Prince of Caligo and loyal to the king
Prince Morax "Mor" Ormaenus - Middle son, Prince of Caligo
Prince Phenex "Phen" Ormaenus - Youngest son, Prince of Caligo

PAWNS & PLAYERS

Belfegor - daemon, King of the Novo Mountain Tribe, deceased
Gremory Cerravaux- daemon, loyal to Morax and Phenex

Delphine Bellinor - powerful witch, of The Mal-Regia
Nuriela Ramas - lumen, intimate friend of Lailah Valdis
Lo Rigby - human, presumed dead

Ouriel - lumen hybrid, deceased
Foras - daemon, loyal to Belial
The Malefica - akin to witches, living in Tellisa
The Mal-Regia - royals of The Malefica

Audrey Kingston - human, student at Law School, attends classes with Seraphina
Mr. Edward Kingston - Father of Audrey Kingston, potential Obscuritas member
Ryan Lancing - Lead Bartender at Noircoeur, Obscuritas member
James "J" Azer - Gym Manager, close friend of Ty, Umbra Noctis member
Dominique - Owner of Noircoeur, Obscuritas member
Otis Redford - Operations Manager of Noircoeur, Obscuritas member
Josie and Lottie Hayes - Twins, Dancers at Noircoeur, friends of Sara Braun
Jade Dawlish - Professional boxer, employed at Ty's gym, allegiance unknown
Xavier Saladino - Fireman at firehouse, member of unnamed gang, allegiance unknown

IMPORTANT PLACES

Vespertine Hall - Estate located just outside city of Boston, owned by The Obscuritas
The Cabin - Michaela and her father's current residence
Blackbyrn Manor - Estate located near Asheville, North Carolina, owned by The Obscuritas
Noircoeur - Burlesque Club beneath restaurant downtown Boston, owned by The Obscuritas
The Towne House - Home of Andras, Typhon, and Leviathan, located near Harvard University
P4 Fitness - Gym owned by Typhon, located near The Towne House
Stella Terra (Stel-uh Tare-uh) - Planet of the daemons and lumens
Tellisa (Teh-lee-sah) - Country of the daemons and lumens
Caligo (Cal-ee-go) - Capital city of the daemons territory
Caelum (Kay-lum) - Capital city of the lumens territory

WORDS & PHRASES

The Obcuritas - Exclusive cult seeking otherworldly power
Umbra Noctis - Shadows of Night, secret sect of The Obscuritas created by the Princes

Daemons - monstrous creatures of myths and legends, varying degrees of magic/power relating to the elements
Lumens - ethereal creatures of myths and legends, varying degrees of magic/power relating to the elements

stellatium (stuh-lay-tea-um) - a rare metal created from a dying

Resurrection

star, powerful enough to kill a daemon or lumen

luxenite (lux-eh-night) - rare stone, magically charged to harness the power of a lumen's essence

tenebrite (teh-neh-bright) - rare stone, magically charged to harness the power of a daemon's essence

Vis-el (Veez-elle) - elemental power of the daemons and lumens, different from the spells wielded by The Malefica

truxen daemon - type of daemon with the ability to shift into any creature and communicate with animals

Mae domina - my lady/master
Diabla - (she) devil
Mi diosa - my goddess
Belle femme - beautiful woman
Mera dil - my heart

PROLOGUE

Seraphina

I bit into the stolen hot dog aggressively, annoyed that we were once again eating old ass hot dogs. But the good news was we were leaving. South Carolina would be a bad dream after tonight. Tibby and I were able to steal enough cash to buy a computer, and within a few hours we had train tickets and new identities. She was a real whiz with computers, and she was teaching me too. I didn't have the same natural talent as Tibby, but I was a fast learner.

We met not long after I burned Mr. Rigby's gym to the ground, with him in it. I was hiding in a shitty homeless shelter. Neither of us trusted anyone but ourselves, and somehow that bonded us. Now here we were, two years later, finally getting out of the gutters we hid in and starting fresh. New York City, the perfect city to disappear amongst millions of people.

The endless ocean with its crashing waves stilled the rumbling storm within me. I scrunched my toes, digging them into the sand as I ate the last of the stale food and contemplated our future. Tibby plopped down next to me.

"I've got all our things packed in the rental car." Tibby smiled. "All two bags of stuff."

I snorted a laugh. "We'll have lots of stuff soon. Clothes. Weapons…"

Tibby laughed. "I can't wait for the weapons. What should I get first?"

My simple pocketknife stuck out of the sand in front of me. I kept it with me at all times. Too many bad things happened to us both and I refused to go anywhere unarmed. Not long after Tibby and I met, I told her about my plans for revenge. She was all in and had her own plans for revenge too.

"I want a dagger. Something sharp as shit and easy to conceal."

Tibby nodded. "I want a gun. With a silencer. So I can catch my stepdad off guard when I kill him."

My face scrunched in anger over my friend's suffering. "I swear I will help you get vengeance, Tibby."

She stared back at me, her silvery blonde hair swaying with the ocean breeze. "I swear it too."

Something tingled beneath my skin, and I picked up the pocket knife. Without thinking, I sliced into my hand. Tibby held out her hand instantly, and I sliced into hers as well. We pushed our bloody palms together and threaded our fingers. Heat rushed through my veins, making me gasp. Tibby's eyes went wide with curiosity.

"I will always have your back, Tabitha." I said the words as a massive wave splashed against the sand.

Tibby's eyes were full of wonder. "And I will have yours, Seraphina."

I didn't know what was happening, but something shifted as we swore our allegiance to each other under the stars. A storm was coming, and the future was fully uncertain, but we were in this together. I loved her like a sister, and I would do everything to protect her, just as she would do the same for me.

CHAPTER ONE

Seraphina

A low voice whispered to me in my dreams. Or was this real? *"Don't give up on them,"* the shadow murmured. *"Trust what you feel, not what you see."* Something sharp pricked my skin, and the endless darkness returned.

For about the millionth time in my twenty-three years, I was certain death had come for me. My brain felt fuzzy, and my limbs weighed a thousand pounds. I didn't dare move, knowing someone was likely watching me. I took a long, slow breath. The air was damp and smelled of dirt. I was definitely underground. Water trickled from the ceiling somewhere nearby, the sound of each drop hitting the gravel echoing in my brain like a church bell. This was so much worse than a hangover. Why wasn't I healing? How long had I been out? My mind raced with questions as memories flooded in.

Devon. He looked furious. *And he shot them.* Ty and Levi. Their bodies crumpled and bleeding. Everything had gone so horribly wrong. And where was Tibby? Andras? I needed to heal and get the fuck out of whatever hole I was tossed in. Dev shot me with something, some kind of tranquilizer. The drug flowed through my veins, subduing me. It must have been strong, because even my natural ability to heal was taking too long. The vague memory of the voice came crawling back. I moved my arm slowly, feeling for the sore spot on my shoulder. A needle prick, but not the one from Dev. What did the shadow give me?

"Is she awake yet? I brought another dose," a voice bounced off the walls around me, sounding far and close all at once. *Was I in a tunnel?* Footsteps echoed on the uneven ground.

"She was murmuring in her sleep, but doesn't seem to be fully awake." Another male voice. Neither recognizable.

The first male whistled. "She sure does go through this shit fast. I've never heard of someone waking up after that many doses." He sounded impressed, and the part of my brain that worked felt entirely too smug.

Darkness surrounded me, just deep enough to make it difficult to take in my surroundings. Light filtered in as the voices grew closer. I was definitely in a tunnel or basement of some kind, and I needed to get out the fuck of here before they drugged me again.

I wiggled my fingers and toes, willing my body to move and the drug to fade from my veins. Whatever the shadow shot me up with seemed to be counteracting the other drug. My insides buzzed with adrenaline. The footsteps were much closer. I opened my eyes fully, trying to adjust to the near pitch-black room. My hands and feet were only tied with rope, but the knots came apart easily. I stumbled to my feet and braced my weight against the wall, feeling my way toward the tunnel entrance where the two males drew closer. The rope scratched my skin as I wrapped it around my hands and waited. I might not have been at full strength, but I could handle two low-level cult guards easily enough.

"Let's get this over with," the first one grumbled. "She's just over—"

The asshole had no time to finish his sentence before I wrapped the rope around his neck as soon as he appeared. The flashlight he carried fell to the floor as he cursed and scrambled for the rope tightening around his throat. I turned and tugged hard, strangling him as the other one drew out a weapon. Probably more of the tranquilizer. Forcing his body in front of mine, he took the shot and the dart slammed into Guard Dumbfuck's gut. I released the rope and snatched the baton at his side. I leapt over his limp body and smacked Guard Asswipe in the head with the metal baton. A loud crack of bones sounded as he dropped to the floor, probably dead. Maybe not. But probably.

Well, that wasn't as difficult as I expected. I snatched up the flashlight and took the knives from their belts, stuffing them into my boots. Thankfully, I was still fully dressed in my leggings and sweater. I had no idea how long I'd been out, but the way my body ached told me it was at least a couple days. Leaving the idiots behind, I followed the tunnel the two males came out of, hoping to find an exit and some daylight.

At the end of the tunnel, a massive wooden door blocked my path. But these guards were stupid, so when I turned the handle, the door swung open, unlocked. Bright fluorescent lights shone down from the long set of concrete stairs. I dropped the flashlight and took out one of the knives, the baton still in my other hand. There was no telling what I would find at the top of those stairs. Hopefully, more bad guys to kill.

Blood thrummed loudly in my ears in the silence and I held my breath as my head popped up over the threshold. This was some kind of...dungeon? Jail? Several rows of cells, no bigger than small bedrooms, with thick metal bars to keep prisoners locked up lined each side. I closed the heavy as hell door the guards left open, locking it and looking around. My eyes adjusted to the low lighting running down the center of the room. A much more secure looking door stood at the far end. I started toward it, glancing into the cells as I went. My breath caught when I peered into a cell about halfway down and found my monster man curled up on the floor.

I darted to the cell and reached through the bars. My outstretched hand could barely brush against his arm. "Ty? Ty, wake up."

He murmured something but didn't budge. I had a feeling he was being dosed like I was.

"Seraphina?" a deep voice that made my insides warm called out from a cell across the room, and I sprinted to Levi.

As soon as I slammed into the bars, Levi pulled me close, crushing me to him as much as he could with the barrier. His hand gripped my hair, and his mouth found mine before I could say anything. His tongue demanded entrance, and I opened for him, my heart melting for this man of mine. The kiss was rough and passionate.

My body relaxed a fraction now that they were here before me. I pulled away and stared into his navy eyes. "You're alive."

He smirked. "As if a few bullets could keep me down."

"You looked very dead." I pinched his shoulder through

the torn fabric of his shirt.

Levi shrugged, brushing the loose hair from my face and examining me closely. "A flesh wound, *diabla*. Are you hurt?"

Relief flooded my system at his teasing tone. "No, just a little woozy from the drugs, but it's fading. I left two guards down there." I flicked my eyes to the heavy door. "One of them is dead, I think."

"Should have killed them both." Ty's voice was rough and harsh.

I let go of Levi and ran to him, reaching for his muscular arms.

"Ty," I choked out his name. I was not a weepy girl, but these men did things to me I didn't fully understand. "You okay, monster man?"

"Are you? You're absolutely filthy. It's getting my dick hard." Ty's arms barely fit through the bars as he gripped my waist and growled, his eyes fierce and ravenous as he pulled me close. "I'm going to rip Devon's head from his body."

I squeezed his arms and shook my head. "No, you are not. Something's not right here. He would never have done that unless he was forced."

Ty's grip tightened, and he shook his head. "There is nothing on this Earth that could force me to do what he did to you and my brothers. He betrayed us."

He wasn't wrong, but something in my soul just couldn't believe Dev would do that to me, to us, without some kind of catalyst. I reached up and placed my hands on his face, bringing him closer and kissing him slowly. His unkempt beard tickled my cheeks.

I pulled away before he could deepen the kiss. "Let's at least try to figure this out before we kill him. Alright?"

Ty frowned but nodded his acceptance. "Fine. I'm still going to punch him in the face for shooting Levi and me."

"Fair enough." I blew him a kiss as I turned away to look down the hall and survey the other cells. "Is Andras here?"

A voice suddenly called out from the speakers in the ceiling. "Andras is with me, Seraphina. Guards will be down shortly to escort you upstairs. If you choose not to follow them, Andras will be punished."

I stuck out my tongue at the speakers the voice bellowed from. I knew that voice. I'd heard it plenty of times in my nightmares, reciting incantations while my sister screamed. Laszlo Blackbyrn.

"Fuck you!" I shouted into the air as footsteps echoed behind the door at the end of the hall.

"Seraphina." Ty's voice was strained, and I turned to him instantly. He rarely used my name, and I didn't like his serious tone. He was afraid. "Don't do anything stupid. Play along for now. Alright?"

I rolled my eyes and crossed my arms like a child about to throw a tantrum. Because I so was.

Levi chuckled behind me. "*Diabla*. Don't make me spank your ass. I'll have Ty bind you up, and we'll really make it hurt. We cannot protect you locked up down here. And only we are allowed to make you hurt."

"Fine! I won't do anything stupid. Yet," I huffed. They were such downers.

Ty growled and slammed his arms into the metal bars. "I

Resurrection

will do more than spank you if you get yourself killed. I'll bring you back and strangle your pretty throat myself."

I blew him a kiss and crossed my arms over my chest. "I know the assholes above are listening, but figure out how to get out of those cells soon, you got it? I need backup."

The heavy wooden door opened, and six guards walked in with tasers. They all wore skeleton masks and plain black clothing. Fucking sheep.

"Six big and bad guards just for me? I'm flattered. Or should I be insulted? I could've taken ten."

The guards didn't speak as they caged me in and turned back toward the wide staircase leading into the unknown above. I didn't have a clue how I would get out of this, so I would play nice. For now. But when the opportunity came, the Kings of The Obscuritas and those who betrayed me would suffer my fucking wrath.

CHAPTER TWO

Devon

The Great Hall was exactly the same as it was the last time I entered it over a decade ago. I hated this room. Everything terrible in my life began in this stupid room. The first time my father and I visited Blackbyrn Mansion, I was only five years old. We were invited to the mansion by a mutual friend from the Exchange. My father was somewhat of a genius with numbers. My parents moved to New York for his new job before I was born. Sometimes I missed the life I never had growing up in England, where my father was born and he shared a whole other life with my mother. Everything about their life in New York seemed depressing.

Blackbyrn Mansion felt like a castle all those years ago. With over 200 rooms and hundreds of acres of land, the beauty of it dominated Asheville, North Carolina. I was deposited in a playroom with other children, including Ty, Levi, and Andras. The four of us became friends instantly, which suited our fathers. Even before their little ritual, something bonded us; something even the four of us didn't understand. I thought it meant we could survive anything together. But I was wrong. Seraphina proved that.

She was responsible for my father's death. And they knew she was the culprit. *They fucking knew.* But they let her in

Resurrection

anyway. Fell for her. Let me fall for her. The woman who killed my own father. When Tibby first told me, I refused to believe her. But she had video evidence of the night he was killed. The fire Seraphina trapped him in. I went to the Kings shortly after seeing the videos, and Samuel Delano confirmed what I saw.

I shook away the memories threatening to drown me. They bled together. My father's screams as he burned in Seraphina's fire. Her mother appearing during the ritual and chanting, trying to stop it. Our father's chanting louder, and Lailah's screams of agony as it began to work. And my brothers and I were trapped within the circle, unable to do anything to stop it.

It was all too much. I wanted out of this shit. But Laszlo made it perfectly clear I was stuck with my traitorous brothers until his final ritual was completed. The tattoo connected to my relic burned, and I grimaced. We couldn't do anything to stop Laszlo while he had our relics. Our powers belonged to him. I supposed that was my own doing, since I returned mine to him freely. But when this was finally over, I would be free of it. Free of them all.

"Welcome, Devon," Andras called out, his arms crossed and his face furious. "How lovely to see you here. My father's new errand boy."

I kept my shoulders back and head held high as I walked toward the center of the room. The dining table had been removed. Servants hurried about, preparing for the party in the coming week, when the moon was full.

"Fuck off, Andras." I didn't care what he thought about me, not anymore. Mostly. "I'm doing this for my father."

Andras narrowed his eyes. "You're an idiot if you believe

anything the Kings told you."

"It wasn't just them. I saw what she did with my own eyes. Tibby sent me the video. And you fucking knew about it."

Andras leaned back and uncrossed his arms, smoothing the creases of his suit jacket. The fancy prick always wore a suit. I knew Laszlo preferred us dressed up, but ripped jeans and a T-shirt was my preferred style and I wasn't changing it for anyone.

"Yes, Devon, I saw the same video you saw. But I also know Tabitha has exceptional skills with technology. And she is working for my father, for reasons I have not yet discovered. I believed that video was fake. I wasn't going to create discord in our group over a fake video. I was going to tell you when I had my proof."

"You should have told me before your father did!" I shouted at him, letting him see the betrayal I felt.

Andras sighed. He looked exhausted and afraid. Two things I rarely saw from him. "I am sorry he got to you first. But I am surprised how easily you believed him. I know your feelings for her are strong, just as strong as my own. She didn't do this, Devon, and on some level, you know that."

"I don't know it," I snapped and turned my back on him, refusing to think about what he was saying. I couldn't. If he was right… No. I know what I saw. I chose my path and that was that.

The double doors opened at the far side of the Hall, and I sucked in a breath. Several armed guards escorted Seraphina. She was a dirty, bloody mess. Her hair was filthy and plastered to her head. Grime and gore covered her clothes. And she looked absolutely beautiful.

My heart broke as the thought entered my mind unbidden. Because god dammit, I couldn't just wish away the feelings I had for her, as much as I tried. I wanted to tear apart everyone who hurt her, if only to inflict upon them the pain she caused me. She was a villain. And I refused to think otherwise.

CHAPTER THREE
Seraphina

My eyes darted around the room, barely registering Dev and Andras. My skin crawled, and my mind shattered with memories of this room. The room where my sister and mother were killed. Images and voices pierced my mind, and I wanted to scream. I couldn't breathe. I needed to get out of here. I needed to burn this place to the fucking ground.

"Seraphina. Sweetheart." The sound of Andras's steady voice pulled me from the fog.

I looked up at him, desperately hoping for a cure, a way out of the darkness inside me.

"You are in desperate need of a bath."

A laugh bubbled out of me, and oh gods, I loved him for bringing me out of my terror. "I rather like this look. Although the blood of the Obscuritas lackeys I killed is starting to stink."

My body slammed to the ground as a guard shoved a taser into my side. I gritted my teeth, refusing to scream as the pain seared through my limbs. Andras shouted. And I thought I even heard Dev's voice demanding they stop. My ears rang as the assault continued.

"Enough!" Laszlo Blackbyrn's voice boomed as he entered the Banquet Hall, and the sharp pain subsided.

Resurrection

I took several long breaths, willing the ache to leave my body faster. I needed to be coherent for this exchange.

Laszlo's fancy dress shoes appeared near my head, and I forced my arms and legs to move so I could stand before him. He looked so much like his son it hurt. I didn't want to see any of Andras in him, but it was impossible not to. He wore an obviously expensive, tailored suit. His nose was straight, like his son's, and he looked down at me with cold, calculating eyes. His head was shaved smooth, and his full mouth crooked into a smile that made me shiver.

"Welcome to my home, Seraphina. Or should I say welcome back? It's been quite some time." His deep voice mocked me.

I wanted to stab him in the heart. And the dick. And everywhere else. Just stab, stab, stab.

Laszlo touched his temple with a subtle smirk. "Don't forget. Any sign of resistance from you results in punishments dolled out to the boys you have enthralled." His face contorted with jealousy, but smoothed back into indifference almost immediately. "I commend you for that. Be it your wit or magical cunt, who can say?"

"Laszlo." Andras growled his father's name, fury in his eyes. "Do not speak to her like that."

Laszlo didn't even flinch at the rage in his son's voice. This man feared nothing and no one. "I have heard you can sing. You will perform at the party next weekend. I think it will be fitting to have your voice heard one last time."

I kept my mouth shut. I was so furious and unprepared I didn't know what would come out if I spoke. And I wouldn't do or say anything to hurt my men.

"What are we doing here? Why was I summoned?" Dev cut in, and I finally looked at him. My heart felt broken, a piece missing, at his betrayal. I was so confused how he could turn against me so easily, how he could betray his brothers.

Laszlo stepped away from me and toward the bodyguards he arrived with. One of them carried a small wooden box. He opened it and pulled out my mother's key. *Shit.* "This key was spelled by Aurora, and even dead, her power is great. There is a safe deposit box in Seraphina's name and inside is another box, which this key will open, but only Seraphina can retrieve it."

I hated the careless way he spoke of her death, as if he wasn't the cause of it. I pictured Laszlo's body strapped to a gurney. Stab, stab, stab.

"What's in the box?" Dev asked, crossing his arms and refusing to look at me.

Laszlo turned to him and held out the key. "A relic. Speaking of, Devon. You will bring us Typhon's relic as well."

Andras's eyebrows shot up in surprise, and he eyed Devon.

Devon frowned, his bright-green gaze colored with confusion. "I don't have it."

Laszlo turned to me with dark, narrowed eyes, his jaw clenching in annoyance. "I know you were the one who killed Bullseye and raided one of our outposts, Seraphina. Where is the relic?"

I couldn't help the smug smirk on my face. "No idea what you mean. Must've been someone else."

Laszlo stalked toward me, and Andras stilled, his face etched with fury and fear as his father approached me. Laszlo's arm snapped out, and his smooth fingers gripped my cheeks, pinching my face hard enough to make my eyes water. "The more you resist, the worse it will be for those you love. You may pretend to be a heartless cunt, but I have a noose around each of them. Your sister. Tabitha. My son. Now tell me what I want to know."

His threats irritated the hell out of me, but I refused to cower to this asshole. "I. Don't. Have. It. I don't even know what it is."

Laszlo's icy gaze leeched under my skin as he absorbed my words. "It is a weapon. A mace."

My mask slipped before I could stop it as I recalled the unique weapon.

Laszlo smiled like a slimy cartoon villain. "So you have seen it."

The mace was in my safe, which currently sat in the basement of The Towne House. I jerked my head back, and Laszlo released my face from his grip.

"If I tell you where it is, you will give me something in return."

The devious King arched an eyebrow. "And why should I agree to that? You are in no position to make deals."

I glared up at him. "No one knows where the mace is but me. Go ahead and torture me. You won't get the answer."

Before I could blink, Laszlo smacked my face hard enough to bruise and my knees slammed into the floor as I fell. Blood coated my tongue and adrenaline zipped through my body. A sigh of pleasure nearly escaped my lips.

"Laszlo!" Andras shouted, his voice as cold as his father's. "I know where it is. Leave her alone."

Laszlo Blackbyrn smiled victoriously at his son. "Good. Go and retrieve it, or I will beat her near to death in front of you. Over and over again." He smiled as his son's eyes filled with hate. "Several guards will accompany you."

He turned to Devon, his expression hard and unyielding. "Seraphina's relic is the final piece needed for the ritual to connect her essence to ours. We will finally finish what was started so long ago. And you will escort her."

"Fuck no," I blurted out the words before I could think. But no, I would not be doing that.

Laszlo smirked, and I knew it meant nothing good. The double doors opened again, and we all turned to see three men enter the room. I knew all three of them. Ty's father, Darren Radnor. He was almost as muscular as his son. His eyes were dark and cold, though. Merciless. This man enjoyed inflicting pain more than anyone. The second man was Levi's father, Samuel Delano. He was harder to read. Mercurial. And a full-blooded lapdog of Laszlo's. But the third man, the one who nearly brought me to my fucking knees, was my father.

I couldn't hold back the strangled sound that left me when I saw him. What was almost worse, he looked…fine. He wasn't dirty or bruised or beaten. He wore a tailored suit like the others. He walked ahead of them, and when he looked at me, I nearly dropped to the floor. His eyes were infinitely sad. My mind flashed back to that moment he left me, a decade ago. When he gave me the key and told me it was safer this way, for us to be apart. He was so sad then, and I wanted to help. I wanted to make that sadness go away. And yet it was still there, all these years later.

He didn't seem surprised to see me, and I wasn't sure how to feel about that.

"What a lovely little reunion," Darren's mocking voice cut through my thoughts, and I wanted to strangle him.

"Indeed." Laszlo nodded. "There is another special someone here as well. But for now, Seraphina, the reunion with your sister will have to wait."

I lunged for Laszlo, but six sets of hands pulled me back. "Where the fuck is my sister, asshole?!" My blood boiled in my veins. She was here, somewhere in this massive stupid mansion. I would die before I let another of my sisters be used by this cult.

"She is resting." Darren smirked, his light-blue eyes filled with lust. "In her condition, she needs it."

My eyes caught my father's. He looked near to tears.

"What condition?"

Laszlo frowned at Darren. "It's not the time, Darren. Take Mr. Bronwen back to his rooms. If all goes well at the bank, you can see your sister when you return."

My mind whirled with the implications of what was said. Darren looked entirely too pleased, and it terrified me. If he hurt my sister, I would give him a death so painfully glorious, the devil himself would cower before me.

"Fine. I'll get the stupid relic." I ground out the words, and Laszlo smiled knowingly.

"Of course you will." He turned to the guards. "Escort the obedient prisoner to her room. She has forty-five minutes to look presentable." Laszlo spun away without another word.

Andras and Dev stayed, watching as the stupid guards shoved me away and out a separate set of doors. I didn't even have time to speak to my father. A part of me was furious with him. Why was he here? How could he let them take Michaela? I hated him for being weak. And I hated myself for not finding her first.

CHAPTER FOUR

Devon

I leaned against the SUV in the circle drive, waiting for Seraphina. Every part of me hated seeing her hurting. When the guards tased her, I wanted to kill them all. My thoughts were a mess. Everything Andras said to me in the Great Hall echoed in my mind. I became increasingly less certain of what I knew to be true. But what was I supposed to do? Ask her to tell me the truth? She would lie to me. Tell me what I needed to hear.

The memory of that night at the party flashed in my mind. I was so rough with her, furious as I fucked her. And she didn't fight me. She moaned for me and told me I was hers and she was mine, even as I gave her pain. Seraphina took it all willingly.

The girl filling my thoughts stepped out with her guards, the sun catching in her silvery blue hair. She wore fitted black jeans, and a charcoal gray sweater hung loosely off her toned arms. Her shoulders were pushed back, and she held my gaze without flinching. Her sea-blue eyes pierced through my soul all too easily, and I swallowed thickly. I needed to know the truth, and I needed to hear it from her.

Two of the guards shoved her into the SUV while I walked around the other side. The remaining guards filed into the second car while these two climbed into the front. As we made the thirty minute journey to the bank, Seraphina stared out the window in silence. I didn't want to speak to her in front of these assholes. They were sheep, loyal followers of the Kings, and I knew they'd report anything I said back to their masters like the good little pets they were. We were going into the bank alone, though, while the guards waited by the exits to make sure she didn't try to run.

The general public didn't know the most powerful and deadly cult was gathering soon to change the world. The Kings required discretion, at least until the time came for their power to become known. I was all mixed up about that too. My father didn't want to be part of this. He wanted out, I was sure of that. At least I thought I was. And then she killed him, so I would never know what he truly wanted from me. From all of this.

When we arrived at the bank, I took the keys from the guard and uncuffed her wrists.

She finally looked at me. "Thanks." She spoke the singular word with only a hint of sarcasm, and I savored the small bit of attention she offered.

I pulled her arm through my own, needing her close even when I wanted to throttle her. "Let's go."

The bank wasn't overly busy, and as soon as I dropped the Blackbyrn name, we were whisked away to the heavily guarded area where the vault and boxes were located. An unremarkable bank manager escorted us to a small room where her box rested on a table at the center.

"Let us know if you need anything else," the pudgy manager mumbled and bowed awkwardly, unsure of us, before finally leaving.

"Here." I pulled out the key and passed it to Seraphina.

She turned to me, ignoring the box. Her bright and clever eyes captured mine. "Why are you doing this?"

It was time. I returned her hard stare, needing to see the truth in her eyes when I spoke. "I saw a video of you killing my father. You set a house on fire. He was in Seattle brokering a deal for the Kings. They found his body bound and tortured and burned. There were cameras outside, and they caught you entering the house after him and rushing out as the fire spread."

Seraphina's eyes widened, never leaving mine as I spoke. The pain and sadness in them mirrored my own. She licked her pink lips and reached for me. "Devon. I swear on my sister's life I did not murder your father."

She seemed so sincere. I closed my eyes, searching my memories for that video of her setting the fire. It was strange, they didn't feel like my memories anymore, and I was starting to think Andras was right. Seraphina's delicate hand reached for mine, and I opened my eyes once more to take her in. Our fingers twined, and I held my breath. Her bright eyes held me captive as she spoke.

"I cannot say that if I had the opportunity, I would let him live," she murmured, hurt and anger flitting across her beautiful face. "He was one of them. He was there when my sister and mother were murdered."

My brows pinched together. She was right, of course. He was there, and he didn't stop it from happening. And I hated that. Hated that someone I loved could hurt her so badly.

"I know."

She squeezed my hand. "I also stalked them all over the years. Your father seemed to distance himself from the others. He would disappear, and even Tibby couldn't find him. But it was always on his own, without the Kings. When we found out he was dead, I suspected the Kings. I think you did too."

Of course I fucking did. I hated The Obscuritas. The other Princes and I all hated the cult as soon as we were old enough to understand it. And especially after that fucking ritual.

The truth in her words hit me like a fucking freight train. She didn't kill him, and even as she said as much, I realized I knew that all along, but was just too stupid and angry to see it. The memories of my father's death began to warp and fade. A familiar pain pierced my mind.

The Kings began training us to withstand mind control when we were children. They needed heirs and soldiers who wouldn't be compromised. And yet, I let them in. In the years I spent away from The Obscuritas, my mental shields grew weak. These weren't my memories. These images of my father being burned weren't real. The video was fake, just like Andras said. Somehow I was so careless, and Laszlo or Samuel got into my head, making me believe the lies. *Fuck. I shot my brothers.*

I dropped to my knees, the weight of my actions from the last week crushing me like an avalanche, threatening to swallow me whole. "Seraphina." I choked out her name. "I've fucked everything up."

She patted my head like I was a child. "You really did."

I looked up at her, and she smirked down at me. But I couldn't smile back, not while I was still wallowing. "Sassy woman. I'm serious. How can I fix this? You're a prisoner. You're

Resurrection

all prisoners because of me. I don't know what to fucking do now."

Seraphina gripped my biceps and pulled me from my knees. I gazed down at her as she placed her hand against my cheek.

"You're going to keep playing the part of hating me. Right now, The Obscuritas Kings believe you follow their orders. Let's keep it that way until we can come up with a plan to save us all." She turned back to the safe deposit box and pressed the key into the lock.

I grunted in agreement and watched over her shoulder as the old box opened easily at her touch. A beautiful blade with a ruby fastened in the hilt rested inside. She picked it up and gasped.

"Holy shit. What is that?" She could barely get the words out as the power of the blade vibrated the air around us.

"Your relic. We each have one. See the symbol near the ruby? Do you recognize it?" I watched as her mouth popped open.

"I dreamt of that symbol one night, maybe five years ago. I got it tattooed on my side the next day. What is it?" she whispered, her voice laced with curiosity.

"It's something related to the power we have. It's not in any language we know. Our fathers used the books to find the relics then forced the tattoos on us. The relics give us power, healing abilities. Access to some strange magic, like having wings."

Seraphina shook her head. "But why do I have one? Why did my mother hide this for me to find?"

I shook my head, because I truly didn't know. "We got ours after that first ritual. Maybe you had one then as well. The books they have on these rituals, it's all strange. I didn't want to believe any of it. It was all fairy tales and magic and shit when we were younger. But when they killed your sister and your mother…it all became very real. And I left. I tried to leave it all in the past. I tried to get my father to leave then too. But he was too deep in it. And they promised him things."

"What things?" She looked up at me, her eyes searching.

Nerves and emotions bubbled up with the memories. My feet anxiously propelled me across the room, unable to remain still. "They promised him my mother and sister could come back."

When I turned back, Seraphina's pretty eyes were filled with sadness. "Oh, Dev."

I shrugged, trying not to think about it for too long. "It's not true. I don't care what kind of magic they have access to. The dead are dead. I've lost them all now, and they aren't coming back."

Seraphina walked toward me and wrapped her arms around my waist. I circled my arms around her immediately. She was so small and so fierce. I let her strength feed into my own.

After several minutes, she pulled away and stared down at the blade. "If my mother hid this for me, then maybe she knew things the Kings didn't. Maybe it will help us."

Her hopeful tone latched onto my heart. I wanted to believe that. For her and for my brothers. I couldn't handle losing anyone else. Not at their hands. From this moment on, I would do whatever she asked of me. Be whatever she needed me to be. I would never doubt her again. "I will do whatever you need me to do. I'm yours to command, *mera dil*."

Seraphina looked up at me and smiled. The sight made my

knees weak. It had been so long since I saw her smile. "What does that mean?"

Staring into her captivating eyes, feeling things I'd never felt for anyone else, I knew this was it. Without a doubt, I would do anything for this woman. "It means my heart. It is yours. It's always been yours. I'm sorry for hurting you, *mera dil*. I will do anything and everything to make it up to you."

I brushed my fingers across her lips, and the blood in my veins heated at the look in her wicked eyes. A plan was forming in her brilliant mind.

"Then follow me." Seraphina stuffed the blade in the back of her jeans and grabbed my hand, pulling me to the door. She peered out. No one waited for us. We stepped into the hall, and she dragged me toward a staircase going all the way up to the roof. I followed her, enjoying the view of her ass swaying with each step.

She pushed open the door, and we squinted into the brilliant sun. "And what exactly is your plan?"

"We're going to fly out of here." She smiled brightly, and I wanted to bottle up the beauty of it.

I laughed, because absolutely not. "I don't use my wings like the others. I don't want anything The Obscuritas gave me."

She walked toward me, the winter wind whipping her hair and a smile playing on her plump lips. She was a goddess. "I don't think it was from them. I have my own theories on that. But even if your power was from them, why not use it? Make it your own. Fuck them and their rules."

I smirked down at her, this clever creature I had no business wanting and definitely didn't deserve. "I'm not as skilled as my brothers. I don't think I could carry you."

Seraphina wrapped her arms around my neck, and I immediately grabbed her waist. Having her alone like this was making my dick hard and my possessive feelings rage with need for her.

"Don't sell yourself short." She reached up and brushed her lips against my ear. "There's a devil lurking inside you, Devon Parrish. I've seen him, and I am not afraid of his bite. Let him out."

Her words raised goosebumps over my skin, my blood singing for her and her alone. I turned my head to kiss her, but she shoved me back. Before I could recover, I watched in horror as she ran for the edge of the roof.

"Seraphina, no!"

"I trust you!" she screamed before jumping off the edge of the roof.

I sprinted toward her. After everything, this would not be how Seraphina fucking died. I willed my body to change, my power rushing to obey as I leapt after her.

Her arms were spread wide like a soaring bird of prey, and I straightened into a dive, my weight carrying me down faster. The sidewalk below was horribly close. I cried out for her as my arms circled her waist. I pushed all my strength into my power, and my wings snapped open. The wind hooked beneath the dark-gray feathers just before we met the ground and carried us upward. I pumped them hard, pushing us into the clouds and toward the sun. My wings carried us higher, and I held her tightly against my body.

Seraphina laughed and wrapped her arms and legs around

me. "You're incredible, Dev."

I kissed her pretty, wicked mouth. "Everything I am pales in comparison to everything you are, *mera dil*." I kissed her again as we flew through the skies. "I will never betray you again."

"No more talking. Only fucking. Take me to ground and make fucking love to me like you mean it." Her words were urgent, and I growled as she ground her hips against my own, my cock pressing almost painfully in my jeans.

I let the currents in the air guide me as we dove through the sky. We weren't far from the mansion, but I wasn't ready to return her to our prison. They would figure out we left soon enough, but for this brief moment, she was all mine.

CHAPTER FIVE
Seraphina

Flying through the skies wrapped in Dev's arms was unlike anything I'd ever felt. The world was nothing, our problems were far and away, and we were free in this moment. I planned to punch Ty in the face for not letting me experience this when they first kidnapped me. Asshole knocked me out. And now he'd get to be jealous of Dev. I smirked. I couldn't wait for that bit of fun.

Dev soared lower, just above the trees. I could see the mansion in the distance. His hard cock pulsed between us, and I desperately needed his naked flesh against mine. He dropped to the grass, his massive wings slowing us as he took the brunt of my weight. His wings were something from a fairy tale. Like a fallen angel. The charcoal feathers looked soft as silk. I reached out to brush my fingers through them. Dev shivered and groaned.

"That feels amazing, *mera dil*." His voice was rough with desire and made my blood hot.

"Your wings are the most beautiful things I've ever seen." I whispered the words, in awe of this man.

His dark hair brushed across his forehead, and his heated gaze captured mine.

"Now fuck me good, lover."

Resurrection

Dev growled as his lips crashed into mine. His hands were everywhere at once, removing my clothes, squeezing my nipples, gripping my ass. His body moved over mine as he laid me in the grass. The earth was cold, but I barely felt it. Dev stood and unbuttoned his pants, staring down at my naked body. His eyes roamed, and I squirmed.

"You look like the most delicious treat I could ever eat." He dropped his pants to the ground, and I licked my lips at the sight. His cock was stiff, and a bead of cum dripped from the head.

"So do you, Dev." I slipped one hand between my legs, coating my fingers in the wetness pooling there, so ready for him. "Keep your wings out."

Dev lunged. He had my legs up and spread before I could take a breath. In the next second, he was fully seated inside me. "Fuck, baby. I missed your sweet pussy."

His words shot desire straight to my clit, and I moaned. Dev fucked me slowly, thrusting once, twice, teasing me, and I begged for more.

"I missed you too."

He continued the slow pace, his body molding to mine like the last pieces of a puzzle. Dev's bright-green eyes bored into mine, and he brought his hands to brush against my cheeks. "Seraphina, my love. My heart. I am so fucking sorry for the mess I brought upon you. For not trusting you or my brothers. I will never be able to make up for this, but I will spend every waking moment trying to do so."

I smiled up at him, the sensitive asshole making me feel things. And gods dammit if his words didn't make my pussy pulse too. I smirked at him. "You're going to turn me into a sap with all your pretty words, Devon Parrish."

He grinned at me, and my fucking heart melted. I moaned as he continued to fuck me, slowly, his eyes still locked with mine. This was not normal; this was the beginning of something beautiful and raw and real. And I was fucking terrified.

As if he could sense my fear, Dev wrapped his hand around the back of my neck possessively, pulling me in for a searing kiss. Our lips parted just enough for him to speak. "You're mine for eternity, Seraphina. And I will never let you forget it."

"I'm yours." I moaned, squeezing my legs tight around his waist. "Now make me come. Fill me up, Dev. I need it."

"As you command, *mera dil*." His eyes lit up with feral lust, and he growled.

Dev pulled me up into his lap and fucked me hard and fast. My tits bounced in his face, and his mouth captured my nipple, biting and licking them each in turn. The orgasm built inside me as his cock thrust deeper and deeper. I cried out as the wave of pleasure crashed through me. My pussy squeezed tightly, and he groaned, pumping faster. He whispered my name like a prayer as he spilled his hot cum inside me. He held me close, his lips brushing against my bare arms, my shoulders, and up to my lips, his heart beating as rapidly as my own. I stared into his gorgeous green eyes and knew this was forever. Our souls were connecting in a way that no enemy could ever tear us apart again. I would never, ever get enough of this man.

Resurrection

There wasn't anywhere for us to fully clean up in the woods, so Dev—meticulously, I might add—wiped up the cum dripping down my thighs with his torn shirt. When his wings snapped out to catch me earlier, his shirt was basically ruined. All those torn up clothes would get annoying fast if we had to keep making these quick getaways.

Dev held me close and flew to the mansion, taking me straight to my room without any guards catching us. I gave him the relic to hand over to Laszlo. For now, we would play along. Our story was that I tried to escape at the bank. Dev had to chase me down and returned quickly to lock me up before I could try anything else. Laszlo would punish someone for my attempted "escape," but I knew my men would survive. And Dev and I…we needed that time together. I brought him back to us, but so did Andras. Dev told me Andras spoke with him and stood up for me. My cold-as-ice prince was such a softie. I would tease him about that too.

I showered, changed, and grew increasingly irritated. I waited for some time, pacing the room, checking for any items I could use as a weapon. Nothing, of course. And all the windows were barred and nailed shut.

The last of my self-control vanished, and I banged on the door as hard as I could. "If someone doesn't let me out soon I will start breaking things! And this shit all looks old and expensive!"

I listened for footsteps, but none came, so I went to the dresser and picked up the expensive Tiffany Lamp. The beautiful lamp was seconds away from getting tossed when I finally heard the stomping of guards outside my door. *Nah, I'm still annoyed.* I threw the lamp with all my strength and smiled with satisfaction as it shattered against the wall just as they opened the door.

The guards in their stupid skeleton masks stared at me in silence.

I shrugged. "You took too long. Something was bound to break. It could've been your skulls."

One of the guards stepped forward, walking past me, and laid a dress bag on the bed. "Change into this and call out when ready. If you don't, Typhon will be electrocuted."

Another guard placed a small tablet on the bed next to the dress. I swallowed down my angry response as I stared at the screen. The camera was pointed at Ty bound to a chair, a leather strap in his mouth. There was no sound, but rage radiated from him, seeping into my veins.

I glared at the guards, and they collectively took a step back, raising their tasers. "Get the fuck out before I kill you all."

The guard who brought the dress laughed. "Go ahead, whore. The more you fight, the worse it will be for him and the others."

This one was stupid and was going to die. Slowly and painfully. I shook with anger as they left my room. I ripped open the dress bag and sneered at the beautiful gown. The fabric was made of soft velvet and the color was a deep burgundy. The long sleeves ended with slim triangle points and loops for my middle fingers. When I put it on, the sweetheart neckline and fitted bodice accentuated my cleavage. The soft fabric pooled at my feet for a mermaid look. The guards also left a box with a pair of black stilettos. It was fucking annoying how perfectly the entire ensemble fit.

Resurrection

"Fucking creepy know-it-all cult leaders," I grumbled and chucked one of my boots at the door to let the guards know I was ready.

When the door opened, I ignored them and walked out with my head held high. I would not be intimidated by lesser men. Or any man, for that matter. They kept pace with me, one of the idiots hurrying ahead to guide me to the Dining Hall. Andras and Dev were waiting near the long dining table, looking delicious in black tailored suits. Dev had his arms crossed and a frown etched into his face. Andras looked cool as usual, his hands clasped behind his back. His eyes roamed over my body, and I shivered at the attention. I missed his touch. I missed them all.

The guards stopped, forcing me to stay back. The three Obscuritas Kings entered the hall next. Laszlo barely glanced my way as he walked toward the table and stood next to the seat at the far end. Darren grinned at me, and I smiled back. His smirk faltered as I let him see the devil in my eyes. He would pay dearly for whatever happened to my sister. Samuel didn't glance my way at all. He looked bored and walked straight to his seat at Laszlo's right. Darren went to his left.

They shoved me forward, and the chair at the far end of the table was pulled out, waiting. I took the seat less than gracefully, because these asshats didn't deserve my niceness. Andras and Dev each took a seat beside me. Four more chairs at the table remained unoccupied. Laszlo followed my questioning gaze and smiled.

"Another familiar face will be joining us shortly. Leviathan and Typhon will not, however. For the stunt you pulled earlier, they have received severe punishments." Laszlo frowned as if he was hurt by this, and I ground my teeth, my nails digging into the arms of my chair at his casual tone. "Perhaps if you learned to behave, those you care for would not be in pain. Although they do deserve it."

Darren growled and rolled his eyes. "Cannot believe my own son turned traitor for pussy."

Samuel huffed in annoyance. "Agreed. After all the training we put our sons through." He looked to Laszlo with a secretive smile. "Shall we impregnate the new wives? I need a worthy heir."

Andras and Dev both went rigid at the mention of their stepmothers. I knew very little about them, even with all the digging into cult secrets. The wives were rarely seen out in the world. They were all beautiful, though, like pretty dolls, never speaking and always locked away until they were wanted again. This entire cult had very little respect for women.

Laszlo shook his head. "We don't have time for that now. Right now, it's time for a lesson."

I arched an eyebrow. "What lesson?"

The Kings' heads all turned in my direction, and I resisted the urge to flinch under their collective gaze. Before anyone spoke, a door opened across the room and a man I didn't recognize strode toward us, flanked by two guards. He wore a custom brown suit, and his graying hair was styled neatly. He gave the aura of confidence, but his eyes betrayed him. They darted between the Kings and myself with uncertainty.

Samuel stood and walked toward him with a smile. "Hello, Kingston."

Kingston. I knew that name. Audrey. Audrey Kingston was

Resurrection

in my lecture class. We rescued her friend from that horrible professor. I stared at the man as Samuel patted his shoulder roughly. Was this her father?

"You, guard," Samuel barked at one of the men. "Bring me my toy."

The guard walked swiftly across the room to another door at the King's command. Something was happening here, and I had a horrible feeling about it.

Laszlo turned to me once more. "Today is a lesson about choice. The power to make decisions and the burden of dealing with the consequences."

"Laszlo, what is this?" Andras snapped at him, his cool demeanor cracking.

The cruel King turned to his son and smirked. "The Obscuritas have survived on rules and obedience. When a new member is initiated, they are given a choice. There is power in choices. Today, we will begin with Edward Kingston."

Audrey's father frowned but otherwise maintained his composure as the attention of the Kings turned to him. The guard who left earlier returned at the same moment, but he was not alone. Audrey was with him. She wore a blood-stained white gown, matted against her lithe frame. Her eyes were bloodshot and mascara ran down her cheeks.

"Audrey!" I stood immediately and meant to run to her, but a guard stepped in my way. "What the fuck have you done to her?"

Her father gasped loudly behind me but made no move to go to his daughter. My blood heated and goosebumps covered my skin as she was forced to walk closer. She was barefoot and walking with a limp, her hands chained at the wrist as the guard pulled her along. I couldn't tell where the blood on her gown came from. Her eyes turned up to mine, and the pain in her gaze pierced my heart.

Samuel walked toward her with a smile. He reached out a hand, and Audrey flinched away from his touch. The terror on her face told me Samuel Delano was the cause of her pain. I was going to fucking kill him for this.

"Hello, little toy," he crooned at her. "Say hello to your father."

Edward Kingston stared at his daughter in horror. "What have you done to her?" he whispered, his shoulders shaking.

Samuel smiled, but his face remained cold. His eyes were entirely too dead for a living man. His lack of emotion was terrifying. "Not much, actually. Humans bleed so easily. But I've kept her mostly intact for you. She won't be forgetting our time together though. I've made sure of that."

Laszlo strode toward Edward with his hands clasped behind his back, the smirk never faltering from his smug face. "Today, you have a choice, Edward. Join The Obscuritas and receive all that we have to offer, power beyond your wildest comprehension, or die."

Edward's eyes widened, darting between the Kings and his daughter. "What about my daughter?"

"If you decide not to join us, she dies with you." Laszlo turned to Audrey. "If you join us, she lives, but she is no longer yours. She is property of The Obscuritas."

I wanted to vomit at the horrifying scene unfolding before me. I had to do something. I glanced over at Andras and Dev.

Their faces were contorted with disgust and horror, mirroring my own.

The silence blanketing the room as Edward deliberated was almost unbearable. Audrey looked at her father, her eyes pleading for something I couldn't know. But he was powerless here. This wasn't a choice. It was a show of force from The Obscuritas. Edward's shoulders slumped in defeat. "I will join you."

Samuel clapped. "How exciting."

Laszlo nodded. "Bring in his wife." He called out the words, and instant dread filled the room.

I watched as Edward's wife was brought into the room. She was dressed in a simple black suit, her blonde hair tied back neatly. She didn't look nearly as unkempt or terrified, and I had a feeling this woman had no idea what was going on.

She saw her husband first and started to smile. But then her gaze turned to her daughter, and a strangled sound left her throat. "Audrey!"

Two guards held her back, holding her arms down and forcing her toward Edward.

Laszlo turned back to Edward. "Another choice. When you join us, you begin life anew. Connections from your previous life must be severed."

Another guard approached and held out a gun to Edward Kingston. The man stared at it, unmoving.

Darren grinned, his face entirely too pleased with the situation. "Shoot your wife in the head, Edward. Do this and you will have more power than you can imagine. And plenty of women too."

Mrs. Kingston began to sob silently. She slumped to the

ground, and the guards stepped away from her.

"Either you all die, or she dies," Darren growled.

Mrs. Kington's eyes widened, and her gaze turned to her daughter. "Save her, Edward," she whispered softly.

Emotions boiled inside me as I stared at this woman, unafraid to die if it meant her daughter would live. The Obscuritas were so fucked up for this. I knew Audrey would not be saved. Not when she was in their clutches. But I wouldn't let her suffer for long. I refused to let her become a toy for the Kings and their fucked up games.

Edward trembled as he took the gun from the guard. He looked defeated and horrified. His arm slowly drew up, and he pointed the gun at his wife's head. The silence went on for what felt like hours before he pulled the trigger and his wife slumped to the floor, blood pooling around her head.

Samuel clapped again and turned to the guard holding Audrey in place. "Take my toy back to my room."

"Welcome to The Obscuritas, Edward Kingston," Laszlo's low, menacing voice drawled.

CHAPTER SIX

Devon

Everything about this situation was the fucking worst. I knew the Kings were murderers, liars, and so much worse, but seeing them force a man to murder his wife was something else entirely. Their cruelty knew no limits. And I was beginning to see how little control we had here.

I was furious with them for the memories and images they planted in my head to turn me against Seraphina. Furious at myself for letting it happen. I checked my mental shields again, having reinforced them since Seraphina set me free. How she managed it, I wasn't sure. I doubted she was either. But when I was with her, everything else faded away and my soul felt tethered to hers completely. I fought it for so long, afraid to trust and unable to let go enough to fully let her in. But that was all behind me now. I was fully committed to Seraphina Valdis.

Several guards escorted Edward Kingston from the room, and another crew came in to remove his dead wife. The Kings seemed incredibly pleased with themselves, and the look in Laszlo's eyes as he turned to me was deeply unsettling.

"Devon. Enjoy your little tryst in the woods?" Laszlo drawled, and I stiffened. "Did you think the guards you can see are the only ones I have?"

Shit. Of course he'd have eyes everywhere. How could I be so careless?

"It seems even with proof, one taste of the little whore's cunt has you turning against us once more," Laszlo mused.

"Don't fucking talk about her like that," I growled at him. "I know you tampered with my mind. My memories. It won't happen again."

"We'll see." Darren chuckled.

The sound was almost similar to Ty's. I hated that. I crossed my arms, staring him down as Laszlo stalked toward me.

"Now it's time for you to make a choice." Laszlo's dark eyes challenged mine, but I refused to look away, even as unease sank to the pit of my stomach.

"Get on with it then," I spat at him, holding his stare.

He turned away first, and for a moment, it felt like I won something.

The sound of another door opening caught my attention, and I turned. A woman stalked into the room with two guards at her back. She wasn't chained or bloodied. She walked in with confidence. The woman was curvy, with brown skin similar to mine and dark hair braided down her back. She wore black leggings, boots, and a maroon sweater. Her face was blank as she stalked toward us. There was something familiar about her.

When her gaze turned in my direction, I gasped. Startling green eyes matching my own stared into my soul.

"Leyja?" I rasped, stepping toward her.

She cocked her head but said nothing.

"It can't be. You died. You're... This isn't real." I strode toward her and reached out, unable to stop myself.

Before I could touch her, she twisted my arm behind my

back harshly and kicked out my knees. Seraphina shouted my name, but was held back.

"Hello, traitor," Leyja murmured.

This was beyond confusing. How could she be here? I wanted to cry with joy that my Leyja was alive, but what she called me stuck in my mind. *Traitor.*

"Devon, it's been many years, but I believe you remember your sister?" Laszlo cut through my thoughts. "She has been a loyal member of The Obscuritas for some time now."

"Laszlo. What is this?" Andras cut in, his body rigid.

Laszlo Blackbyrn walked slowly to my sister and placed his hand on her shoulder. I snarled and scrambled to my feet, hating him being anywhere near her. Guards prevented me from stepping closer to them.

"When your mother was tragically killed, we were able to save your sister. Your father was going mad, even then, so we kept the knowledge of her from him." Laszlo squeezed my sister's shoulder affectionately.

Everything out of this man's mouth was a fucking lie. But what haunted me most was the idea of my only sibling being in the hands of the fucking Kings for the last fifteen years. Doing the math, she would be around twenty years old now. I hadn't seen her since just after her eighth birthday. I thought she died with my mother. But now she was here, alive. Elation and terror flooded through me in equal parts. No one survived that much time with The Obscuritas without going insane.

Laszlo stepped in front of her and glared at me. "Unlike the other members of the Parrish family, your sister has remained loyal and true. She is quite gifted too. A quick learner and very skilled with a variety of weapons." He smirked. "And Samuel has trained her to feel very little pain. She is truly a sight to behold."

I processed his words slowly. Samuel Delano. I knew of his sick desires. He liked to see how much pain his victims could take. The idea of my only sister on the receiving end of that torture was enough to make bile rise in the back of my throat.

"What the fuck do you want, Laszlo?" I ground out the words. He said I had a choice to make.

Laszlo smiled. "Yes. It's time to choose where your loyalties lie. To your sister, to us. Or to the whore. Seraphina Valdis would surely kill your sister if given the chance. She wants us all dead, and Leyja is one of us."

"Father," Andras cut in once more. "What exactly are you making him choose? You have us all here. You've won."

"You see, my traitorous son, you all need a lesson in power. And the realization that you've never had any," Laszlo snapped. He turned back to me. "Choose, Devon. Your sister or Seraphina. Whichever you do not choose, will belong to me."

"Father!" Andras bellowed angrily.

"Silence!" Laszlo shouted back, a dangerous edge to his voice. "Take my son away."

Before anyone could move, a guard tased Andras from behind and several of them dragged him out of the room.

"Devon," Seraphina whispered, and I looked at her, desperate for an answer. "It's alright. I'll be alright."

The weight of the decision before was suffocating. I just got her back, my heart, my soul. How could I give her up? I locked eyes with my sister. Her face was a blank mask as she stared back at me, her arms crossed and back straight. Leyja reminded me so much of our mother. She was fierce and strong, but now, her mind was fucked. This was not the loyal and caring big sister I knew. I had to get her away from Laszlo. Had to at least try and save her. For my father's sake. For our mother.

My head bowed in defeat at this fucking awful choice. "I choose Leyja."

Another guard immediately pulled out a taser and aimed it at Seraphina. She dropped to the floor as the electricity shot through her body, but my brave queen didn't scream. Another guard stepped forward and stuck a syringe in her neck. Seraphina's eyes drooped as the drug quickly worked its way through her system.

CHAPTER SEVEN
Tabitha

My eyes went wide, and I stopped short as soon as I saw her. Seraphina was strapped to a simple wooden chair in my bedroom, her head hanging down and her silvery blue hair hiding her face. I noted her hands cuffed to the arms of the chair, and my stomach fluttered with nerves when I noticed her feet. Someone had removed her shoes and placed her bare feet in a small bin of water. Some kind of wire trailed from the bin and around the chair. It was hooked up to a machine. I had a horrible feeling about what was to come. This room brought pain to all who entered, except for Laszlo. He was the one in control, the King doling out punishment to his subjects, loyal or not. I had been loyal, and the punishments he gave me were excruciating. I didn't want to be loyal. Everything inside me screamed to spit in his face, but when I tried, my legs bent and I bowed before him, kissing his shoes instead. Laszlo scrambled my brain. I had some awareness that my thoughts and actions weren't fully my own, but the claws he dug in were buried so deep, there was no getting them out. There was no escape. Until him. The guard who gave me a gift.

When he walked me to my room that day, he didn't speak. Didn't threaten me or make gross comments about my body like the other guards did. He was taller and broader than most of them too. I had a strange feeling he could make himself even more threatening but he chose to hide that away and appear weaker. I wasn't sure why, but that was comforting. He was comforting. His presence at my side awoke something needy in me, and I didn't know what to do with that. He spoke softly to me, offering to help me. No one had offered to help me, so I was obviously suspicious. And yet I accepted. I let him touch me, his rough fingers sending shivers through my body. Only Laszlo was allowed to touch me, and others could do so only when he gave them permission. I was breaking his rules by letting this man touch me, and some tiny part of my mind that was still my own cheered at the rebellious act.

I didn't understand the words he whispered but watched in fascination as he pricked his finger and traced symbols in his blood against my skin. The marks tingled and faded, leaving a sense of healing. My body was always in pain, bruised and battered and rarely given time to heal. But the aches dulled as the marks seeped into my skin.

His second gift I didn't notice until the next time Laszlo entered my mind. He snarled and speared words like knives into my thoughts, forcing me to feel things and think things I didn't want to. Tears burned my eyes, and I closed them, wishing for a place to get away. And at the thought, a door appeared in my mind and I went to it. There was only darkness, but once I was in that empty space, Laszlo's power wasn't so sharp. I could feel him there. The guard. And pure nothingness in the most comforting way. I didn't know how it worked or why, but for once I didn't have to take the pain of Laszlo's intrusion so fully.

Seraphina groaned and stirred in her chair. The part of me

that was still me wanted to run to her and rip the chains from her body to help her escape. But I couldn't. Instead, my body walked to the closet and pulled out an outfit. Laszlo liked me to dress in clothes similar to a doll. Little dresses and stockings. It was so weird. I hated it. When I was in this room and he wanted to play, I had to wear the outfits. I tugged a blonde wig with pigtails over my hair and adjusted it to fit.

When I finished dressing, I walked back into the room and climbed into my own seat. The chair I was required to sit in was taller, bar top height. My feet dangled, unable to touch the ground, and I waited for my master. The silence in the room was suffocating, but I couldn't think of anything to say as Seraphina groaned and began to wake. Her head rolled back, and she cracked her neck. Her eyes opened, and she searched the room before noticing me.

Seraphina's mouth dropped, and she stared at me in shock. "Tibby." She said my name with such sadness in her voice. I could sense her hurt. The betrayal.

My eyes watered, but I couldn't comfort her. Couldn't say all the things I wanted, because he wouldn't let me.

Laszlo strolled into the room a moment later, stopping next to me and placing his hand on my shoulder. The part of me that was still me wanted to flinch away, but I couldn't do that either. His control over my mind and body was nearly all-consuming. Instead, I shivered and smiled as if that small amount of attention from him brought me pleasure. And maybe a small fucked up part of me was pleased.

"Hello, my King," I whispered, keeping my head down.

Laszlo's hand brushed over my back and up to my neck.

Resurrection

He squeezed from behind, applying enough pressure to hurt and reminding me who I belonged to.

"My little slave has been so good to her King." Laszlo smirked at Seraphina. "I was told you were the clever one, and yet you had no idea Tabitha belonged to me."

Seraphina spat at him, snarling with rage. "Fuck you. She didn't go willingly and we both know it. What have you done to her?"

Laszlo stepped to my side and stared down at me with his dark and hateful eyes. "Whatever I wanted." He looked back to Seraphina with a smile. "She was easy to turn. When I dangled her stepfather as bait, she came to kill him, just as I thought she would."

Seraphina's eyes widened, looking at me. "When was that?"

I couldn't respond. I looked to Laszlo, and he continued taunting her. My insides burned with shame for keeping secrets from my only friend. Maybe if I hadn't, we wouldn't be in this mess.

"She didn't tell you, because you were too busy whoring yourself out to my son and his friends. Too busy to care about something so important to her. So she went alone, as I hoped. I thought about interrupting her little plan and letting him fuck her one last time, but I was enjoying the show too much. Tabitha thought she was so clever and powerful, sneaking into the house and blowing him to bits."

My eyes burned with tears at the memory. It didn't feel as good as I wanted it to. After I shot him, all I could think was, I wish Seraphina was with me. But then Laszlo showed up instead, and I was lost to his power.

The terrifying Obscuritas King patted my head. "I made sure to keep her fears alive and well, though. We played often, repeating those filthy things her stepfather used to do. She's quite fond of it now. I bet her little cunt is getting wet just hearing my talk about it, isn't that right?"

He turned to me with an arched eyebrow, and I nodded. I hated him so fucking much because he was right. The arousal was low, but it was there as I thought about the pain I would witness and receive. I could no longer orgasm unless I was in pain and watching someone else being tortured. Bile rose in my throat even as the blood rushed to my clit in anticipation. I hated myself.

"I am going to fucking gut you and your stupid cult for this. You have no fucking idea the pain you will suffer at my hands," Seraphina snarled, pulling against her restraints.

"I'm shaking at the thought." Laszlo chuckled and waved a hand dismissively. "But until that time, let's play a little game of choice. Devon didn't choose you in the end, and Tabitha chose her father over your friendship. What will you choose, I wonder?"

He walked between us, bringing his hands behind his back and clasping them as he took measured steps, circling us both like the predator he absolutely was. He eyed Seraphina with obvious lust. I wanted to move, to go to her, but my body refused to do anything but obey him. His gaze turned back to me, filled with satisfaction at my obedience.

"Women are good for two things in this world. Satiating our lust, and our bloodlust. Often the lines between are blurred." He smacked my face enough to sting and smirked. "And when

Resurrection

your mind and bodies can no longer satisfy those urges, what use are you?"

Seraphina raged in her chains. "As if anyone would willingly lust after you, asshole."

"Be. Quiet." Laszlo turned back to her with a snarl, his cocky smirk slipping. "Did you honestly believe you could infiltrate *my* domain? As if the greatest kings of your lifetime could be outwitted by a twenty-three-year-old *girl*. Your hubris is nearly as bad as my son's. I know all about their little sect of defectors. I am always one step ahead of everyone else."

A knock on the door interrupted his snarling speech, and Laszlo barked at the guard to enter. My mouth twitched as I recognized the guard who helped me. My blood began to sing, and I desperately wanted to run to him for comfort.

"Who are you?" Laszlo snapped.

The guard stood at attention. "Greg. Tony sent me."

Laszlo's eyes narrowed at the guard. "And where is Tony? He usually plays with my toys."

The guard's eye twitched like the comment bothered him, but he hid his distaste well. "He thought I'd enjoy this… Whatever this is."

Laszlo stared at the guard for several moments before speaking. "Very well. Go to the table and choose a blade and a vibrator." He moved closer to me, placing his hand back on my shoulder. "Seraphina, shall we have Greg use these on Tabitha, or yourself?"

Seraphina's eyes filled with rage as she stared at him, grinding her teeth and refusing to answer. "Fuck you, Laszlo Blackbyrn."

Laszlo nodded to the guard. "Cut Tabitha's wrist."

The guard walked over slowly. His bright-blue eyes connected with mine, filled with uncertainty. But I nodded, giving him permission. He cut a thin line across my wrist, and blood dripped over the side. It hurt but wasn't the worst pain I'd experienced in this room.

"You imbecile. Don't you know how to inflict pain properly?" Laszlo snatched the blade from his hand and grabbed my wrist. He held my hand down on the arm of the chair as he cut a longer line from my wrist to my elbow.

I couldn't help the whimper that escaped as my skin tore open under the sharp knife and a steady flow of blood left my body. Dizziness tickled at my brain as the blood dripped to the floor at a steadier pace.

"Stop it!" Seraphina yelled. "You'll kill her!"

Laszlo wiped the blood from the knife with my dress. "I know. She doesn't have much time with a cut like that. Will you let Greg here play with you, or shall we continue with Tabitha?"

"Me, motherfucker. Just leave her alone," Seraphina snarled, her eyes filled with fury as she stared at my bleeding arm.

"Even knowing Tabitha betrayed you over and over, spilling all your secrets to me, touching herself for me? You don't want to watch her writhe in pain?"

"She didn't betray me. You forced her. You're pathetic. The only power you have is what you take." Seraphina's voice was full of rage, and she looked close to losing her shit.

Laszlo smirked. "All power is taken. If you cannot keep it, you're weak."

"Whatever, asshole. I chose me so get on with it and help her."

"No, I don't think so." He shook his head and handed the

blade back to the guard. "Now, spread her legs and use the vibrator on her whore cunt while you deliver tiny cuts to her arms and legs. Do not stop until I tell you to do so."

"No!" Seraphina screamed.

Laszlo's hands clasped behind his back as he walked over to Seraphina. "You will watch. See how she enjoys it. She needs the pain only I can give her to finish."

Seraphina began to thrash in her chair, nearly knocking it to the side, but Laszlo smacked her across the face and forced her to be still. He pulled a strange remote from his jacket pocket and pressed a red button. Seraphina screamed as sparks shot up from the water, and I realized he was electrocuting her.

Silent tears escaped as I was unable to shout and beg for him to hurt me instead. I could take it. This was all my fault, and watching him hurt her was tearing my heart into a million pieces. The guard distracted me from her grunts of pain when he knelt in front of me with the blade and sex toy. I whimpered, unable to hold back the needy sound at the sight of those two items. The guard looked up at me with anger in his eyes. He didn't look like a Greg to me. He was too beautiful.

I nodded at the toy and knife. "Please." I whispered the word, and I swore his eyes glowed for a moment.

"Begin or I will call Tony in here to do it for you," Laszlo snapped at the guard.

Greg turned the vibrator on, and fresh tears fell down my cheeks as my pussy throbbed with desire. I closed my eyes and searched for that door and the darkness that would welcome me. But when I entered the small corner of my mind where I could hide, I could feel him there too. The guard. I couldn't see anything, but I knew it was him brushing against my thoughts.

Fuck this. Don't be afraid. I'm going to save you.

His words reverberated in my mind like an oath. I opened my eyes, unsure how to respond, but there wasn't time to do so anyway.

In the next moment, the guard turned and flung the blade at Laszlo. My eyes widened as the knife sunk into his neck. He dropped to the floor, choking and holding his hands to the bleeding wound. The guard lifted me gently into his arms, as if I weighed nothing. He turned to Seraphina, but she shook her head.

"No. Get out of here. Take care of her." Her voice was laced with pain as she spoke, but her eyes were sharp and commanding.

My guard didn't say a word, only nodded and walked to the window. He whispered a few words, and the glass exploded outward. He stepped to the ledge, and before I could think to scream, he jumped.

I wrapped my arms tightly around his neck and buried my head against his shoulder, waiting for us to smash into the earth. But we didn't. We were going up and up, into the sky. I peaked out and gasped at the sight of monstrous, breathtaking wings. His wings were a combination of black scales and deep-green feathers. His arms held me tight as his wings flapped powerfully against the wind.

Blackbyrn Manor faded away, and we swiftly left my prison behind. My arm throbbed, and my head drooped suddenly. I was losing too much blood, and my mind grew cloudy.

"I've got you, Tabitha. Stay with me, love. We'll be there soon," the guard spoke quietly, his deep voice a caress against my ear.

But I couldn't respond. I was fading fast. At least if this was the end, my guardian was here, holding me and making me feel safe. I tried to murmur a thank you, but the words came out jumbled. My eyes closed, and I let the darkness swallow me.

CHAPTER EIGHT
Andras

I stalked through the manor, glaring at anyone who attempted to speak to me. Many of the guards I knew, having been forced to grow up in this terrible place. Our fathers each had five personal guards who existed solely to protect them. Those fifteen or so men had been with The Obscuritas for years. They were almost as cruel and unfeeling as our fathers. Tony, one of my father's favorites, accompanied me back to The Towne House in Boston to retrieve Typhon's relic. Seraphina may not have known what she took, but I did. After she was taken from me, I was finally able to break into her safe. There wasn't much of importance, besides the relic. If only I had known Typhon wasn't bound by them sooner, this could've played out differently. It's no wonder Typhon was the first to be taken out. Our fathers needed to neutralize the one Prince they couldn't bring to heel. And with Seraphina within their grasp, he wouldn't dare attack them. We were outmaneuvered here, and we all knew it.

We took my father's private plane, and the entire excursion took approximately five hours. Tony attempted to speak to me several times, but eventually gave up when I ignored him. He had a thing for Michaela. Seraphina was going to murder this one when she had the chance.

My dark angel was at the forefront of my thoughts every minute I was away. Not knowing what my father would do to her while I was gone made my skin crawl. She was strong, the strongest woman I'd ever met, but he was ruthless. And the whole of his wrath was focused on her.

When we returned, Tony informed me Seraphina was with my father and they would both see me at dinner. This was deeply unsettling, but his guards blocked entry to the entire floor. They weren't in his rooms, but in the room he kept Tabitha. I hadn't seen it, but I was certain it was something out of a nightmare. Laszlo treated Tibby like she was an insect he couldn't wait to smash. My fury at the woman dissipated as soon as I discovered how deeply Laszlo controlled her mind. She was a shell of herself. My own mind was wracked with guilt over it. *How had I missed that?* I let the girl into my home, studied her, looked into her background, and still didn't realized how fucked the situation was.

If I couldn't see Seraphina before dinner, I would at least visit Typhon and Levi. Devon had his own cell down here as well, but I wasn't as keen to visit him. I knew my father put him in an impossible position, but I was still so angry with Devon for falling for our fathers' mind games in the first place. He should've come to me. I could have made him see sense. Or tried, at least. His failures only added to my own. Devon wouldn't have been so susceptible to their mind control if we stayed in touch. After his father died, he pulled away and I let him go. That was a mistake. Many years ago, the four of us were something fierce. Our bond was strong, making our power even stronger. We were a force to be reckoned with, and in that time the plans to overthrow our fathers emerged. Without Devon, the plans changed and everything became so much more difficult.

The two guards standing before the door leading to the cells where my brothers were being held were new. I stared them down, and their eyes flicked back and forth uneasily.

"I need to speak with the prisoners." My voice was sharp and threatening. I could sound like my father when it was necessary.

They hesitated for only a moment before unlocking the door and letting me pass. I descended into the darkness, only for motion-sensor lights to pop on as I arrived at the base of the stairs. Levi's cell was closest, and I walked to him quickly. He was lounging on the concrete bench at the back of the cell, leaning against the wall. They weren't much bigger than a small bedroom, with even less amenities.

"Comfortable?" I quipped.

Levi looked over at me with a lazy smile. "It's practically five star." He stood, coming to the bars, and we clasped hands, his eyes searching mine. "You're looking dapper, Andras. Pleasant afternoon?"

I rolled my eyes. "I went to Boston and retrieved Typhon's relic. They have them all now."

"Fucking hell," Ty snarled from his cell across the room. "Where's our girl?"

I shook my head with a frown. "I am not sure. I think she is in Tabitha's room. With my father."

Ty growled, his eyes darkening. "I need to get the fuck out of here so I can murder that motherfucker."

"Good luck with that," Devon mumbled from his own cell.

Resurrection

Ty slammed his forearms against the bars, his muscles bulging. "This is your fault, you little shit."

Devon jumped to his feet. "And what exactly have you done to help, asshole?"

"Stop it. Both of you," I snapped at them. "This won't help us or her."

Devon slumped back against the wall, his head drooping. He was hurting, and it killed me that we couldn't all come together to save our woman. Ty growled, his anger still raging. Without even his gym as an outlet, my volatile brother was going to come apart at the seams soon.

We all stiffened at the sound of someone coming down the stairs. When the figure descended enough for me to see them, I resisted the urge to sneer. Darren Radnor. What the fuck was he doing down here?

"Father," Ty growled. "I'm itching for a fight. Why not let me out so we can spar like old times?"

Darren smirked, the act unlike his usual dangerous smile. "Maybe another time, boy."

My eyebrows shot up, and Ty looked at him curiously. Darren Radnor never called Typhon "boy."

The next moment, Darren snapped his fingers and the lights flickered before going out.

"I have a very limited amount of time, and I am taking a risk here. Try to keep up." His voice startled me in the pitch-black room.

"What the fuck?" Ty growled.

The next moment, the lights came back on and standing before us was a goddamn monster. A true daemon. I jumped back, prepared to fight. My brothers all stood, rattling the bars of their cells in outrage.

"Who are you?" I demanded, and the daemon's glowing eyes turned to me.

He was close to seven feet tall, with black feathered wings and horns protruding from his dark hair. His feet were that of a beast's, with sharp claws on his fingers to match. He snarled, and the glint of sharp canines caught my eye.

He took a step toward me, and my brothers cried out in alarm, but something about him wasn't exactly threatening.

I cocked my head at him. "Where is Darren Radnor?"

The daemon stared at me for a moment before answering. "He is dead."

"Bullshit," Ty snarled.

The daemon growled back, and the sound was a bit more intimidating. "I found him assaulting Michaela. I tore him into pieces. He is dead."

Several seconds of silence passed before Typhon let out a low chuckle. His smile was dark and depraved. "Good."

The daemon nodded. "I am Morax. And I need your help to save them both."

I assumed he was speaking of Seraphina and her sister. When he spoke of her, the daemon softened. He had some connection to her.

Devon spoke up next. "How can we help, locked down here?"

The daemon eyed him before speaking. "You will be let out. The Kings plan to have you all at dinner this evening. They're putting on a show… Seraphina will see her sister for the first time. It will not go well."

Levi slammed his fists against the bars. "Did you hurt her sister?"

The daemon snarled, and his skin shone red as his eyes glowed a darker shade of gold. "Never. She is my mate. I would die before causing her harm."

That little revelation was less shocking, after his reaction, but still curious.

"I will repeat Devon's question, how can we help?"

Morax turned back to me. "The ritual your fathers have planned for Seraphina. It needs to happen as planned."

"Why the fuck would we do that?" Ty growled.

Levi frowned. "Are you asking us to let Seraphina die?"

Morax shook his head. "No, she won't die. My brother has seen to that. He has tainted their power, and when the ritual is completed, your relics will be destroyed and we can escape."

"Why not fight them then?" I asked curiously. "If we are free and able, we can take them out."

Morax shook his head. "No. It is not time. I cannot say more than that, but you have to trust me."

My trust was shared with very few people, and three of them were locked in cells. Trust would be difficult. But I did believe him. Hurting Seraphina would hurt Michaela, and if he was truly mated, as he said, to her, he wouldn't risk that.

"Can you save my sister?" Devon whispered, his voice low and hopeful.

Morax frowned and crossed his arms, tattooed biceps straining at the movement. He truly was a beast. Even with our abilities and wings, my brothers and I could not shift into daemons. I was a little envious. This is what my father sought, a true transformation. And Seraphina's sacrifice was supposedly going to make that happen.

"I cannot reach her mind. But we should bring her, when we escape," he offered, his voice kinder than it had been thus far. "Given some time, I may be able to help her. Or one of my kind that is more gifted with healing."

Devon nodded, his expression determined. "I will make sure she comes with us."

Morax studied Devon for a moment, a flash of emotion crossing his face. "Devon Parrish. Several months ago, Michaela and I saw something. A message recorded in secret by your father."

The room went deathly quiet. Devon's eyes bored into the daemon's, and we waited for him to continue.

"He said to tell you he loved you. And that he was sorry." Morax turned from Devon, his face kinder.

No friend of my father's would offer this kindness, and I decided then that I would trust the daemon. And in our current state, it might be the only option. "Alright—"

Before I could continue, a loud boom sounded, shaking the walls and rattling the windows.

"What the fuck was that?" Levi voiced the question first.

Morax stared up at the ceiling, as if he could see or hear what we could not. "We are out of time. I must go."

Screaming sounded through the manor and seared into my mind. The others began shouting. We all knew that voice.

"Seraphina!" Ty roared, rattling the bars of his cell and trying to force his power to obey him. But we were weakened when our fathers had our damn relics.

Morax turned for the stairs. He flicked his fingers, and the lights shut off and on once more. He was hidden again, and Darren Radnor stood in the daemon's place.

"Trust no one. Not even your own eyes. You have each other, that is it." Morax mumbled the words and stormed up the stairs.

I was eager to follow him and find our girl. She was in pain. More pain than I could handle standing idly by. And yet we had to be smart. I needed my brothers out of these damn cells, and we had to be there for the ritual. If we were to trust the daemon, our own inner monsters needed to slumber a little longer.

"I will see you soon, brothers," I stated, eyeing each of them.

Devon looked more like himself. His green eyes were fierce, and there was something of the man I knew many years ago staring back at me.

CHAPTER NINE
Seraphina

Guards flooded into the room a few moments after the guard leapt from the window. I don't know why I trusted him to take Tibby, but I did. Laszlo lay on the floor behind me, and I was honestly bummed I couldn't turn enough to watch him bleed.

From my peripheral, I watched as he pulled the knife from his neck and began chanting. Heat radiated around him as he huffed and leaned forward to sit up.

"Go fucking find them!" he shouted at the guards as they all stared dumbly at their bloody King.

Laughter bubbled out of me, and I couldn't stop it. Laszlo jumped to his feet, grabbing the stupid remote, and pressed down on the button angrily. Pain shot through me like wildfire. The electricity coursed through my veins and sizzled with enough force to knock out a regular person. But I refused. I forced my mind to stay coherent as the electric heat invaded every inch of my body. When it ended, I sagged against the chair, my body already trying to heal itself. I laughed again, and Laszlo grabbed my hair, tugging my head back to look up at him.

"All powerful King. Do you still feel like you're in control?" I laughed in his stupid face, not stopping even as he pressed the button and the electricity set my insides on fire again.

Resurrection

The girls screamed as I watched the gym burn. *The fire was out of control. I doused the entire place in gasoline. And the girls were screaming, begging me for help. Begging me to save them. But I just stood there, smiling.*

No. That wasn't right. It didn't happen like that. I cried when I heard them.

I didn't try to save them. I knew I wouldn't burn, but I still refused to save them. I let them scream.

No. That wasn't right either. I didn't know I could heal from that. I thought the fire was too much. I didn't know. I swear I didn't know.

Their screams grew louder and more piercing as their bodies burned. I didn't save them. I knew I could, but I didn't save them.

Someone was screaming. Something wet was on my face. Wait, *I* was screaming. I opened my eyes, and the images and sounds of the dream faded. That was just a dream. It didn't happen like that.

A dark chuckle sounded behind me, and I tried to move but realized quickly I was chained to a table. I was also almost naked, covered in only my black lace bra and underwear. A man walked around the table so I could see him. His face was passive, and his eyes were dead. More disturbing than Laszlo or Darren. This was Samuel Delano. I hated seeing the similarities between him and my Levi. Levi was so full of life and emotion. His father was dead inside.

I narrowed my eyes at him. "Stay the fuck out of my head, you sick fuck." *How did he even get in there?*

Samuel cocked his head to the side, studying me. "Me? I think you should be looking inward, daughter of Aurora. You're a murderer. They were children, and you left them to die." He tsked at me, shaking his head in mock sympathy. This monster had no actual feelings. "How do you think they felt, knowing someone they trusted left them to die? Burning alive is quite painful."

"Shut the fuck up!" I raged at him. "It was an accident. I didn't know they were in the building."

"Are you certain?" He walked casually around the table, running his hands up my leg, and I resisted the urge to vomit. "I think you knew. But it didn't matter, did it? Their father was your target, but taking them all out made it easier. No loose ends. Very clever."

I ground my teeth, seething. "That. Is. Not. What. Happened." Rage and guilt warred inside my mind. He was wrong.

"Tut tut." Samuel shook his head, his fingers walking lightly up my arm and across my chest. "You're just like us, Seraphina Valdis. Ruthless. Vile. Powerful. You could be a queen here."

Something shifted in his voice. It was soothing, forcing my rage back into its cage. He spoke softly as he traced his fingers over my skin. But it wasn't revolting, it was nice. He murmured words I didn't know between his comments of my rise to power. My chance to join them. Rule the weaker men. Take from them.

Part of my mind screamed to ignore this, ignore him, but I was so tired. His voice was a lullaby. "You can save them all. Join us. Claim your power, your true nature. A hunter. A killer."

"No." I tried to shake my head, but everything felt heavy,

weighed down by his words and my failures.

Seraphina. You're stronger than this.

The voice whispered from the depths of my mind, and I strained to hear it. I knew that voice.

"You're a killer. You will kill again. For us."

"No."

You can save them, Seraphina.

"You are one of us."

Save them. Save them all.

"Join us."

Save us.

"Join us."

I screamed, unable to take it any longer. The voice. My mother. It was my mother. I screamed and screamed, heat radiating out of me as a power exploded through the room. Samuel Delano flew through the air, his back slamming into the wall across the room before his body dropped to the floor.

The feeling of power and warmth faded quickly, and I lay there panting, confused, angry, and wracked with guilt.

Samuel groaned, picking himself off the floor and swiping away the dirt from his suit jacket. The Kings were always dressed in suits, entirely too self-important. He smiled as his blue eyes, too much like his son's, locked with mine. "How curious."

"Fuck you up the ass with a hot poker, Samuel Delano," I snapped at him. My brain throbbed like the worst hangover in the world. I needed a damn drink. And I had the strongest urge to stab someone.

"I have found that particular bit of torture to be quite effective, actually. Turns men into mewling babes." He slipped his hands into his pockets and cocked his head at me once more.

I wasn't even surprised by his response. "Perhaps you should try it out."

He chuckled. "Perhaps."

I pulled against the chains keeping me locked to the table. "Where the fuck is my sister? I demand you let me see her."

Samuel moved closer to the table and reached out, tracing circles across my stomach. "You will see her this evening. We have much to plan before the big event. Your full cooperation will be required."

I rolled my eyes, jerking away from his disgusting hands roaming over my skin. "Good fucking luck with that."

His hand snapped out and gripped my cheeks hard, nearly enough to make my eyes water. Sadistic lust filled his gaze. "If you do not, your sister will be given to me next."

"If you fucking touch her, I. Will. Kill. You." I growled through the pain of his fingers digging into my face.

"We will see." Samuel smacked my cheek like the jackass he was and left the room.

Guards entered a few moments later. I let them pull me along through the manor, back to my own room. My mind was reeling. I heard my mother's voice. I knew it was her. How did that even happen? And that heat. The power that exploded out of me. I never felt anything like it, but how could I summon it again? My back tingled and itched like my skin was too tight and something needed to escape. There was something powerful building inside me, something hiding beneath the surface. And I needed to find a way to let it out.

CHAPTER TEN

Michaela

I paced my room, waiting for Morax to return. He had to play the role of King Darren Radnor. Every moment he wore the guise of that monster was hell. I craved Morax with every fiber of my being, but when he had to touch me as Darren, I wanted to vomit. I knew it was worse for him, though, even when he said it wasn't. He was forced to degrade me, taunt me, and claim my belly was filled with his child. Morax was clever, though. He found ways to avoid hurting me or assaulting me too severely when the other Kings demanded it. And with the ruse of my pregnancy, they were willing to be gentler. At least until the fake baby was born. Then I was promised to Samuel. I shivered. Samuel Delano terrified me. His soulless eyes were far more terrifying than the heated violence Darren had.

The nervous energy that had me pacing the room didn't come from waiting for my daemon, though. In a short time, I would see my sister. She'd been captive in this stupid place for days, but tonight we would finally be reunited. It was a bittersweet moment, considering the Kings would be there. I was nervous. Would she remember me? Did she think about our childhood as often as I did? And her seeing me pregnant... I had a bad feeling about that.

The door to Darren's room opened, and Morax stepped

inside. He couldn't drop the illusion, unfortunately. The magic was courtesy of our new ally, Gremory Carreveaux. Grem was a daemon, like Morax. He was the highest ranking General of the Royal Army in Caligo, their home. Morax was skeptical of Grem's allegiance, but over the few months I'd been captive here, he'd proved to be our friend.

"How did it go?" I asked, rushing to him anxiously.

Morax dropped to one knee and took my hands in his. He brought them close to his lips, barely brushing against my knuckles. He refused to kiss me while in this form. And I hated that I agreed with him.

"*Mae domina.* Gremory has escaped with Tabitha." Morax whispered the words. Even with his heightened senses, he wouldn't take the chance of others hearing our conversation. "She was badly hurt, but he got her out. He will heal her."

I sighed with relief. Tabitha deserved this, more than anyone. The torture and mind control she faced from Laszlo was disgustingly intrusive. "I'm so glad. Hopefully that little incident will keep their minds occupied and away from us."

Morax nodded. "It should help. Your sister, they tortured her too."

The sound of her tormented screams was branded within my mind. I swallowed audibly. "I heard her cry out several times. What did they do?"

He frowned, staring into my eyes with uncertainty. My fierce daemon didn't want to cause me pain, even with this. If souls could speak, mine would sing with pleasure for the care Morax had for me. I nodded encouragingly, and he sighed.

"Laszlo was electrocuting her. The amount of electricity

would have killed a human instantly. She is quite strong. She laughed at them even as she screamed."

Tears burned my eyes, my fury needing an outlet, but I smiled. "Damn, that's badass. I hate that she was hurting. But at least she gave them hell."

Morax wiped away my tears. "She is…chaotic. I can see how one male is not enough for her."

I barked a laugh, and Morax smirked. "And I'm what, simple? Maybe I need another boyfriend."

He stood, snarling and towering over me. His alluring eyes glowed, turning gold with power as his possessive nature emerged. I smirked at him, backing away slowly. Morax's shining eyes tracked my movements like a predator's.

"You are mine, little doe," Morax growled. "Mine to hunt. Mine to feast upon. *Mine.*"

My back hit the wall, and I stared into his stunning daemon eyes. The flesh of Darren Radnor faded as I got lost in my daemon's liquid gold gaze. I reached out and ran my hand along his sharp jawline.

"Yours."

Morax released a pleasant sound, like a growl mixed with a purr. "I do not have it in me to share you with anyone else, *mae domina.*"

I smiled at him. "I don't want anyone else. You're everything I could ever need."

He made that sound again, and I wanted desperately to curl up against his daemon form and press my ear to his chest. "And you are anything but simple, Michaela Valdis. You are fierce, brave, determined, and filled with more compassion for others than anyone I have ever known."

My cheeks flushed at his words. "Time to use some of that bravery."

Morax frowned, and his eyes returned to the dull brown of Darren Radnor's. He nodded and walked to the dresser, pulling out the stupid collar and leash I always wore around the other Kings. His hands were gentle as he clasped the collar around my neck. Tonight, I wore a bright-blue, floor-length gown with an empire waist. The gown worked with the baby bump I was now sporting, mimicking a five-month long pregnancy. The illusion was simple enough. Gremory taught Morax the words he needed to create it each time we were outside of this bedroom. It did feel strange, almost real. I wrapped my hands around the bump, comforting my non-existent child. Someday, when the Kings were all dead and life was easier, children might be nice.

My daemon held out his arm, and I slipped mine through. He gave my fingers a squeeze and let his eyes glow just enough for me to be sure that my daemon was still here. It was time. I was finally going to see my sister.

CHAPTER ELEVEN
Seraphina

The pain from my afternoon of torture was gone, but the dull ache of Samuel invading my mind still persisted. It was really fucking annoying. His intrusion was the first time I felt someone inside my mind and that would never be happening again. The Kings and even the Princes of The Obscuritas were far more advanced in the use of their powers, that was obvious. Up until a few months ago, I didn't even know I *had* powers, other than fast healing. The maddening part of it all was I had no control over my own. I healed myself without thought, and anything else was beyond my reach. Knowing what I do now, there were so many moments I could recall feeling something. Some other thing filling my veins and writhing beneath the surface, desperate to get out. But I couldn't access that power. It wouldn't answer me—not until that fantastic moment when I tossed Samuel Delano across the room. My power came to me then, and the rush was unlike anything I had ever felt. Well, almost anything. Thoughts of my men slithered into the forefront of my mind and sent shivers down to my overzealous clit. Since the stolen time in the woods with Dev, I was practically fiending for their touch.

It was also easier to focus on them instead of the impending meeting tonight. My sister. I was finally going to see my baby sister. Almost a decade apart, and here we were, back where it all began. Maybe that was a good thing. Like a full circle moment. But how would she act? What would she think of me? If I saw so much as a hint of a bruise on her, I'd burn this fucking place to the ground with everyone in it, myself included. I don't think I could handle seeing her hurt by the cult that already took our other sister and our mother.

The fact I hadn't even thought of my father did not go unnoticed. I was too angry with him. Angry that he let this stupid cult get their hands on Michaela. Angry that he couldn't save our mother and sister. And angry that he left me and never looked back. Why should I care for a father who never cared to find me?

Angry tears burned my eyes, and I shoved thoughts of my father and any other messy emotions deep, deep down. I stalked into the bathroom and checked my hair and makeup. The Kings left several dresses for me, via their guards. I wished for my leggings and boots, but apparently women could only dress like slutty debutantes in this fucking place.

The gown I slipped into now was made of the softest velvet. The fabric clung to my curves especially well, and the deep shade of red looked like blood. I found a red lipstick to match the dress. The dark smokey eye makeup paired well. I was going for goddess of death vibes and really thought I nailed it.

I slipped on the black stilettos last, smoothing out the beautiful gown in annoyance. Why did evil assholes give good presents?

A guard tapped on my door but did not speak. I smirked,

opening the door and stepping out. Two guards backed away, giving me a wide berth. They were all mildly terrified of me.

"Shall we go to dinner?" I smiled, showing far too many teeth and making them fidget awkwardly. I didn't bother waiting for their reply before charging down the hall and through the maze of doors to arrive at the Dining Hall.

This place was massive. Tibby and I had studied the building plans extensively. I knew this day would come eventually, and I at least wanted to know my way around. Thinking of my only friend sent a piercing hurt directly to my soul. Laszlo had fucked her up so royally, and he would pay for that. I didn't even get to tell her I loved her before that crazy ass guard, who was definitely not a guard, whisked her away. I hoped she was safe somewhere now.

Two more guards stood before the doors of the Dining Hall, opening them slowly as I approached. I was growing utterly bored of only seeing guards dressed in riot gear and The Obscuritas Kings. When the doors opened and I turned my gaze to the table at the center of the room, I smiled something fierce to see my men waiting for me. They were all there, dressed impeccably in tailored suits.

Ty stalked toward me. His eyes narrowed as he licked his lips and examined me from the swish of my dress against the floor to the silvery blue curls on top of my head. He wore a black, three-piece suit with a black shirt beneath. Ty looked like a wild animal forced into submission. I wanted the beast to come out and play. He growled as he approached, snaking one arm around my waist. The other gripped the back of my neck possessively.

"My pet," he purred, his lips so close to mine. "You look fucking edible. I'm about to rip this dress from your flesh and fuck you against the wall."

His words melted my insides, and I licked my lips, loving his eyes raking over me. "Are you expecting me to say no, because that's a fuck yes."

Ty chuckled, and I heard Levi's laughter collide with it. I leaned around my monster man and smiled at Levi. His suit was a deep navy blue and matched his eyes perfectly. He wore a crisp white shirt beneath it, the top buttons undone and informal, the flames tattooed on his chest just barely peeking out.

He cocked his head and brought his rough hands against my cheek. "*Nuestra Diosa de la Muerte*. Have you come to collect our souls?"

I leaned into his touch. "I am quite hungry for souls. Specifically those of the four devils I see before me."

Andras joined us then, his cold mask melting only slightly as his eyes locked with mine. "Only you could look so tempting when the world is burning, my dark angel." He leaned in close. "Do you like the dress?"

My mouth popped open, and I laughed. "More now that I know it was you and not the fucking Kings who knew my tastes so well."

Andras smirked. I noticed then the rouge pocket square tucked into his charcoal jacket was the exact shade of my dress. Before I could let loose another sassy comment, Dev walked up to us, more slowly than the others and looking reserved. I thought of his sister, and my heart went to him.

"Hi, Dev," I whispered, studying his gorgeous face. "How

are you?"

Dev's head dipped, hiding his beautiful green eyes from me. "You look beautiful, Seraphina."

He turned swiftly and went back to the table. His suit was similar to Ty's, but with a white shirt beneath. The tailored pants did wonders for his ass, and I bit my lip, watching him walk away.

I wanted to go to him, to tell him it would be alright and we would fix this, but I didn't even know if I believed that.

"He will come back to us. We will get through this. Together." Levi rubbed my back gently, offering comfort.

I nodded, forcing my emotions down once more. There was nothing else to say in that moment, not with so many villains among us. We walked to the table as one. It was a large dining table, set for twelve people. I was curious to find out who would be filling the extra seats.

A member of the kitchen staff directed us to our assigned seats. We were not allowed to sit, but made to stand behind the chairs and wait for the oh-so-important Kings. Ty was placed next to me, at the middle of the table. An empty seat was on my other side. Andras was seated diagonally to my left, at the right of the head seat. I assumed Laszlo would be there, the entitled prick. Dev took his place next to Andras. Levi was moved to the same side of the table as me and Ty, but at the far end, closest to the end seat. I had a feeling his father would be seated there, which was a bit unnerving. This was going to be the dinner party from hell.

Chapter Twelve
Leviathan

Keeping my thoughts civilized when Seraphina looked like a goddess of the dark and dangerous variety was nearly impossible. Fuck, I was in love with this woman. She radiated strength and power so forcefully, I almost dropped to my knees when she entered the room. She was a queen, and I would follow her through the gates of hell if she asked.

We only waited by our seats at the table for a few minutes before the men we were forced to call our fathers entered the room. They swept in like a hurricane, commanding the attention of everyone. I hated them so viscerally, and my daemon roared, eager to be unleashed. But while they held our relics, we could not harm them directly.

I heard Seraphina's intake of breath when she spotted her sister. I could see the resemblance. Michaela had a lovely face, with a mouth shaped like her sister's. She was slimmer than Seraphina, with long golden hair that reminded me of their mother. Michaela's eyes were her most striking feature, one sky blue and the other a golden brown. But it was not her lovely face that caused my girl to gasp.

Michaela had a crude collar around her neck, with the leash attached to it held by Ty's father, Darren Radnor. Darren wore an easy smile, his eyes watching Seraphina as she took in the state of her younger sister. But it wasn't Darren. It was the daemon, Morax, I reminded myself. Unfortunately, our girl didn't know that yet.

Seraphina snarled and, before we could stop her, ran at Darren. Guards jumped in front of her, and in a matter of seconds, she stole a gun from one and had both bleeding at her feet. She stepped over them and pointed the gun at Darren. More guards poured into the room and aimed their weapons at Seraphina.

I roared at them, rushing to her side with my brothers and ordering them to stand down. Laszlo and my own father watched the scene unfold with bored expressions.

"What the fuck do you think you are doing with my sister?" Seraphina snarled at Darren.

Darren leaned forward, tugging the leash and pulling Michaela closer to him. "Whatever the fuck I want."

Michaela reached down suddenly and cradled her belly, which I hadn't noticed was sporting a swollen belly. She was pregnant. Oh shit. Morax left that bit of information out when he came to us in the cells.

Seraphina seemed to notice this at the same moment, and in seconds she spun and kicked out, knocking Darren to the floor and releasing his hold on her sister. She aimed the gun at his head. "Fuck you."

Michaela dropped suddenly, her body covering Darren's. "No!" she shouted, raising a hand and staring down her sister.

Seraphina paused, her eyes widened in shock. "Kaela." She whispered her sister's name. "What the fuck are you doing?"

Darren rolled over, awkwardly getting to his feet. He looked furious and took a dangerous step toward our girl. I had to actively remind myself it wasn't Ty's horrible father any longer.

Ty stepped in front of Seraphina, his chest level with his father's. He growled, a dangerous edge to the sound. "I will kill you before you touch her."

My father's laughter caused everyone to pause and turn their gazes in his direction. Samuel crossed his arms, and his naturally blank face looked positively amused. "Darren. Is your captive in love with you? What a spectacle that was."

Darren chuckled, plucking the leash from where it dangled at Michaela's side. "Yes, I think she enjoys what I have to offer. My cock is her favorite toy."

Seraphina screamed, attempting to plow through Ty and attacked, but he grabbed her around the waist and held tightly. "Not now, Seraphina. Not now." He whispered the words against her ear.

She looked miserably at her sister, the devastation plain on her face. My heart broke for her, but there was nothing any of us could do in that moment. She didn't know what we knew about Darren's death. The man her sister protected was her mate. We needed to find a way to tell Seraphina this news before she inadvertently killed the love of her sister's life.

"Now that that's done with, everyone take your seats." Laszlo's sharp voice cut through the tension, forcing us all to listen.

Ty kept his arm around Seraphina's waist as he guided her to her seat. Staff appeared, pulling out each chair and tucking us in against the table. Several seats were still empty, I noticed. My father sat to my right, eyeing me with amusement.

"Don't worry, the others will be in shortly," he said, taking a sip of the bourbon a servant brought to him.

My father's smirk was more unsettling paired with the endless nothing in his eyes. I did not like the way he spoke, and I knew Michaela's pregnancy was only the first surprise of the evening.

The doors against the far wall opened, and I cursed beneath my breath when I spied who the remaining guests were. Dev's sister stalked toward us, her head held high. She wore a simple black dress, and her dark hair was braided down her back. Her gaze remained above the table, refusing to look at her brother who was staring wide-eyed at her.

Leyja took the seat to the left of Laszlo's, next to Seraphina. She didn't speak, and Seraphina eyed her curiously from the side. But her attention was quickly turned to the final guests.

"Audrey!" Seraphina shouted her friend's name and stood from her seat.

Ty grasped her wrist, forcing her to stay at the table.

Her head snapped to Laszlo, and she snarled at him. "Let her go. She doesn't deserve this."

Laszlo leaned back in his chair with an easy smirk. "I have done nothing. It is her father who made the choice."

I turned to the man walking behind Audrey. He looked like a sub if I'd ever seen one. Why our fathers wanted him in The Obscuritas was beyond me. He took the seat across from me, his graying hair disheveled and his suit slightly wrinkled. Mr. Kingston did not look like a man capable of attaining power of any kind. But he must be important for him to be seated at this table. Audrey, I was sure, was only here to keep her father compliant.

The scheming of our fathers was something I never wanted to be part of, and yet I was always roped into it. My part in their plans was obvious from boyhood. I shared my father's eyes, but it was my mother who granted me a striking face. She was a beauty, my father told me, and I inherited that beauty, turning me into the handsome Prince our fathers needed to draw men and women alike to their stupid cult. I was forced to feed desires of all kinds in the name of The Obscuritas. When my brothers found out how truly used I had become, they banded together with me and ended it. Seraphina was the first woman I gave myself to of my own free will. She drew me in so fully, made me feel safe and seen and wanted in ways no other person had.

I picked up my whiskey and took a long pull of the harsh liquor. These thoughts were too heavy, and I needed to keep my shields fortified against my father. I glanced in his direction, but he was staring at Audrey.

The girl was silent and rigid in her seat next to mine. I didn't see any obvious bruises, but my father preferred to fuck with people's minds first. I pitied the girl. If we could get her out of this, we would.

"Father." Andras spoke first, after the final guests were seated and served drinks. "I am somewhat surprised to see we are having this dinner, after the events earlier today."

Andras eyed his father with a smirk, and I was equally satisfied to see Laszlo's cold mask slip. His eye twitched, and I swore he almost growled.

"My slave will be found and returned to her place at my feet soon enough. We are confident of that."

"Are you?" Seraphina cut in, leaning forward. "I'm not. Did you see that thing? He had wings and shit. Do you have some flying monkeys hidden away to chase them?"

I snorted a laugh, earning a raised eyebrow from my father, but I could care less what he thought. Even less about the repercussions of my actions. We were not strangers to torture at the hands of our fathers.

Laszlo ignored Seraphina as the servants brought out the first course. Darren picked up a spoon and scooped out a small bite of the cucumber soup and fed it to Michaela. His gaze turned to Seraphina, and he winked.

In the next second, Darren had a fork lodged in his upper shoulder. He snarled, ripping it out as Seraphina seethed from across the table.

Ty chuckled. "You shouldn't provoke her so, father."

"Next time, it will be your eye," Seraphina raged at Darren, holding her butter knife.

Darren leaned toward her, his eyes narrowed. "If you cannot keep your little psycho in check, boy, I will."

I smiled broadly. "There is not a soul on this Earth who can keep our diabla in check. And even if we could, I would never do so."

Seraphina's gaze turned to me, and she smiled. Her eyes still held fury and sadness in equal parts, but I would do whatever I could to take both away.

"When the full moon is upon us, the ritual that was meant to be so long ago shall commence." Laszlo's sharp voice forced everyone at the table to listen.

Except for Seraphina. "And what exactly does this ritual

entail? Another lame attempt to gain power that doesn't belong to you? Killing more women because they won't sleep with you?"

Pride filled my soul at her defiance. Our girl was brave and refused to cower to the men who created us. But Laszlo was not easily deterred. And with the disruption earlier, he seemed more determined than ever.

"Your life, like your mother's and your two sisters', is meaningless." Laszlo's words were cold, and his eyes filled with icy fury as he stared at Seraphina. "The power running through your veins belongs to me. To The Obscuritas. To men who understand it and will wield it the way it was meant to be wielded."

Seraphina shook with rage. Michaela's eyes dropped to the table, her lips set in a grim line. Darren tugged at her leash. No one else was looking at them, and the look in his eyes was strange to see on the man I knew who only brought pain. He wanted to comfort her. The look faded quickly, and the evil smile returned as Laszlo turned to Darren.

"Take your toy back to your bed," Laszlo started, but Seraphina interrupted.

"No!" She snarled at them, slamming her steak knife on the table. She brought it up to her throat. "I will kill myself and ruin your fucking ritual right now if you send her back to that fucking monster."

Ty moved to take the knife, but she growled at him, her aquamarine eyes blazing with fury.

CHAPTER THIRTEEN
Seraphina

I was fucking heartbroken and filled with more rage than I could imagine. Morbid images of Darren Radnor raping my sister flashed in my mind. And now she was pregnant with his child. I had thought of a million scenarios for how things would go the first time I saw her again, and none ended like this. An inferno was building inside my soul. I needed to unleash it on the Kings. I would flay them alive and laugh as they screamed. My sister, my baby fucking sister. I failed her. Our father failed her. *Where was he?* He said leaving me behind would protect her. But he was wrong. Her barely swollen belly proved that.

The blade of the knife shook as my fury grew, and I barely registered the blood beginning to drip down my neck from the cut.

"Seraphina," Andras snapped, and the sound of his fear pulled me back. "Don't."

My eyes shot up to meet his, and I paused. "I will die before she spends another moment alone with him."

Andras frowned and looked on the verge of speaking, his eyes drilling into mine. In them, I saw anger, fear, and something else. As if he was begging me to understand something beyond what was happening here.

He turned to his father. "Perhaps you should consider giving Seraphina some time with her sister? You do need her alive to perform the ritual, do you not?"

Laszlo's lazy smirk was beyond irritating. I snarled at him, refusing to back down. He merely watched me with mild annoyance and amusement. As if I were a wild cat he cornered and decided to keep as a pet. But I would not be stuck in a corner created by the Kings.

I sliced the blade another centimeter across my neck, and Ty growled beside me.

"Stop it." His voice was deep and demanding.

But I would not stop. Not for him. Not for any of them. My entire plan of revenge against this fucking cult was falling apart.

"Very well." Laszlo finally spoke, his tone commanding attention whether we wanted to give it or not. "The guards will escort Seraphina and Michaela back to Darren's rooms. You will have ten minutes to speak to each other in private. Then Michaela will stay with her King."

I wanted to scream. There was no way I would leave her alone with him. But Michaela stood before I could speak and bowed her head.

"Thank you. We will go now." She walked slowly around the table until she was at my side. "Please, sister."

I couldn't refuse her. I dropped the knife, and it clattered loudly against the floor. "Fine."

Michaela threaded her arm through mine and forced me to move. We walked in silence, heavy with so much emotion I wanted to hurl myself through a window. Or maybe I would just hurl us both through a window. Perhaps there was another winged man disguised as a guard who would come and save us. Thinking of the stranger and Tibby shattered my heart into even smaller pieces. I continued to fail everyone I cared for. The Kings were always one step ahead. I let the Princes claw their way under my defenses and in falling for them, I failed to save the ones I cared for most.

My heart was being caged once more. I could feel the walls around it building back up, brick by brick. These feelings were a weakness, and I refused to be ruled by weakness.

"Sister," Michaela whispered as we walked closer to her prison. "It is not what you think. Do not trust everything you see."

Her words brought up a memory. A voice whispering to me in the dark. *Trust what you feel, not what you see.*

How could I trust what I felt? All I felt was rage and sorrow.

Don't give up on them. The other words uttered to me in the dark sank into my bones. Did the voice know I would try to push them away? Try to cut the feelings I had for the Princes from my heart?

A guard stood at the door of the bedroom and opened it for us. Michaela went in first, pulling me behind her. She gripped my hand, dragging me into the bathroom. She turned on both faucets of the double sink and turned back to me. Worry filled her mismatched eyes. And then she smiled. Michaela threw her arms around me and hugged me so fiercely I could do nothing but hug her back.

"Sister," she whispered. "I am so freaking happy to see you."

I snorted a laugh. "Not exactly how I wanted our reunion to go. I was hoping to have the dead bodies of the Kings at our feet."

Michaela pulled away and grinned. "Soon. You will. I know it."

I stared into her eyes, so full of life and determination. "How are you so sure? After everything, after what's been done to you…" Bile rose up in my throat, and I could not finish the sentence.

My sweet sister shook her head. "It is not what you think. I promise."

We both turned as the bedroom door opened. I searched for a weapon, but unless I could kill Darren Radnor with a bar of soap, there wasn't much for me to do but let this all play out, one way or another.

"Stay behind me," I growled, forcing my sister back.

Darren strode through the room and leaned against the frame of the bathroom door, assessing us both. "Time's up."

I was on the verge of screaming at him when a small laugh from Michaela made me pause. I turned to her in shock. "Why in the hell are you laughing?"

But she wasn't looking at me. She was staring at the King, her eyes twinkling with secrets. "You first."

I looked back at Darren, only it wasn't Darren at all. In the doorway stood a massive creature. The suit he wore was practically bursting at the seams now that this thing wore it. His skin was tinted red, and horns protruded from his dark wavy hair. His eyes were golden, and when he smiled, the sharp glint of fangs caught my eye. He was a daemon. A fucking daemon was standing in front of me.

"Hello, psycho girl." The daemon chuckled. "Can't say I

Resurrection

am surprised you tried to kill me. Or Darren, rather. But you should know, I have already had the privilege."

Words evaded me as I processed what the daemon was saying. Michaela grabbed my hand and brought it to her now very flat belly. I looked at her with so many questions on the tip of my tongue.

"We had to make them believe it, sister." Michaela squeezed my hand. "And there was no time to tell you sooner. But it's not real. I'm not pregnant."

Relief flooded my system like a drug I desperately needed. "So he didn't hurt you? Didn't...assault you?"

Michaela's face fell, and the anger returned. "He did. But Morax arrived before he could actually get his gross dick anywhere but my mouth."

My own mouth dropped open at my sister's blunt and vulgar words. Anger writhed inside me like a living thing, and the daemon behind me growled his own fury. My sister and I both looked at him.

He dropped to one knee and bowed his head. "I will forever be shamed that I did not arrive before that filth could harm my mate."

"Morax." Michaela whispered his name softly. She walked around me and went to him, placing her hand on his shoulder.

"I'm sorry. Your what now?" Alarm bells rang out in my brain.

The daemon looked up at me with a smirk. He stood, pulling my sister in close and bringing her hand to his lips. He kissed her palm gently, staring into her eyes as he answered. "I am Morax Ormaenus, Royal Prince of Caligo. And your sister, this perfect being at my side, is my mate."

My eyes were practically bugging out of my head. "So like, you love her? You're together?"

Morax rolled his eyes at me, and I really wished there was a utensil in here to stab him with. "Michaela Valdis owns my soul. My heart is hers for eternity. So yes, I love her and we are 'together' as you so carelessly put it."

Yeah, I wanted to stab him again. I crossed my arms instead. "Listen here, daemon guy. She is *my* sister, and I claimed her for life long before you got here. Besides, you let them hurt her. Why didn't you stop them if you're so fucking powerful?"

Michaela frowned at me, but I kept my gaze level. If he was so badass and loved her so much, he should have saved her sooner. Morax let go of her and stepped before me. I had to crane my neck to look up at him; he was so fucking tall. And fucking massive. He was even bigger than Ty.

"I will accept any punishment you see fit to give me for failing your sister."

He bowed to me, and I flicked my eyes to my sister. She stared at me, pleading with her wild eyes for me to do something. I wasn't sure what. But I could see she cared for the creature, and he for her. And he did kill Darren.

I rolled my eyes. "Can you bring that fucker back to life so I can kill him?"

Morax gazed down at me with a smile so dark. "I wish, psycho girl. I would enjoy watching you cut him to pieces."

"Well on that, we are in agreement."

He chuckled.

I stared at him, recognition dawning. "It was you, wasn't

it? The one who spoke to me down in that dungeon?"

He nodded. "Yes. And I gave you a stimulant to counteract the drug you were given."

I leaned against the counter, listening to the water still rushing from the faucets. "Seems I have a lot to catch up on."

Michaela came up beside the daemon. Morax, as if sensing her every movement, turned to the side and wrapped his arm around her waist. This bathroom, although massive, was much too small with a big fucking daemon in it.

"We don't have time to reveal all, but there is one thing you must know," Morax began, and his serious tone had my thoughts scattering. "You must go through with the ritual."

The blood drained from my face. "What the fuck are you talking about?"

Morax leveled a sharp look my way. "There is so much more at stake than the corrupt plans of The Obscuritas Kings. When I have the time to tell you, I will. But know this, my brother has manipulated things from Caligo. You will not die in the ritual. But your blood will bring Phenex forth. And to survive this, to save us all, we need him. And we need you." His voice was so determined I wanted to laugh.

"Michaela and I watched our sister, our mother… We watched them both die in one of The Obscuritas' rituals."

Michaela's face fell, but she recovered quickly. "It will not be the same. I believe him, sister. I trust him."

Her eyes were wide and insistent. Part of me believed her, and the other part was certain my death was inevitable. I sighed. "Do the Princes know any of this?"

The daemon nodded. "I revealed myself to them recently.

When Gremory took Tabitha away."

My head snapped up at his words. "He was like you? He saved her?"

Morax nodded, and Michaela smiled. "Yes, he is a daemon. Not a royal, but the General of the Royal Army. She is safe and he will protect her."

Emotions threatened to bubble out of me. Tibby was safe and away from the horrors of this place. What would happen next, I wasn't sure. But I had to trust my sister and these daemons who were apparently on our side. My shoulders slumped, and I was suddenly exhausted. This clusterfuck of a day needed to end. A strong drink and a twelve hour nap sounded magical right now.

I stood, crossing my arms once more. "Alright. Well, I think that's enough for today. Don't want anyone getting suspicious of us."

Morax nodded. "I will call for the guard to escort you to your rooms."

Michaela hugged me close as her daemon went to the door, disguising his voice to sound like Darren. She was a few inches taller than me and slender where I had muscle. I hugged her back more gently, unwilling to hurt her in any way.

"We're going to get through this, Seraphina," she whispered. "Together."

CHAPTER FOURTEEN
Typhon

I paced Seraphina's rooms, waiting for her to return. Now that the Kings thought we were compliant, we had a bit more freedom. Freedom was a strong word, though. The Kings still held us by the balls while the fuckers had our relics hidden somewhere in the manor. Morax revealed to us the relics would be destroyed through the ritual, and since we were royally fucked right now, his word was the only one we trusted.

"Will you desist?" Andras growled, leaning against the far wall. "Your pacing is irritating."

"You know I enjoy irritating you, brother." I smirked, continuing my tour of the suite given to our girl. Of course, our fathers flaunted their money and power by putting her in a suite instead of a dungeon cell. Giving her a bedroom was meant to make her think she wasn't powerful enough to bother locking up. The day she proved them all wrong would be especially sweet.

"Where the fuck is she?" I snarled, irritated that others were keeping her from us.

Andras sighed. "It's only been fifteen minutes. I'm sure she will be back soon."

I stopped and cocked my head, letting my daemon out to listen for any approaching footsteps. A devilish smirk lit up my face. "Perhaps we should hide. I want to taste her fear when I pounce."

Andras, the cold bastard, turned his head to hide, the mirth threatening to show on his face. My brother needed his freedom from this life even more than I did. I missed the smiles and laughter he often shared with us in youth. In fairness, none of us laughed like we did back then. Our fathers took whatever measures they could to ensure happiness was always out of reach. Until she arrived.

Seeing her at dinner, pressing the knife to her own throat, made my heart freeze. I understood why she did it; the devastation was plain on her face when she saw her sister with Darren. We could do nothing, say nothing, as she processed the illusion Michaela and her daemon played out in front of the Kings.

I hoped after speaking with Michaela and her daemon just now, she wouldn't be so willing to die. When the blood trickled down her neck, fear and lust warred within me. I wanted to lean over and lick the nectar from her perfect skin. And throttle her for thinking she could leave this Earth without me. My very being was tethered to hers. If she thought for a moment I would survive without her—that any of us would—she was severely wrong.

The door opened, and I immediately grabbed her throat, pulling her into the room and shoving her against the wall. I snarled in her face. Seraphina didn't even look scared. My little pet stared back at me with equal measures of anger and lust. Her monsters were just as eager as my own to come out and play.

"Did you think you could get away with that little stunt at

dinner, pet?" I growled, bringing my face down so it was level with her own. "If you ever, *ever*, threaten to take your own life again, I will follow you into the afterlife and torment you for eternity." I squeezed her throat tightly, cutting off any air supply to let her know how serious I was.

Her nostrils flared, and she bared her teeth at me. Fuck, I adored this woman. I slammed my lips to hers, forcing her mouth open and claiming her with my teeth and tongue. She fought me, her nails digging into my biceps as I released her throat just enough for her to breathe.

Andras walked closer to us, and I felt his presence a moment before he ripped Seraphina from my arms. He held her tightly, his large hands cupping her cheeks. She was breathing heavily, looking up into his dark eyes. They stared at each other for several moments. Seeing my brother like this gave me hope. Our girl had no idea how reserved Andras was, how few people he trusted. How many women tried to get close to him, and how many of them he shut down. Seraphina carved her way into our souls, and she would never be rid of us.

"Did they tell you everything?" Andras whispered, the slightest hint of concern in his tone.

Seraphina nodded, closing her eyes. "Yes. I know about the illusions. And the ritual."

Andras straightened, his mouth a grim line. "I don't like it, but I do believe Morax and his plan. He cares about your sister, and killing you would hurt her."

She shrugged. "I would die for my sister, especially if it would save her life."

Andras tensed, his emotions coming through at her careless

words. "Oh really, sweetheart? Did Typhon not make it clear to you how important you are to us? And you would leave us?"

Her face scrunched, and her eyes darted between mine and his. "Don't make me choose between you and my sister."

Andras let go of her and stepped back. "I would never, my angel. There will never be a day where I would make you choose. But know this. If you die, we will follow you. In this life and every other. You're ours."

Seraphina's eyes blazed with emotion, and she licked her lips. I tracked the movement, needing to taste her. Every inch of her.

"I'm yours." Her voice was low and filled with lust.

"Get on your knees," Andras commanded, and my dick jumped to attention.

Seraphina smiled like the Cheshire Cat, and I knew she was eager to play. "Make me."

Andras chuckled. "Typhon."

I was already moving, knowing what he wanted. Seraphina's eyes widened moments before I prowled behind her. I slipped my hands in her hair and tugged her head back. In the same instant, I kicked out her knees and forced her to the ground. My grip tightened in her hair, and she gasped, looking up at us with those mesmerizing aquamarine eyes. Her tongue slipped out and licked her lips once more, and I growled possessively.

"Very good, sweetheart. Don't you look lovely on your knees for us," Andras purred, his voice as sharp as the edge of a blade. My brother could weaponize words like a pro.

Seraphina's hand snapped out, and she grabbed his belt to tug him closer. "As if you could put me here"—her words were soft, forcing us to lean in and listen—"against my will."

Resurrection

Her nimble fingers quickly unbuckled his belt. She pulled it through the loops, but before she could discard it, Andras held out his hand. Seraphina smirked up at him and placed the leather belt across his palm. My dick throbbed at the simple act. She was right. Seraphina might be the one on her knees, but she held us in the palms of her pretty little hands. She could ask anything of me, and I would give it.

I held her hair up while Andras slipped the belt around her slender neck. He slipped it through the buckle and slid the leather tightly around her throat. He tugged the leash, forcing her to stand.

"Typhon, our girl is wearing too many clothes." Andras smirked, his dark eyes boring into hers as he gave me the not-so-subtle command.

The dress Seraphina wore was stunning, but it also came from this house and our fathers, and therefore I hated it. I pulled a slim knife from my pocket and began slicing down the back of her dress.

She laughed as I cut the soft fabric away from her body. "Who let you have a weapon?"

I chuckled in her ear and nipped at her jaw. "As if they could stop me from having a little fun. Or stealing a weapon or two."

The dress was officially offending me, so I knelt down behind her and cut away the last of the fabric. She wore no lingerie beneath, and I couldn't resist biting into her lush ass. Seraphina yelped, and I gripped her thighs, forcing her to stand still. A possessive growl rumbled within my chest at the sight of the pink teeth marks on her ass cheek.

"I'm getting my teeth tattooed onto your ass, pet." I decided instantly. "I want to see my mark every time I fuck you from behind."

"Fine." She laughed, her aqua eyes twinkling wickedly. "But I want mine tattooed on your dick."

I barked out a laugh. "Deal, little vixen."

She smelled so delicious, and I could practically taste her arousal. I slid my hands up the back of her thighs and squeezed her ass cheeks, pulling them apart. Andras tugged on the belt, and Seraphina bent at the waist. Her perfect pussy and tight pink hole were stunning. My mouth watered, and I leaned in to lick her from cunt to ass. She moaned, and I buried my face between her cheeks, devouring her.

I heard a zipper as our girl moaned for me then Andras's deep voice. "Open your mouth. Suck."

God damn, my brother was a sexy motherfucker. The commanding tone had me ready to suck his dick too. Instead, I slipped a finger inside Seraphina's pussy just as she took Andras's dick down her pretty throat.

Her moans were the sweetest music to my ears while I toyed with her cunt.

"You're dripping, pet. My beard is covered in your scent. I fucking missed this pussy."

Seraphina whimpered, unable to speak as Andras fucked her mouth. Her nails dug into his thighs where she held on to keep steady bent over between us. He pulled the belt tighter, forcing her to take him all the way in. She choked and gagged, spit dripping down her chin, but she didn't stop. I fucking loved her for it. Andras pulled back, allowing her to take a breath.

"Such a good girl for us. You look stunning with your

mouth wrapped around my cock, sweetheart," Andras praised her, and her pussy tightened around my fingers.

I chuckled. "She liked that. Her sweet cunt just gushed for you, brother."

Andras grinned like a fucking daemon, lust filling his eyes. "Tell us what you want, Seraphina." He pulled out of her mouth, and she took a deep breath, staring up at him.

"Fuck me. Please. I need it." Her voice was equally low and desperate.

"Fuck yes, little vixen," I growled, licking my lips.

Andras tugged the belt, forcing Seraphina toward her bed. "Typhon, on the bed. I want to watch our little slut ride you."

Seraphina's eyes dilated, and I stalked toward the bed. I stripped out of the stupid suit our fathers made us wear and dropped the clothes to the floor. My dick was rock hard and aching for our girl. Her ravenous gaze dropped to my cock, and that wicked tongue slipped out to lick her lips.

"I want to taste you first," Seraphina demanded, her eyes crawling up my flesh like a greedy slut.

"Get the fuck over here then." I growled at her.

Andras kept hold of the belt around her neck as my naked queen walked to me with all the grace and power of a feline on the hunt. Her eyes blazed, and my throat went dry at the sight of her. Her perfect, pink nipples hardened, and I desperately wanted to watch her tits bounce in my face.

I want to pierce those pretty nips. The thought popped in my mind and stuck. Oh fuck yes, I'd be getting some metal in my girl very soon.

Her silvery blue hair was a mess as she leaned over my prone form and dragged her nails up my thighs. She grinned as her hands gripped my cock and pumped slowly. Her soft hands felt amazing, and my dick twitched in her grasp. Andras pulled the belt tight around her neck and gripped her hair, taking control. She complied, smirking before opening her mouth and dragging her tongue over my Prince Albert piercing. Goosebumps pricked across my flesh immediately. Her mouth felt fucking amazing, and I needed more of her.

I thrust my hips, forcing her to take more of my cock down her throat. "Yes, pet. Take it all."

She moaned, spit dribbling down the sides of her mouth as my piercing grazed the back of her throat.

I dropped my head back on the bed and groaned. "Fuck yes. You're such a good fucking slut for us."

The next moment, Seraphina gasped when Andras pulled the belt and forced her off my dick. He wrapped one arm around her waist, his hand trailing across her abs and down between her legs. She leaned back, resting her head against his chest.

CHAPTER FIFTEEN

Andras

My self-control was slowly etched away by the debauchery taking place before me. This fucking angel before me was taking every ounce of restraint I had and tossing it out the window. The icy cage I built around my heart was melting to nothing in her presence. Watching her bent over Typhon and sucking his dick was the most beautiful torture. But I couldn't wait any longer. I needed to be inside her.

I slipped my fingers between her thighs and smiled against her throat at what I found between them. "*Belle femme,* you're soaked. Taste it."

My dick throbbed when she opened her mouth willingly and I pressed the soaked digits against her tongue. She licked and sucked, moaning for us, knowing exactly the power she held.

"Now you've had your mouth filled by us both, I need more."

Seraphina smiled, her devious eyes flicking between the two of us. "I want to feel you both filling me up."

Ty grinned something wicked, and I chuckled softly. "Our very own naughty little angel. Or are you a devil?"

She turned her head to the side and looked up at me. "The devil, attempting to be an angel but knowing it's hopeless. I like the taste of sinning too much."

I yanked the belt down, forcing her head back, and brought

my lips to hers. She tasted like sin and starlight. Fire and ice. She was my damnation and my redemption. I stopped the kiss, nipping her lip to remind her who she belonged to.

Seraphina smiled at me, her eyes blown wide with lust. Before I could give her another command, she turned from me and climbed into Typhon's lap. In one swift motion, she grabbed his dick and slid her sweet pussy down on him. I watched, transfixed by her toned body as she rode Typhon's cock. Ty and Seraphina moaned in unison as she started to roll her hips. She was a vision, a work of art.

I stepped up behind her, between his legs, and tugged on the belt around her throat. "Lean forward, sweetheart, and I'll give you what you need."

Seraphina complied, leaning forward and pressing her body fully against Ty. He wrapped his arms around her and kissed her fiercely as he fucked her. It was messy and sexy as hell to watch. I wasn't much for porn, but seeing Seraphina fuck Ty with pure ecstasy on their faces was almost enough to make me come.

Stepping out of the last of my clothes, I stroked my dick, watching them. Ty's muscular arms moved down Seraphina's body, and he slowed his pace. His hands came down over her ass, and he spread her cheeks, baring that perfect pink hole for me. I leaned over her ass and spat directly over it then brought my thumb down and pressed my spit into her plump ass. She moaned huskily as I massaged her ass with my thumb.

"I'm going to fill this tight little hole with my cock, angel," I murmured, my own voice practically shaking with need for her. "But first, you're going to come for us."

My hand tightened around the belt, and I tugged hard, forcing her to sit up. She leaned against me as I crowded over her, and I pressed two fingers inside her tight ass. The sounds she made for me were pure fucking sin. Typhon continued to fuck her slowly and brought his calloused hand down over her swollen clit. He began rubbing her clit with his thumb, and her body jerked with tension.

"Fuck," Seraphina moaned, her body glistening with sweat.

"Come for me, pet," Ty demanded. "I want to feel your sweet cunt tighten around my dick."

Ty's hips thrust into her harder and faster. I dipped my fingers into her ass again, matching his pace. Her body began to shake, and I knew she was close.

"Come for us, angel." I whispered the command into her ear and bit down on her neck.

Seraphina screamed, and her body squeezed my fingers.

The sight of her soft flesh marred by her very own devils made my dick throb. I smiled, licking at the mark left behind by my teeth. "Good girl. Now I'm going to fill you up, and you're going to give us another."

I shoved her forward, and her arms snapped out, landing on either side of Typhon's head.

He grinned up at her. "Hurry brother, I'm ready to fill our girl up with my cum."

"Are you ready for us, sweetheart?" I asked, tugging on the belt again.

Seraphina nodded, her voice low and breathy when she responded. "Fuck me like the world is ending, boys."

Her response pulled a groan from my lips. She was a constant surprise in all of the best ways. Seraphina lifted her hips and presented her edible backside to me. I rubbed my dick against her ass cheeks, moving lower to coat the head in the arousal leaking from her sweet pussy. My dick brushed against Typhon's, and he shivered. I didn't hate the sensation either.

I pressed the head of my cock against her tight hole, eliciting a moan from her sweet lips. "Relax, angel. Take a breath and let this sweet ass suck me in."

She listened to my command, her body relaxing and allowing my cock to ease inside her. The guttural sound that escaped me as I fully seated myself in her ass was truly daemonic.

"Fucking hell, Seraphina," I groaned, pulling out halfway and pushing in slowly as our bodies connected. "You feel amazing, *belle femme*. You take us so fucking well."

Seraphina whimpered as Typhon and I found a rhythm, fucking our girl in perfect synchronicity. She was the most stunning creature, writhing between us and making the sexiest sounds I'd ever heard.

My dick throbbed, and I knew I wouldn't last long. My body curled over hers possessively, controlling her movements with the belt in one hand and the other gripping her hips. Typhon continued to thrust into her from below, one hand rubbing circles over her clit as he said the filthiest things in her ear.

"So. Close." Seraphina panted, barely able to speak as we brought her body to ruin. She moaned loudly when I tightened the belt around her throat.

"Come for us, our dark angel. Our queen."

She screamed our names as her body shook with the force of her orgasm and her pussy tightened around my cock. I could feel Typhon's dick throb through the thin barrier of her body. As he thrust in one final time, he growled her name, pumping hot cum inside her. I squeezed her hips with a bruising grip and followed them both into oblivion.

CHAPTER SIXTEEN
Seraphina

The scalding water in the shower heated my skin in the best way while I mulled over everything that happened in the last twenty-four hours. Andras and Ty managed to turn my body and mind into mush for the better part of an hour. And fuck, had I needed that. We all did. Being here in this horrible fucking place with the wannabe kings controlling every fucking thing was driving us all insane. Tibby's escape had them rattled, and I smiled thinking about it. The electric chair I endured because of it sucked, but it was worth it. I would take any amount of torture if it meant the people I cared about were safe.

Speaking of safety. My sister was tangled up with an honest-to-shit daemon. The guys told me all this shit was real, but seeing a full-on daemon was weird as hell. And I hated seeing him wearing the face of Darren Radnor and pawing at my sister with his sticky fucking fingers. I knew it wasn't him and the prick was dead, but it was seriously difficult not to keep throwing knives at him.

I also did not believe for a second that Laszlo Blackbyrn let me go off for a chat with my sister out of the goodness of his evil heart. That fucker was always up to something. He was always a step ahead of us, and I would not underestimate him.

Having us all seated together at the world's most uncomfortable dinner table was purposeful. Dev was tortured with his sister while I was taunted with mine. Levi was forced to sit next to his father, Andras beside his. And poor Audrey and her father. They were pawns in a game of Kings with no hope of coming out of this unscathed. I would do whatever I could to help her. And yet, I knew I would choose Kaela first, if I had to. But that was the whole point, wasn't it?

Laszlo liked giving us impossible choices. He wanted us to feel the pain of those choices. Fuck that fucking guy. Samuel Delano too. He wasn't outwardly awful the way Laszlo or Darren were. He was sleazy and gross in a whole different way. Recalling his slimy presence inside my mind made my skin crawl. I wished for my mother. The need to rage at her for not telling me about all this was overpowering. If only she had, maybe I could've protected myself. Protected Kaela.

I realized once again how little I thought of my father. He'd been absent since that day in the Great Hall. He gave up on us. He got Kaela kidnapped. Joseph Bronwen was supposed to be the parent, the protector. His inaction was like a punch in the gut over and over again. *He was just as bad as the Kings.*

Alright, fine. He wasn't just as bad. But I did seriously want to punch him and ask why he did nothing when he could have done anything else.

I shook off the anxiety building inside me with all the negative thoughts bubbling in my mind. How was I supposed to sleep in this fucking place? The room was too quiet without my Princes. The moon shone high in the cloudless sky, casting shadows across the bed. I climbed into it and stared at that moon. It would be full soon enough, and when it was, the ritual would finally take place. Would it hurt? Did Lailah feel pain when they killed her for power?

Morax said I wouldn't die. And I would be helping bring his brother here. Phenex, he called him. Strange name, but I kind of liked it. Would he be monstrous? The daemon form Morax had was badass. I bet the Princes would look tasty as hell if they had daemon forms. My mother was a lumen, though. Were their forms so different? Would I be like her?

I lifted my hand into the moonlight, gazing at the slim fingers, wondering. So far, I only had the ability to heal, but what else could I do? Something inside me pulsed, and I begged the feeling to come forward. My skin tingled, and I could've sworn my flesh was glowing. The feeling left as quickly as it came. Whatever power surged in my veins, I couldn't access it. Not yet. But I would. Soon enough, I would have the power to fight back.

The Kings weren't afraid of men or weapons. They weren't afraid of the Princes. But I would make them fear me.

The next few days leading up to the ritual passed in a blur. The Kings were oddly absent. Andras said his father remained distant and dismissive. Extra guards were posted at every door, and my men and I rarely had a moment alone together. I needed them badly. Not just for orgasms. But also definitely for orgasms.

Typhon was able to get me access to the gym, and working out was one of the only pleasures of this stupid haunted prison.

Resurrection

Of course, there were guards watching us the entire time. I smiled, remembering how my monster man knocked out two of the guards for staring a little too closely.

My sister was kept away from me, even more thoroughly guarded than my princes. Morax, aka Fake Darren, kept her locked away in their room. The illusions he kept up were exhausting his strength, and he was almost out of Darren's blood. The other daemon, Gremory, had access to a witch, apparently, and that was how he had the power to create the illusions. Witches. Who knew? It made sense, though, their existence. All the creepy ritual shit was very witch-like.

I was a little bummed I wasn't one. Even before I learned about daemons and lumens and the absolutely bonkers existence of other worlds, I wished for it. There were moments when I felt it too. That pulsing power in my veins. The way Lailah's skin would sometimes glow before our mother would give her a look. I was beginning to think she forced Lailah to hide her power. If it was to keep us safe from The Obscuritas, her plan failed spectacularly.

My face scrunched up in frustration. No, there must be more to it. Our mother was anything but stupid. She wouldn't let this happen without reason. I just needed to fucking figure out what that reason was.

A knock at my bedroom door startled me out of the spiraling thoughts, and I suddenly felt like vomiting. Tomorrow was the event that would change everything. But today…today I was going to see my father. Laszlo casually mentioned the happy reunion at another one of our fucked up family dinners. We were all being called to the ballroom where the event would take place for some weird-ass rehearsal.

I wore a long black dress with the V-neck going down to my navel. The fabric was silky soft and hugged my curves to perfection. I wore my hair in waves down my back. The door opened, and a guard was about to speak when he was suddenly ripped from the floor and shoved aside.

My monster man grinned like the daemon he was and stalked toward me. He wore a dark-green suit that complimented his complexion and made his hazel eyes pop. He licked his lips, and my thighs clenched at the hunger in his wolfy hazel eyes. Ty's hand snapped out, and his fingers tightened around my throat as he dragged me close. Our lips were nearly touching, and I sucked in a ragged breath, enjoying the feel of his rough hands squeezing tight. My pussy throbbed, and I nearly moaned. I really really needed to get fucked.

Ty's nostrils flared, his sexy-as-sin face lighting up with wicked desire. "You smell exquisite, pet. I think your sweet cunt misses me."

Smirking back at him beneath dark lashes, I nodded. "Perhaps. Could've been for the guard, though. I did see him first."

Ty growled and squeezed my throat tighter, cutting off the oxygen. "Don't taunt me, pet."

I leaned into his grip, slipping my hand over the massive bulge threatening to break free from his pants, and smiled. Ty leaned down and crushed his lips to mine, forcing his tongue down my throat. I kissed him back feverishly, even as little spots began to appear behind my eyelids from the lack of oxygen. But I wouldn't stop. My breaths were his to take, and I would give every last one to him and the others if they asked. The emotional thoughts were still unnerving. How much I cared for these fuckers still shocked me.

"Stop now!" a guard shouted behind us.

Ty released my throat enough for me to drag in a long breath. He stared at me, our eyes locked in a battle of sexual wills.

"I said—" the guard began, but was cut short by an ominous snarl from Ty.

"Speak to me again and I will rip out your spine," he snapped at the guard, and his little eyes widened in fear. "And if you so much as look at her, I will pluck out your eyeballs with a spoon. Slowly."

I squeezed Ty's cock through his pants, and he turned his attention back to me. "I fucking love when you say sweet things like that."

Ty grinned and forced me to his side, smacking my ass as he pulled me close. "Anything for you, little vixen."

We followed the guard out of my room and through the maze of hallways. I desperately needed to get out of this fucking place. Nightmares found me each night, filling my head with the screams of Lailah and our mother.

There was no rest for the wicked, as they say, and I was absolutely in the wicked category. But like, the good wicked. I killed bad people and was basically making the world a better place.

"Where are the others?" I whispered to Ty as we walked.

"They will be arriving soon." Ty frowned. "Guards took Devon and Levi somewhere, and sent Andras to his father. Only I was allowed to escort you."

"Those assholes sure do love splitting us up," I grumbled, so over this shit.

Ty grunted in agreement.

We arrived at the ballroom, and two guards opened the doors for us. We entered via one of the side entrances, not the grand entrance where guests would arrive tomorrow. The hall was massive. The ceilings were easily fifty feet high. It was similar to the ballroom at Vespertine Hall, with the gothic architecture, but twice as big. Windows decorated the far wall leading out to the courtyards beyond. There was a stage at the center of the room on the opposite wall, and dozens of staff flitted about the room setting up cocktail tables and decor.

I might actually enjoy attending a masquerade ball if it wasn't for the Kings hosting it. Speaking of cockroaches, we headed closer to the wall of windows where the Kings stood. My grip on Ty's arm tightened as I absorbed the scene before us.

CHAPTER SEVENTEEN
Morax

Something was very wrong. Even the minds of the guards were blocked from me, and I could not figure out how they were able to do so. Laszlo and Samuel were constantly away, and I was left behind—seemingly to guard the prisoners and keep the Princes out of trouble. But it was obviously to keep me in the dark about whatever plans they had for tomorrow evening. My daemon itched to be released, and an unsettled feeling vibrated through me as I walked with Michaela to the Queen's Ballroom. It was apparently named for the mothers of the princes, although other than having a room named after them, the Kings seemed to care less about the poor women. To the Kings, women were disposable vessels at best. Michaela would never be treated as such, not while I lived.

She was silent at my side, as she usually was when I wore the face of her attacker. The sight of her at his mercy played constantly in my mind, making my blood boil. I would never be able to take that moment away from her, and I would punish myself until the end of time for being too late to stop it. Her virginity was intact, but the assault was brutal and degrading. Wearing his visage was a constant reminder of her worst moments, and I couldn't wait to be rid of it.

I squeezed my mate's arm, letting her know I was here,

always. She looked stunning in a navy gown. The illusion of a small baby bump jutted out below the empire waistline. Her golden hair was braided back, and she wore sapphire earrings to match the dress.

"You are stunning, as always, princess," I murmured low enough so the guards walking ahead of us wouldn't hear.

Her cheeks flushed, and her breasts heaved slightly as her pulse quickened. It was my favorite thing, to see her sweet flesh color at my words. My dick twitched, and I had to force away the urge to fuck my mate. The urges were growing stronger each moment I spent with her. When a daemon or lumen found their mate—if they were privileged enough to do so—within days of finding each other, our souls urged us to consummate the binding. But I refused to do so under duress. I would not claim my mate that way; her beautiful soul and perfect flesh were meant to be celebrated. Revered. Our binding would come, and I would wait.

"I'm nervous." Michaela uttered the words so quietly only I could hear them.

I grunted in agreement. "Something is coming. I can feel it."

The guards ushered us into the ballroom amidst a flurry of activity. Staff bustled about, preparing the room for the event tomorrow evening. I caught Samuel's eye as we walked toward the Kings, and he gave me a lazy smile that didn't reach his eyes. I grinned, tugging on the leash around Michaela's neck. Darren was ever the jackass, and I must play the part.

Laszlo's face was a mask even I could not penetrate. I paused several feet from them, keeping Michaela at my side. "Evening, Blackbyrn. Delano."

Resurrection

"Evening." Samuel spoke first. He was shorter and less muscular than Darren, but no less dangerous. His mind was darker than most. "Ah, but what shall we call you?"

His question caught me off guard, and my daemon stirred uneasily. "What?"

Laszlo pulled one of his hands from his pockets and held out his palm. "Give me the leash."

I hesitated. I knew I shouldn't, but I did. How could I hand her to them? Michaela kept her head down, and I knew if she looked at me now, I would lose my shit. Instead, I nudged her forward and gave the leash to Laszlo.

"We are equals, are we not? I won't do anything to your toy, at least not without letting you watch." Laszlo smirked.

I nodded, crossing my arms and doing my damndest to appear unphased. "Of course we are."

A door opposite us opened, and Seraphina and one of her Princes, Typhon, walked toward us before he could respond. At the same moment, one of the glass doors built into the wall of windows opened, and Devon walked in, his hands and feet chained and his sister holding the leash. Yes, something was very, very wrong.

"What the fuck is going on here?" Seraphina snarled, her eyes glued to the leash in Laszlo's hand.

"A moment, please. Others will be here shortly." Laszlo's lips barely moved, his face showing only the slightest irritation at Seraphina's outburst.

The next moment, his son, Andras, and Samuel's son, Levi, joined us, surrounded by several guards. Both Princes looked angry and uneasy.

"Where have you been?" Ty growled as Levi walked up next to him.

"Forced to watch my father's brand of torture on the Kingston girl," Levi murmured, his voice laced with fury. He was nearly vibrating with his anger.

"Easy, brother." Andras touched Levi's arm.

"Now that you're all here," Laszlo called out, forcing our attention back to him. "This is how things will go tomorrow. You will all participate in the ritual as required. If you choose to disobey my orders, there will be punishments."

"Take your best shot, asshole," Seraphina snapped.

The next moment, Laszlo ripped the leash around Michaela's neck and forced her to the ground. She cried out in shock, and I snarled. My daemon was nearly to the surface when I felt a prick to the back of my neck. A weight descended over my limbs, and I dropped to the ground. I couldn't move, couldn't call upon my power. I rolled my eyes to the side and stared in shock at the creature holding the needle. He was a daemon, or at least a hybrid. His eyes glowed violet with power, and I felt the familiar touch of an old enemy.

"Yes, my Kings, this one is not what he seems." The daemon smiled and knelt down beside me. "Morax, is that you? Your scent is mixed up with the meat suit. When did you come to Earth?"

"Foras?" I stared hard at the creature before me.

He smiled. Foras was one of the stronger daemon hybrids my father recruited. While he didn't have wings, he possessed abilities my father found useful, such as the one he used on me. Foras could see beneath illusions.

I ignored him, my eyes snapping to Michaela, still on the floor at Laszlo's feet.

Samuel walked toward my prone body and cocked his head. "How long have you been impersonating Darren?"

I smirked, refusing to give him anything.

Samuel's gaze flitted to Michaela and back to me. "I could make you talk."

"Like fuck you can." Seraphina stepped toward us, but was immediately surrounded by guards. She crossed her arms and smiled. "Haven't we done this before, boys? If you want to die, just ask."

"Silence," Laszlo snapped, his mask of indifference slipping. "Here's how this will go. Michaela will remain with me. And if any of you fuck with my plans in any way before this ritual begins, I will hurt her. I will make her scream. Whatever she endured at Radnor's hands will pale in comparison to what I am capable of."

My daemon raged, but was caged by whatever concoction Foras gave me. I stared at my beautiful mate in anguish, unable to protect her once again.

Her sister fumed, the power within her vibrating the air with electric energy. If only she could have unleashed it now, this would have gone down differently. The thought brought an errant memory to the surface. The necklace. The powerful stones left by Aurora for her daughters. I kept them hidden, even Michaela knew not where. But it was time. Fucking hell, I hoped Phenex was ready, because things were about to get interesting.

CHAPTER EIGHTEEN
Devon

Fucking get it together, Dev. I couldn't get it together. I was struggling. When the guards came for me and my sister stepped in front of them, I wanted to weep. I wasn't exactly the type to cry, but seeing her like that was enough to bring me to my knees. Leyja was barely herself. The eyes I remembered being so full of life even as a baby were cold and unfeeling. She wouldn't speak directly to me, only ordered the guards to cuff me and force a fucking shock collar around my neck.

Of course, I wasn't going to fight them. If I did, they would hurt Seraphina, or my sister. Until we had something to fight against the Kings with, any outbursts would just get people hurt.

Reuniting with Seraphina had been the spark I needed to regain my own mind. I was furious with myself for letting them get inside my head and scramble my memories. How many months they took from me, I wasn't entirely sure. And Leyja…she had been in their grasp since she was a child. They had been controlling her mind for decades. Morax spoke of others capable of healing, and I held onto that hope with all my fucking heart.

I assumed when Leyja arrived and ordered the guards into the room that we weren't going for an afternoon walk in the park. The scene that played out in the ballroom was also not what I expected. Now that it was over, I shouldn't have been surprised, none of us should have. Of course, the Kings had other daemons working for them. Creatures we didn't know about. They wouldn't thrive the way they did without power.

What was interesting was Andras's reaction, or lack thereof. He didn't seem surprised by the daemon showing up to do his father's bidding. Did he know this was coming? He must have known more than I did, at least.

I paced my cell, still wearing the fucking shock collar. Leyja and the guards led me back here without a word spoken. I caught Seraphina's eye as we left. My queen. Her beautiful aquamarine eyes ensnared my soul. I would do anything for her, be anything for her.

The door to the basement banged open, and I turned toward the entrance, waiting to see who would descend from above. Andras stalked toward me, no guards in sight.

I raised an eyebrow. "No bodyguards?"

Andras sighed. "My father knows I won't do anything to ruin his plans, not when he has everyone I care for placed fully beneath his boot."

I nodded and tugged at the collar. "I know the feeling."

"I'm not certain why he has you in the collar. Seems excessive. You're clearly not going anywhere." Andras cocked his head to the side, ideas swirling in his dark eyes.

"How is Seraphina?" I whispered, missing her.

Andras smirked. "Furious. Breaking everything in her room that isn't bolted down. Laszlo won't hurt Michaela for that, I don't think."

I sighed, shoving my hands in my pockets. "So, now what,

we just sit here like obedient little dogs?"

Andras nodded. "For now." He pulled something small from his pocket and handed it to me. "I was told to give you these. I don't think anything good will come from listening to whatever they are connected to."

Andras passed the earbuds through the bars, and I took them. The hairs on the back of my neck immediately stood on end. He might have been right.

"I'll see you soon, brother," Andras murmured, his voice almost tender.

He walked back up the stairs and left me to my thoughts. And the earbuds. Everything in my body screamed in alarm. Whatever I would hear, it wouldn't be good. But I had to. I needed to know.

I stuffed the earpieces into my ears and waited.

Samuel's voice filled my head. "Your brother is listening to us, my dear. Do you want to speak to him?"

"No." My sister's cold voice cut straight through to my heart.

Samuel laughed, an empty awful sound. "You're such a good girl, Leyja. So obedient. I want him to hear something tonight, though, so we're going into the vault."

There was a beat of silence.

"Yes, sir." My sister's voice sounded less confident. She seemed unsettled.

What was the vault?

"Close your eyes, Leyja." Samuel's voice dipped into a hypnotic cadence. It was his sleazy sales guy talent, amplified by the daemonic power he possessed.

My blood heated at the sound. I remembered how he used

it on me, and I would never let him inside my head again. But Leyja, she was willingly letting him in, and that terrified me.

"Go to the door and open the vault," Samuel ordered, his voice deep and melodic. "What do you see?"

Leyja started to breathe heavily. "My daddy. And my brother."

I sucked in a breath and fisted my hands to keep from ripping out the earbuds.

"What are they doing?" Samuel asked quietly.

"Inviting me to sit with them. To have dinner. They're smiling at me." Leyja sounded close to tears.

"Ah yes, they love you, don't they? In here, they love you. Protect you." Samuel goaded her. "If you agree, press the button, Leyja."

A second later, a shock zipped through my body, knocking me to my knees. The collar vibrated with electricity, and I sucked in a breath.

"Good girl. And you love them too, don't you?" Samuel continued, his voice forcing her to obey. "Do you agree?"

A second bolt of electricity shot through my body, and I fell to my hands, grinding my teeth and breathing through the pain.

"Yes, you love them. But this isn't real, is it, Leyja?" Samuel sounded sad.

She whimpered. "No. It's a lie."

"Press the button when you agree, Leyja," Samuel snapped, his voice booming in my ear.

The zap of electricity knocked me to the ground, even when I knew it was coming. Samuel went on and on, forcing her to answer him, and in doing so, shocking me over and over. Tears blurred my vision as I forced myself to take the pain. Did she know this was happening? She ordered them to put the collar on. Did she know what she was doing?

"Who lied to you, Leyja? Who tortured you and hurt you?" Samuel asked, his voice soft again.

Leyja was crying. "My daddy. He sold me. My brother. He left me. They killed my mother."

"They did. They never cared for you like you did for them. Isn't that right?" Samuel sounded so sincere, like he really cared for her.

The collar shocked me again, and my heart broke for my sister and the lies the Kings fed her.

"And you know what you must do now, Leyja?" Samuel cooed.

There was an edge to his voice I didn't like. It was almost as if he were excited, and since he never showed emotions, it was fucking disturbing.

"I know what I must do," Leyja responded like the soldier the Kings turned her into.

"Who cares for you? Who do you serve?" Samuel's voice sounded louder, more powerful.

"Master Samuel. Only him. Can I leave the vault now?" Leyja's voice was quiet and pleading. She sounded so young, so alone.

"Very well. You did well, my Leyja," Samuel cooed, and my sister whimpered.

The earbuds went dead, and I ripped them from my ears. My body ached, and every muscle screamed in pain. I lay on the floor, unending anger and sadness flooding my mind. Samuel

Resurrection

Delano would fucking die, and I would be the one to kill him. Before this shit finally ended, I would see the light leave his eyes and feel the blood draining from his body. He would pay for this with his fucking life. And I would get my sister back, no matter the cost.

CHAPTER NINETEEN
Michaela

Several guards led me to Laszlo's bed chambers, and I was doing my best not to let terror overcome me. I never visited this part of the mansion, and I most definitely didn't want to. His rooms were elegant. Muted grays and warm browns dominated the walls and furniture. His king-sized bed was nestled between a canopy of creamy velvet and sheer fabrics. His bedding was also cream colored, and if this wasn't the bedroom of the world's most vile villain, it would almost be nice. The chill in the air stayed with me as the guards closed the doors and left me to my thoughts.

All I could think of was Morax. I'd never seen him look so helpless. We were stupid. We should have known they would figure out the illusion. Of course, the Kings would have evil daemons and lumens working for them. Why wouldn't they? Morax could usually sense them, and I was sure he was feeling all kinds of guilt right now. I wished he was here so I could comfort my daemon. My mate.

It still felt weird to say that word. Probably because we'd been prisoners of a stupid cult for the entirety of our relationship. Calling it a relationship also felt weird. Because it was more than that, so much more.

I paced the room, trying desperately to sense him, but that

connection I sometimes felt was dimmed to a whisper, and I didn't really know how to access it.

The bedroom door opened, and my body went rigid. Laszlo stepped into the room, his dark eyes landing on me instantly, and I wanted to vomit.

His gaze traveled down my body and back to my face as he stalked closer. I was frozen to the spot, screaming internally. My fight or flight was clearly broken.

Laszlo reached out and grabbed my cheeks, turning my face side to side and examining me.

He frowned. "You do resemble your mother so closely. You and Lailah both carry much of her in your faces and slim frames."

I was pretty sure he didn't want me to answer, so I remained silent and waited.

"Unlike Seraphina." His hand left my face, and he stepped back, eyeing me like a jungle cat. He smirked and began circling me. "You, I could break so very easily. But luckily for you, you're not the one I truly want to break."

I swallowed, and heat flooded my body. Not from embarrassment, but from fury. "My sister—"

"Your sister," Laszlo snapped, interrupting me. "She has your mother's beauty and more. There is something truly wild in her. And I want to break it. Consume it. Feel her wither beneath me."

"You will never break her," I spat at him. Apparently, I was feeling courageous.

Laszlo stopped his circling and stared at me, his eyes like two endless black holes eager to destroy everything and everyone in their sight. "Take off your clothes."

My eyes widened, and I almost choked on my next breath. "What?"

Laszlo stepped closer, his height casting me in shadow. "If I have to repeat myself, I will have someone in here to do it for you. And it will not be gentle."

My cheeks flamed, and I was suddenly back in that room with Darren. Morax wouldn't be here to save me this time. No one was coming. I swallowed and slipped out of my dress. I wasn't wearing a bra and quickly crossed my arms to cover my chest.

Laszlo watched me with a lazy smile. "Your underwear. Off."

Shame trickled down to my toes as I slipped the panties down my legs and to the floor. I hated him so damn much. Laszlo walked closer to me and grabbed my wrists, forcing my arms to my sides. He stared and stared at my body, saying nothing. The silence was deafening, and my heartbeat thudded in my ears as blood rushed to my cheeks. He let go of one of my wrists and reached up to flick my nipple. I refused to make a sound.

His hand moved down across my stomach, and he inhaled. The next moment, he shoved me away and I smacked into the wall, my eyes wide.

"Not nearly good enough. Only she will do." Laszlo frowned and began to undress. "Get into the bed. Arms above your head."

Laszlo Blackbyrn's obsession with my sister might help me tonight. There wasn't much for me to do besides obey, unless I wanted things to get worse. But getting in that bed felt all kinds of wrong. I slipped beneath the covers and lay on my back, bringing my hands up to the tufted headboard. Laszlo

Resurrection

came around the bed and pulled out chains hidden behind the headboard and locked my arms in place. He ripped the covers off of me and produced more chains, trapping my ankles. My body was completely on display for him. He gazed down at me, still silent. I hated it, the silence almost as much as the starring.

"Still a virgin, Michaela Valdis?" Laszlo smirked.

My stomach dropped, and I forced myself not to squirm at his dangerous tone.

"The ruse was clever, and it took us longer than I care to admit to discover something was off." Laszlo walked back to the other side of the bed. "Darren would have enjoyed humiliating you more in public. I surmise your daemon pet wouldn't allow too much of that."

He was right, of course, but I refused to respond. Instead, I kept my gaze on the copper tiled ceiling.

Laszlo's hand drifted across my abdomen. "Perhaps I'll have a guard fuck you while he watches. Tony has a thing for skinny blondes. See how quick we can have a bastard baby in your belly."

He chuckled, and the sound was horrifying. His hand drifted down further, and he tapped his fingers over the soft mound between my thighs. My body was rigid, and I was so very close to sending my mind away.

"No. It won't be the guards. It will be Foras," Laszlo continued, drumming his fingers agonizingly close to my entrance. "We want a hybrid baby, after all. The more creatures we can create, the stronger our future will be. Foras will be first for his loyalty. And then others. So many others. You'll be a good little broodmare."

He smacked my pussy, and I let out a gasp at the shock of it. Then Laszlo rolled away from me and left me there, chained and naked in his bed. My arms went numb after a while, and I continued to stare at the ceiling. I didn't send my mind away tonight. Anger flooded my body, and I welcomed that rage. The Kings were poisonous and needed rooting out. He thought his words would break me. Scare me. And maybe they did a little. But my anger was stronger than my fear. I was no fucking broodmare. For him or anyone else. And when I could finally unleash the rage inside me, these assholes better run.

CHAPTER TWENTY
Leviathan

Even though I knew we had to continue with this stupid ritual, every fiber in my body was shouting in alarm. We weren't allowed to see Seraphina after the shitshow in the ballroom yesterday. Ty and I went to the gym and worked out. Andras went off somewhere. But all three of us paced the halls and ended up in front of her door during the night. There were five guards in front of it, which made me laugh. The Kings were threatened by her, even if they wouldn't admit it. Once there were four, now only two Kings remained. Although, I wasn't so sure Dev's father deserved the same fate as our own did. The very brief moments we spoke with Morax, he mentioned Ezekial Parrish wanted to save his family. We were fairly confident our fathers killed him before he could take action. And all these years, they had Dev's sister.

I never had a sister, or any close female companions. Our fathers forbid relationships unless they benefited The Obscuritas. I rolled my eyes, buttoning up the ridiculously expensive dress shirt. Tonight, all of the important members would be in attendance. There would be celebrities, politicians, and various other important people with deep pockets and shady connections. They were to witness the true power of the Kings when they sacrificed Seraphina. But hopefully, that's where everything would go tits up for the Kings. We all had a lot of faith in this mysterious brother of Morax.

"You're practically shouting, Levi." Ty chuckled.

I hadn't said a word. "Stop feeling my feelings. It's not my fault you're in love with me."

Andras sighed as he exited my en suite. "Will there ever be a time when you two aren't close to fucking?"

"It's hard to say." I grinned and winked at Ty.

We hadn't technically fucked, but came close while enjoying a female or two together. Perhaps that was simply because the chemistry between us as brothers was stronger than the feelings we had for whomever we were fucking.

Even as the thought formed, I knew it was a lie. Ty and I… there was something there. Something that was maybe worth exploring, but could cost us everything. My brothers meant the world to me, and I would be lost without them. But denying these feelings was beginning to make me uneasy.

Every man I had been with was at the direction of my father. I'd never fucked a man for my own pleasure. And I think I wanted my first time to be with him. But would it break us? I shook my head, forcing the heavy thoughts out. I caught Ty's gaze. His hazel eyes captured mine, and I could see a question in them. A concern.

I looked away first and grinned. "Besides, you assholes fucked Seraphina without me. My dick's been hard ever since."

Ty chuckled, running his thumb over his bottom lip. "I miss her. I miss the taste of her on my tongue. Fuck."

Andras adjusted his maroon bow tie, attempting to hide the restlessness we all felt. "Soon, brothers."

Resurrection

The door opened, and Dev's dashing form slid into the room. We were meeting for the masquerade from hell in my rooms. They were the farthest from our fathers.

"Soon what?" Dev asked, cocking his head to the side and leaning against the wall.

He looked fantastic in the forest-green, three-piece suit. He wore a crisp white shirt and a black tie clipped beneath the crisp vest. His green eyes shone brightly, and I smiled.

"Soon we will enjoy the delectable treat that is Seraphina's pussy." I winked at him, and he rolled his eyes. But he didn't scowl, and that was something. Dev was officially coming around to this whole sharing thing.

With Dev's attention focused my way, he didn't see the beast of a man launch himself before tackling him to the ground. Ty reared back and punched Dev in the face, breaking his nose. Blood pissed from the broken appendage.

"What the fuck, man?!" Dev shouted, his voice laced with pain.

Ty leaned down, his face menacing. "That's for shooting me in the gut, you little asshole." Ty stood slowly and offered his hand to Dev, which our brother took.

As soon as Dev stood, I leapt at him, jamming my fist into his stomach. He doubled over, cursing and spitting mad.

"Fuck! What the hell, Levi?" Dev groaned.

"That's for hurting Seraphina. And helping the Kings." I patted him on the back. "You know you deserve worse."

"Alright!" he snarled, shoving my hand away. He straightened, fixing his suit while blood continued to drip from his nose. "I fucked up. I know. And I'm so fucking sorry for it. I'll spend the rest of forever on my knees apologizing to our girl."

I locked eyes with Ty and smiled. "It's a start."

Andras walked toward Dev. He pulled out a handkerchief and offered it to him, his eyes glittering with dominance. "There will be punishments in due time, Devon. And you will take them, on your knees or otherwise."

Dev's handsome face fell, and his green eyes darted between each of ours. "You guys are going to tie me up or some shit, aren't you?"

Ty grinned like the devil he was. "You can count on it."

Dev's eyes narrowed, and he pointed a finger at Ty. "Nothing goes in my ass."

I laughed out loud and clapped Dev on the shoulder, giving it a squeeze. "Brother, there are no limits here. No walls between us. No holes denied. Are you in?"

Dev rolled his eyes to the heavens, as if searching for a way out of this, but there was only one answer. He rubbed his face, his broken nose already healed. "Gods above and devils below. I'm in."

The hottest fucking fivesome ever was most certainly in my future, and my dick pressed against my pants at the thought.

Andras smirked, adjusting his bow tie and nodding his approval. "Now finish getting cleaned up. We have Kings to destroy and an angel to claim."

Dev went to the en suite to clean the blood from his face, and I turned to the full-length mirror in the room to check my ensemble for the party. My suit tonight was navy, a shade darker than my eyes. I paired the three-piece with a bow tie, similar to Andras's. I tucked the white shirt into the pants and quickly slipped on the vest. While Dev's hair was styled to perfection, I left my surfer boy waves to do what they willed.

Ty's man bun was not quite as messy as he usually left it, and his beard was trimmed. He wore black from shirt to shoes. Fuck, the man was sexy as hell. I licked my lips, and his eyes flicked to mine, his gaze zeroing in on my mouth. I almost groaned out loud.

Andras cut through the sexual tension, stepping between us and tying my bow tie.

"Thanks, papi." I blew him a kiss.

The stubborn bastard let loose a hint of a smile.

"Watch it, Levi." Ty chuckled darkly. "You know Andras likes it when you call him daddy."

"Fuck off, Typhon," Andras snapped with little venom.

Dev laughed, and we all turned to him. He stared back at us, almost as shocked as we were to hear him sound so…happy.

"What?" Dev kicked off the wall and shoved his hands in his pockets.

I looked at Ty and then Andras. "Did you guys know he could do that?"

Andras smirked, his eyes soft as he looked at our lost brother. "I am glad you are with us, Devon."

Ty stood and wrapped a thick, muscled arm around Dev. "It's been too long. And while the timing of this reunion is absolute shit, I am glad you're here too, brother."

I stepped up to Dev and rested my hand on his other shoulder, giving it a squeeze.

Andras came toward us quietly. He wore his signature charcoal gray suit, with a black shirt beneath. The touch of color from his bow tie was new and fitting for this night. He looked around our little circle and slowly brought his arms up, resting a hand on Ty's shoulder and mine.

"So," I started, keeping my voice somber. "Should we have a theme song? Or like a band name?"

Andras barked out a laugh. Ty grinned and Dev cracked a smile. Exactly what I wanted.

"Let's get this fucking night over with," Ty growled.

We all knew whatever happened tonight, it would change everything.

CHAPTER TWENTY-ONE

Morax

Three guards stood inside the room I was being held captive in while Foras dosed me with another round of his vile toxins. My daemon itched to come out, raging beneath the fog created by this poison.

"I'm going to rip out your heart, Foras," I snarled at him, and he simply smiled.

"I highly doubt that, Morax." Foras stepped away, crossing his arms. "Belial will be here soon, and I'm quite certain he will kill you first."

I smirked. Phen would be the daemon joining this party, but he didn't know that. "Whatever you say."

Foras frowned and cocked his head. He was lean, and his skin was pearly white, almost as white as his hair. Even in his more human form, he looked all wrong. He was always a wiley fucker. The lesser daemon had no wings and limited power. He couldn't even summon fire. And yet he climbed through the ranks and became important enough to work for my brother and this gods forsaken cult.

"Do you have a secret, Morax?" Foras grinned, and his eyes glowed violet. "Are you perhaps thinking your crazy younger brother Phenex will save you?"

My head snapped up, and I bared my teeth at the weaker

creature. "What did you just say?" If my hands weren't chained behind my back, I'd wring his neck.

Foras laughed, his teeth sharp and gleaming. "Did you really think Phenex, that absolute loose cannon, would be able to plan some kind of heist without Belial finding out?"

I didn't respond. My mind was reeling. Was he telling the truth? Where was Phen?

Foras grinned like a smug weasel. "Poor Morax. You really have no idea what's going on."

I scoffed. "You're an imp. A leech. A low-level daemon to use and toss away when your usefulness runs out. I can't imagine you know much of anything, Foras."

The daemon snarled, his eyes glowing violet as his control slipped, just as I hoped. He came at me, claws extended, and swiped out, leaving deep gashes across my cheek.

I laughed. "As if you could truly hurt me. You're a pawn in a game meant for kings. Why don't you leave now before Belial laughs in your face."

Foras swiped at me again. "I am his FAVORITE! I have been by his side every step of the way, planning your demise. I have been in the ears of The Obscuritas Kings. When he comes, I will be the one to receive the royal blood."

He spat in my face, and I grinned. Belial was making promises he most definitely couldn't keep. Only the King of Caligo could offer blood to a lesser daemon to enhance his power. Our father would never do this for Foras. Is this what The Obscuritas Kings hoped for? To taste the blood of my father and become daemons themselves? I chuckled.

"Oh, you fools. My father wants slaves, not equals. He will

never give you what you seek."

Foras heaved angrily, staring down at me as he registered my words. But instead of anguish, I saw only mirth. "Once more, Morax. You know nothing."

The slimy daemon turned and quickly left the room, leaving me to ponder his last words. The guards stepped out after him, and I was alone once more, unable to do anything but rage at my own insignificance.

I lay on the floor, wrapped in chains, my power subdued and unavailable to me. I could hear the music playing in the ballroom. The mansion vibrated with energy. Even in my weakened state, I could feel it. Sense them. There were other creatures here now. Lumens, daemons, hybrids…and witches. I sniffed the air, and the scent of a witch invaded my nose. This one was nearby. What was a witch doing so far from the party?

Muffled sounds suddenly drifted through my closed door. Bodies dropped to the floor. I narrowed my eyes, waiting for whoever was out there to come for me. The double doors opened, and in sauntered three females. My eyes widened. A witch, a lumen, and a human. How curious.

The witch came forward, her hazel eyes taking me in, assessing. She had light-brown skin, and dark curling hair flowed down her back. She wore black leather pants and a fitted dark-green sweater. The witch was clearly not here for the party.

The lumen, however, was dressed in a brilliant gown of blue silk. Lumens held a natural grace that daemons often envied, and this one held herself well. She was young, but experienced. I could sense her strength even now. Her silver eyes glowed brightly, but her face remained grim. Her black hair was braided back, and she flicked the long braid off her shoulder as she stepped up next to the witch.

The human with them was equally fierce, in her own right. She too had long black hair, but it was styled up and twisted around the crown of her head. She had green eyes, murky and haunted. This one had seen things that scarred her soul. I noted the scars on her neck and down one side of her body. Her emerald-green dress had strategic cutouts to showcase her curves, and her tattoos. Her body was covered in scars, and her scars were covered in tattoos. This human was nearly burned alive. It was easy enough to recognize where the flames had licked her skin.

"Don't look at her," the lumen snapped, her eyes glowing and her hands balled into fists.

I raised an eyebrow. "And who are you, young one?"

The lumen raised an eyebrow. "I am Nuriela."

I narrowed my eyes. The name was familiar, but why, I wasn't sure. I turned to the witch, who was now crouching in front of me. "And what brings you ladies to my chambers?"

The witch rolled her wolf-like eyes. "Getting you out of here and ready for what comes next."

"And what comes next?" I pressed, watching her closely.

She pulled a small bag with several small vials from her pocket. She opened one and held it to my lips. "Drink this."

As if I would trust a witch. I pressed my lips together.

"Drink this if you want to help your mate," she snapped.

I opened my mouth and allowed the clear liquid to slip down my throat. I grunted, feeling whatever it was enter my bloodstream and attack the poison. My daemon snarled as the fog inside began to dissipate.

"Thank you." I bowed my head to the witch. "Who are you?"

She smirked and stepped back without a word. The lumen, Nuriela, came forward and easily ripped the locks off the chains wrapped around my arms and legs. I stood, shaking them off and already feeling my power returning.

I breathed in deeply, and another scent caught my attention, making me smile. "You're Gremory's witch," I stated.

The witch crossed her arms and smirked right back at me. "I see your power is returning." She held out another vial. "Before the ritual, make sure each of the Princes and Seraphina drink one drop each. As soon as your brother arrives, you all need to get the hell out of here. Do. Not. Hesitate." She turned to the lumen. "And don't engage. If you fight, you will die."

The lumen frowned but nodded. "I understand."

"And where are we going?" I asked, memorizing all of her instructions.

"Vespertine Hall. It's warded and ready." The witch gathered her small pouch of vials and pulled out one more, handing it to me. "Drink this, it will keep you mostly undetectable from other creatures. Foras will sense you, though, so try to stay away from him until it's time to run."

Without another word, the witch left the room. The lumen and human female followed her. My clothes were not masquerade appropriate, so I quickly changed into a black suit, white shirt, and a black tie flecked with gold. I pulled down a pair of dress shoes from the top of the closet and looked inside. The two boxes with Michaela and Seraphina's necklaces were still here, safe. Was tonight the right moment for them? I had memorized the message left behind by Ezekiel Parrish, the one Michaela and I listened to all those months ago.

The darkness that would take over our world and her own world. If we carried on this path, no one would survive. There was only a small window of opportunity to make things right. You and your sisters are that opportunity. Take the gift. I have kept it these many years for you and Seraphina.

It seemed our time here was coming to an end, but whose end, I wasn't entirely sure. I sent a silent prayer to my brother and begged the stars to let him hear me. Foras thought Belial had the drop on Phen, but I knew our wiley brother better than he did. And I had faith he would not fail in this.

As my power fully returned, I closed my eyes and reached out for my mate. I could sense her. She wasn't in pain, and relief flooded my system. While I was filled with that poison, I could not reach her, could not feel her. Knowing she was with Laszlo Blackbyrn all night drove me near to madness. I needed to see her, touch her, hold her, taste her. And once I took us away from this fucking place, she would never be rid of me.

CHAPTER TWENTY-TWO
Michaela

After the humiliating night naked in Laszlo's bed, guards escorted me to another bedroom where my dress for the evening waited for me. I took the world's hottest shower and hummed a song, forcing everything about that horrible night out of my mind. I desperately wanted to find Morax. And I doubted he'd be allowed to come to the masquerade. My stomach was filled with tension, and when I came out of the bathroom to find a tray of food on the bed, I nearly vomited. Eating was the last thing I wanted to do right now.

I nibbled a single piece of toast and continued to prepare for the evening, curling my hair and putting on my war paint, aka makeup. I wasn't super into the stuff, but I opted for a sunrise color pallet and added a bit of gold shimmer to match the threading on the dress. The dress was honestly beautiful, and I wondered who picked it for me.

My hair was not working well with the curls, so I pinned it halfway up and left it at that. Damn you, straight hair. As I walked back into the bedroom, the door opened and I froze in place, waiting for Laszlo to come for me.

Instead, a young woman quickly walked in and shut the door behind her. She had olive-green eyes that flitted around the room, looking for what, I wasn't sure. Her jet-black hair was curled and piled on top of her head. She wore a sexy-as-hell dress, with cutouts to reveal tattoos running down the entire left side of her body.

"Um, hi. Who are you?" I ventured, hoping she was here to help and not to hurt me. I had no weapons. Sure, I took some self-defense classes, but this girl looked tough as hell.

"My name is Lo. I'm here to help you get ready." She spoke quietly, but with confidence. Lo walked toward the bed where I had my dress laid out.

"Okay, sure." I shrugged, hoping my gut feeling was accurate and she was trustworthy. "I'm still working on my hair, though. Curls aren't really working.

She nodded. "I can help."

I followed her back into the bathroom, and she pulled out the stool under the vanity for me to sit. Lo took the pins out and started teasing my straw-colored hair, braiding in two small braids across my head like a headband.

"Wow. You're good at this."

Her hands made quick work of my hair. I glanced up and sucked in a breath. Earlier, I didn't notice what was beneath the tattoos. But up close, I could see them.

Lo's eyes locked with mine. "I survived a fire when I was younger."

I dropped my gaze. "Sorry."

"Why? You didn't start it." She scoffed, and I looked up again to see her green eyes harden. "Your sister did."

My mouth dropped open in shock. "What did you just say?"

Lo dropped her hands, having finished my hair, and stalked out of the bathroom. I followed her. She picked up my dress and held it out.

I propped my hands against my hips. "Uh, no. Explain what you just said."

Lo tossed the dress back to the bed and crossed her arms. "Your sister stayed at the gymnastics club my father owned for a few years. Found out he was doing fucked up things to other girls about the same time I found out he was going to give my little sister to some old creep. Your sister burned the gym down with him inside it. Problem was, he had my baby sister in there too, and I went after her. But I was too late to save her."

I dropped onto the bed, my legs unable to hold me up. Seraphina killed her baby sister. Almost killed her. Tears burned the back of my eyes.

"No use ruining your makeup now." Lo's harsh words cut through my spiraling emotions. "It was a long time ago. And I've…mostly dealt with it."

I knew that was a bit of a lie, considering how closed off she was now. "Do you hate my sister?"

Lo looked away, her mouth set in a grim line. "I did. For a really long time. But I had someone to help me channel the rage into something else."

"What?" I asked, although by her *I'm a badass vibe* I could guess her answer.

She shrugged. "Revenge."

Before I could respond, my door opened again and we both jumped. Relief crashed through me like a hurricane, and I ran at the daemon stepping into my room. Morax scooped me into his arms and growled. I crushed my lips to his, my hands threading in his hair. His mouth opened, and his wicked tongue flicked against my own. I moaned into the kiss, and he chuckled.

"*Mae domina*," Morax purred, pulling back enough to speak. "I fucking missed you."

I kissed him again, every bit of shame from the night before washing away with the tide that was this beautiful, loving mate of mine.

Lo cleared her throat behind us, and I blushed at our display. Morax nipped at my neck and chuckled.

"You need to get ready." Lo sighed. "Can you get her dressed?"

Morax gently set me on my feet and looked over my head at Lo. He nodded. "Of course. Thank you for helping her."

Lo nodded and slipped out of the room.

I looked up at him curiously, and he smiled. "I met her earlier. There is hope for us yet, *mae domina*."

I grinned up at him, feeling something other than dread for the first time in the last twelve hours.

"Finally. Last night was…bad."

Morax dropped to his knees in front of me. I was only in my robe, and the ties slipped to reveal delicate ivory lace lingerie beneath. Morax pressed his forehead to my stomach and wrapped his arms around my waist. I hugged him close, gently brushing my hands through his soft, dark hair.

"You're going to wrinkle your tux on your knees like that," I murmured.

Morax lifted his head, and the anguish in his eyes pierced my soul. "Did he hurt you? I couldn't feel you, your hurt or pain. The poison blocked you from me."

I shook my head. "It was more about humiliation than actually hurting me."

He snarled, his eyes turning to gold. "Tell me."

I knew he wouldn't let it go, so I braced for the hurt I knew I would see in his eyes. "He made me undress. And he chained me naked to his bed. He didn't do anything…just little touches while he talked about all the people he planned to, uh, give me to."

Morax growled so deeply I jumped. His skin glowed red, and his horns shot out from the crown of his head. "I'm going to burn him to ash. And every name he gave you, you will tell me. And they will burn with him."

I half-smiled. "I'm really not opposed to that idea. Foras is on the list."

He snarled, standing tall before me and looking every bit the daemon. "Foras is mine. He will die. Soon."

I shrugged. "No complaints here."

I started to step back to the bed, but Morax dragged me against his chest, making me laugh.

"I need to get dressed."

His eyes glowed, and I gazed up at the creature I was in love with. Shit. I was in love with him. Oh my gods, do not freak out. Morax cocked his head, staring down at me curiously.

"What were you thinking just now?" he whispered, his voice nearly a purr.

I shook my head and attempted to escape his arms, but he held me tightly.

Morax gripped my chin and forced me to look up at him. "Tell me, little doe. Or I might have to punish you."

The blood drained from my face and went directly to my clit. I clenched my thighs together, and his nostrils flared.

My cheeks heated, but something inside me was buzzing with desire and so much more. "I was thinking…I'm in love with you."

His eyes went wide and shone like the sun. A brilliant smile lit up his face, and I gasped at the beauty of it. Morax caressed my cheek, and I leaned into his touch. "I love you, Michaela Valdis."

My skin tingled and my heart soared at his words. "I love you too."

Morax lifted me completely off my feet and crushed his lips to mine in a bruising, all-encompassing kiss. He walked us away from the bed until my back pressed against the wall. Our tongues clashed, his mouth overpowering mine and his tongue dominating in its exploration. This kiss was a claiming, and my heart burst with love for this daemon of mine.

He pulled away just enough that I could heave several short breaths.

"I need to taste you," Morax growled, and I whimpered a yes in response.

He dropped to his knees before me once more, and I leaned against the wall, waiting to see what he would do next. Morax reached up and gently pulled the lace thong down my legs. His hot breath tickled against my naked flesh, and I shivered. He slowly dragged his claws up my thighs, and I continued to shiver and whimper at his gentle touches. Morax gripped my left thigh and hiked it up, propping my knee on his shoulder and exposing my drenched core to him.

He growled again, and his forked tongue flicked out but didn't touch me. His eyes turned up to mine, and my breath hitched at the wickedness I saw in his gaze. "This pretty little cunt is all mine. And I will never get enough of you."

With those words, he dove forward, his nose crushing against the soft hairs above my entrance as his lips sucked my clit into his mouth. I moaned his name, and he growled into my soaked pussy. I leaned against the wall and angled my hips to give him more access. My hands went into his hair, and I tugged hard when his tongue sank inside me. His mouth was everything. It was everywhere. He could never get enough of me, but I would never get enough of him.

My body shook with desire as the orgasm built inside me. It felt like decades since I came for him. His hand reached around to my backside, and he squeezed my ass, his claws digging into my flesh enough to hurt. But the pain was dulled by the constant ministrations of his wicked tongue and teeth eating me alive.

"Morax. Shit. I'm close." I moaned again, practically ripping his dark hair from his head. I caressed his horns, and he started to purr.

"Not yet, little doe. You come when I tell you to come." His voice was deep and filled with desire.

I wanted to listen to him. To accept any command he would give me, but shit, I was so turned on I didn't know if I could follow his rules.

Morax must have sensed this, because he pulled his mouth away, and I nearly growled in frustration. He chuckled, eyeing me like a beast. With one hand still gripping my ass, the other slowly traced up my thigh. His claws on this hand were hidden away, and he brushed his knuckles over my soaked pussy. I whimpered, needing more. Morax nibbled at my inner thigh and slipped his middle finger inside me. The sounds I made as he slowly fucked me with his finger were obscene.

I gripped his horns roughly, and he snarled, but the sound wasn't angry, it was feral. He added a second finger and began moving them in a come hither gesture, hitting that spot inside me in such a way I started to moan even louder. The hand on my ass pressed between my cheeks, and he began teasing my hole with his finger, pressing in and making me gasp.

"I can't wait to fill you with my cock, little doe." Morax sounded wild, his voice rasping. His finger pressed further into my ass. "And then I'll claim you here. Stretching you. Marking you with my seed. Mine. My mate."

I moaned, bucking my hips against his hands as he fucked me. "Morax. Yes. More. Please."

I could barely get the words out, begging for him to let me come.

He bit down on my inner thigh, and I cried out. "Come for me, little doe. Come for your mate."

His tongue fell upon me again as his fingers fucked me harder, my hips gyrating against his face. I could feel it now. I was soaring, higher and higher. His teeth grazed my clit just before he sucked it into his mouth, and I screamed as all the sensations crashed together for an epic orgasm. I shouted his name as my body sizzled with power and pleasure. His movements slowed, but didn't stop. His tongue licked lazily between my legs, lapping up the arousal leaking out of me.

"I'll never tire of hearing you scream my name, *mae domina*," Morax murmured. He gently lifted my leg from his shoulder and gripped my waist to keep me from falling to the floor.

"I seriously feel like a baby deer right now." I rested my head against his broad chest, still fully dressed in his fancy suit.

Morax chuckled. "I will always be here to keep you steady." He lifted my chin and planted a soft kiss against my lips.

I tasted my arousal on his lips, and it sent another zip of pleasure through my body.

"And to chase you down, should you run."

"Oh, I'll run. But only because I know you'll catch me."

Morax traced his thumb across my lips, and the mixture of love and desire in his gaze lit me up from my heart to my toes.

He smirked at me, letting his eyes glow once more. "Until the stars take us, I will always catch you, *mae domina*."

CHAPTER TWENTY-THREE
Seraphina

Once again, I was getting all dressed up for a fucking party I did not want to attend. This was like the theme of my life. Pretty clothes, hot guys, and maybe some people die. Well, definitely people would die. But the jury was still out who would die tonight. I was voting not me. Were ghosts real? If I did die, maybe I could haunt the stupid Obscuritas Kings and destroy the cult from the other side. Fingers crossed that was an option.

Pulling the fancy dress from the closet, I whistled aloud. It was really fucking pretty, damnit. I hoped Andras picked it out again. Then I could like it even more. The dress was actually two pieces. I stepped lightly into the fitted gown and pulled it over my hips. The black velvet was stunningly soft. I pulled the thin straps over my shoulders. Silver was threaded into the velvet, creating an illusion of vines laced throughout. It looked more like lightning crackling, and I rather loved that. There was a high slit down the center, reaching almost to the apex of my thighs. I quirked a smile. That was going to drive the Princes wild. I cupped my tits to hold the dress up and awkwardly moved to the mirror, turning to see the backside of the dress.

I frowned, staring at my reflection. The back of the dress had about fifty buttons, and there was no way I could get them all done up on my own. What was I supposed to do, hobble through the halls and ask for help? I missed having a fucking cell phone, for once.

A quiet knock on the door had my head whipping around. I grabbed the steak knife I stole after the last family meal with the Kings and prepared for whoever was coming.

The door opened, and a stunning woman walked in, her head held high and her eyes guarded. My first thought, she was not human. No fucking way.

"Who are you?' I decided being aggressive was best.

She smirked at me, her eyes glowing silver. "Someone who won't be harmed by that little blade."

I glanced at my stupid knife and shrugged. "I could probably stab you in the eye. It would hurt, I bet."

She rolled said eyes. "I'm here to help you dress."

"And why the fuck would you do that?" This was annoying. Although, I did need help with the dress.

The woman moved closer to me and crossed her arms, the silky fabric of her cerulean-blue dress swishing against the hardwood floors. "Well, Laszlo was going to come and dress you himself, I can leave, if that's what you prefer?"

Bile threatened to ruin this odd moment, and I made a puking face. "Pass. Did he send you then?"

She snarled, and I was starting to trust her. "Hell no. I created a distraction he had to deal with personally. I sent someone to help your sister with her dress and created a similar distraction for Samuel Delano."

Tossing the knife on my bed, I mulled over her words then shrugged. For now, I was going to trust she wasn't part of the cult. "Alright then, weird gal. Do me up."

The gorgeous woman let out a snort, and her eyes widened, almost as if the sound surprised her. Her mask of indifference returned, and she stomped toward me a little less gracefully. She shoved me around to face the full-length mirror and began expertly looping each silk button from the edge of my ass and up my spine.

"So, again…who are you?" I tried to sound casual, but the suspense was killing me. If Tibby was in my ear she'd have the information at the tips of her fingers. Thinking of her made my heart ache.

"My name is Nuriela." Her words were soft, the next spoken barely above a whisper. "Your sister called me Nuri."

I froze, and the woman behind me stopped moving too. Her eyes met mine in the mirror.

"Lailah?"

She nodded. Her eyes hardened, glowing silver again. "I am here to avenge her. No matter who gets in my way."

Well, I wasn't going to disagree with that. "You're not human, are you?"

She shook her head and continued with my buttons. "I am a lumen. Like your sister. We were best friends before you were even born. We were soulmates."

I stared and stared at the woman behind me. A million questions rattled my brain. She knew the real Lailah. She was around when my older sister was still free to use her powers. Nuriela stepped back when she finished, and I turned toward her.

"When we get out of here, will you tell me about her?" The emotion in my voice was embarrassing. But I couldn't help it. She was the closest thing to my dead older sister, and I wanted to know everything there was to know about her. And so would Michaela.

Nuriela's eyes narrowed, and she looked at me, assessing. "I wanted to hurt you. For a long time, I blamed you for her death."

Returning her scrutinizing stare, I squared my shoulders. "So did I." Because she was right. It was my fault. The Obscuritas wanted me, but they got Lailah and things didn't go as planned. At least that's how the Princes thought it went, after the first ritual failed.

The beautiful lumen turned away from me and picked up the second piece of my dress. It attached around my waist like an extended train. The black fabric was a mix of silks and chiffon. Hundreds of tiny silver crystals adorned the chiffon pieces, making it look like an endless starry night. Nuriela deftly carried the mass of fabric to me and easily attached it to the dress, covering the buttons with pieces of fabric until the extra skirts looked seamless with the original dress. The entire ensemble really was stunning.

We looked at each other for a long moment. I was almost the same height as Nuriela in my three-inch heels.

"Well. Shall we go to this party full of pricks and figure out how to kill them all?"

Her lips twitched, attempting to hide her smile. "I suppose. I will be around, but out of sight. There are some who may recognize me."

I nodded, desperately wanting to ask my questions. But I knew they would have to wait. She left the room first, and I schooled my face, straightened my shoulders, and prepared to face the the fucking Kings once more. There were no guards at my door. Whatever distractions Nuriela created, they gave me time to myself, which was rare, and I was grateful. I walked through the halls, hearing the beat of music muffled by the many walls between me and the ballroom.

When I turned the next corner, I nearly ran over Michaela. "Shit!" I shouted, and she yelped, jumping back.

We stared at each other, eyes wide, until a smile broke across her face.

"You look gorgeous, Sara."

My insides warmed at how happy she sounded. "So do you, Kaela. Like a fucking princess!"

She truly did. Her dress was brilliant white silk with a sheer gold overlay. The sweetheart neckline suited her frame, and the dainty sleeves hanging off her shoulders were very Helen of Troy. Her heels were shorter than mine, so we were almost the same height now.

"Well, you look like some kind of dark queen. A goddess of the night, even." She giggled, and I noted her flushed skin and extra cheeky smile.

I narrowed my eyes. "Why are you so happy?"

Her mismatched eyes widened, and she flushed. "What do you mean?"

I grinned. "Did you just get laid?"

"No!" she squealed, and I laughed. Kaela smacked my arm. "It was just…stuff."

I giggled and threaded my arm through hers, forcing her to walk with me. "Well, you can tell me all about the *stuff* later.

Right now, we have to meet the fuckers who shat all over our family and maybe kill them all."

"No big deal." She shrugged, and we grinned.

This was the most I'd smiled in days. Having her at my side was melting the icy cage around my heart just the smallest amount. I couldn't let her in completely, though. If I did, and they took her from me, I don't think I would recover.

We walked in companionable silence, turning the final corner to see the main entrance of the ballroom. The massive double doors were closed, and standing before them with several armed guards were our two most dangerous enemies, Laszlo Blackbyrn and Samuel Delano.

I sneered at the wannabe kings. Fuck them. Samuel's bored expression annoyed me. I pictured his face screaming in agony, and my spirits lifted slightly.

"Michaela, don't you look lovely." Laszlo uttered the words with a deadly smirk. "I much preferred you naked and chained in my bed. But there will be many more of those nights to come."

Fuck this. I snarled and started at him. Before the guards could move in front of him, Kaela pulled me back.

"It's not worth it, Sara." She whispered the words, and I fumed, knowing she was right.

"If you're jealous, Seraphina, you can always take her place." Laszlo arched an eyebrow.

I smiled and let him see the devil in my gaze. "I'd love to. Just to see the bedsheets painted red with your blood as the sun rises."

Laszlo's dark eyes filled with rage, but he said nothing. Instead, he turned away from us, and a guard stepped forward with a pillow in his arms, two sparkling collars resting on it. Samuel picked up the first one and walked toward Michaela.

"A gift." Samuel smiled, his eyes dancing with pleasure.

I was immediately uneasy. Michaela lifted her hair, and he clasped the strange necklace around her throat. He took the next one and presented it to me. I lifted my hair and allowed the slimy prick to lock the necklace in place. We watched as Laszlo pulled a tiny remote from his pocket and pointed it at my throat.

"What the fu—" I gasped as a painful shock of electricity shot through my body. I stumbled, and Michaela grabbed my arm to steady me, her eyes wide with fear.

Laszlo smirked. "Neither one of you will have anything to say this evening. Unless you'd like to feel that again?"

My insides raged, and my blood practically boiled with hatred for these fuckers. But I said nothing, and Laszlo smiled, his eyes filled with delight. And lust. I fucking hated him.

"There's my obedient girl."

"Oh, fu—"

The collar zapped me again, and I wanted to scream. Michaela gripped my arm tightly, begging me with her eyes to calm down.

The music inside the ballroom dimmed, and suddenly the guards opened the doors. A butler stepped forward and announced through a microphone two names.

"Samuel Delano and Michaela Valdis."

Samuel held out his arm for my sister, and I froze in place. She gave my hand a squeeze and stood tall, walking to the stupid prick with her shoulders back and chin high. She was stunningly confident, and I loved her for it. She took his arm and descended the stairs into the ballroom. I knew what was coming next.

"Laszlo Blackbyrn and Seraphina Valdis."

Laszlo held out his arm for me, and I smiled sweetly. Just as I approached him, I swerved out of his reach and took to the stairs on my own. Several gasps and hushed whispers filled the room as I made my way to the bottom of the stairs ahead of my escort.

I surveyed the sea of trashy cult members before me. Several of them looked away quickly when I caught their stares. I wanted them to see my rage. To know how fully I hated them for the part they played in my family's destruction. These fuckers were willing to sacrific innocents for their own personal gain. They were the scum of the Earth. Speaking of, I noted Mr. Kingston in the crowd. He was dressed impeccably and speaking with a curvy woman in a red gown. He laughed at her words, the smile on his face falling when I locked my eyes with his. His beady eyes flicked across the room. I followed his line of sight and fumed at what I saw. Audrey Kingston was locked in a cage, her body on display with only the sheerest scraps of fabric covering her. She was dancing, following the slow beat of the music. My anger grew. She must be drugged or influenced by Samuel Delano, because there was no way in hell she'd do that willingly.

A small crowd of men watched her move, and I noticed a digital board beside the cage with numbers rising as different men raised their arms. They were auctioning her off. That would not be fucking happening. I would get her out of here before the end of this stupid fucking event.

The hungry gaze of a predator at the base of the steps drew my attention away from Audrey. Typhon was waiting for me, looking tasty as fuck in his dark suit. His wolf-like eyes gleamed as he took me in. He held out his arm, and I accepted it immediately. Ty whisked me away into the crowd and out of sight of Laszlo.

"You look fucking gorgeous, little vixen," Ty purred in my ear.

I winked at him then tapped the collar.

His eyes snapped to the necklace, and he frowned. "What is it?"

I rolled my eyes and searched the room for Laszlo but found Andras stalking toward us, forcing the crowd of cult members to part. His eyes narrowed in on the collar, and as he approached, he reached out and caressed my throat.

"What the fuck is going on, Andras?" Ty growled, gripping my waist and hovering behind me.

"My father is an asshat," Andras snapped. "It's a shock collar. She can't speak."

Of course, Andras would use a word like asshat when I couldn't comment on it. Would making fun of him be worth getting shocked? Maybe. Probably.

Devon and Levi appeared, and I smiled at them with the cheeriest grin I could muster. Dev's eyes widened as he took me in. Levi whistled and barged between the others, grabbing my waist.

"Hello, *mi diosa*," he purred, that easy smile I loved so much lighting up his handsome face. "You're stunning. Not that I'm surprised. Andras picked the dress. He chose Michaela's too, in case you were worried."

I smiled and pressed my hand to his cheek. His eyes shaded in confusion when I didn't speak.

"She can't fucking talk without getting zapped," Ty snarled, and guests standing nearby backed away. "Can we kill that fucker now?"

Andras searched the crowd for his father, his mouth set in a hard line. "Soon enough, brother."

I tapped Andras's shoulder to get his attention. How did I tell him to find Michaela? I turned away and made to look through the throws of people. He understood, my dark knight always in-tune with what I needed.

Andras was over a foot taller than me and easily able to peer into the crowds of people to find her. He frowned. "I don't see her. But I'll go find her. Ty, with me. Levi and Dev, stay with her."

He brought my hand to his lips and kissed my palm much too erotically for my liking. Actually, I did like it. His lips on my skin woke up the horny bitch between my legs, but there was nothing I could do right now to satiate Miss Mina. And I couldn't sass him for getting me all worked up, damnit.

Andras quirked an eyebrow at me. "Behave."

CHAPTER TWENTY-FOUR
Seraphina

As if.

Levi's muscular arms wrapped around my waist from behind, and he pressed his lips to my ear. "Shall we go misbehave, *diabla*?"

I grinned and nodded, reaching for Dev. He was coming too. Levi took my hand and guided us through the crowds. I held tight to Dev's hand, the three of us receiving endless looks from the guests. My skin crawled at the feeling of dozens of eyes on me. Cages similar to the one I saw Audrey in were placed strategically throughout the room. One of the dancers was from Noircoeur, and I was grateful not to see my favorite twins, Josie and Lottie, in any of the other cages. The number of people we needed to save after this ritual was growing. I was maybe a little worried not all of us would make it out of this party alive.

The band began to play a lively song, and eyes drew away from us in favor of the dance floor. Of course, a bunch of fucked up people would think this is the time for dancing. Let's party before we murder an innocent woman in a creepy ritual! Okay, I wasn't innocent. But I still didn't deserve to be sacrificed.

Levi opened a slim door, and we slipped into a dark hallway lit only by candlelight.

"Staff-only hallways. Easier to sneak around." Levi grinned, and his navy eyes looked ominous in the dim lighting.

I licked my lips and could feel his eyes tracking the movement. He continued down the hall, tugging me further until we stopped in front of a single door. Levi opened the door and pulled me inside, Dev following close behind.

At first, I thought it was a closet. The shelves were mostly empty, except for a few fancy bottles of liquor. Levi continued into the small room to a second door, and when he opened it, a musty scent filled my nose.

The second door led down a staircase, but before moving forward, he turned back to me. "We should remove the skirts. Don't want to ruin your pretty dress."

Dev flicked on a light, and my two Princes began unbuttoning the heavy fabric. Dev gathered the skirts and stuffed them onto one of the shelves, making me laugh, silently of course.

It's going to look wrinkled as hell when I put it back on. I pointed at the skirts.

Dev shrugged, understanding my train of thought. "The only person ruining your dress will annoy is Laszlo. Fuck him."

I grinned and gripped Dev's suit jacket, pulling him close. I pressed my lips to his and kissed him hard. Would I get shocked if I moaned? I guess we were going to find out.

Dev pulled away, and I smirked at the lipstick smeared on his face. He was so fucking hot.

Levi suddenly grabbed the back of my neck and growled. "Let's go, *diabla*." He went first, holding my hand to make sure I didn't trip.

We descended into the wine cellar, and I was shocked at

how massive it was. Rows and rows of ridiculously expensive booze, and not a good place to fuck in sight. I wondered what his plan was, until he stopped in front of a glass-walled room at the back of the cellar. A tasting room. It wasn't exactly luxurious, but was designed for a small group. An oak wood table and four matching dining chairs sat in the center of the room.

Levi went into the room first and immediately walked to a small shelf to the left, pulling out a bottle of whiskey and three small glasses.

"This bottle is probably a few grand. I'm sure they won't miss it." Levi grinned, pouring us each a glass. He held up his glass. "To misbehaving."

Dev chuckled, and I smiled. We clinked our glasses together, and I relaxed my throat to take the shot all in one. The liquor lit up my insides in the most delicious way. I was so close to moaning out loud. I stomped my foot in frustration instead.

Levi laughed. "Poor *diabla*. Can't make a sound. Should we test that?"

Before I could move, Dev was behind me, deftly undoing the buttons down my back. "We're leaving this on, because you look stunning and I want to fuck you in this dress. But if I don't get one of your pretty pink nipples in my mouth right now, I'm going to lose it."

I gasped and instantly regretted it. The collar sent a shockwave through my body. Dev cursed, stepping in front of me and tilting my chin up to meet his eyes. My own threatened to spill tears, but I held them back.

"No sounds, *mera dil*. No pain tonight. This is only for your pleasure," Dev whispered, his soulful green eyes holding mine, and the world around us faded away.

Well, most of the world. Levi took Dev's place behind me and slowly pulled the thin straps of my dress down my arms. Dev's rough hands pulled the dress down with him, and when cool air hit my nipples, I almost gasped again. Dev's mouth was immediately on me. I leaned back against Levi as Dev sucked and teased my nipples with his tongue and teeth. The buds hardened further at his attention, and it took all of my willpower not to moan.

"Hush, *mi diosa*," Levi whispered as he nibbled my ear. "If you make a sound and the collar shocks you again, I'll have to tell Andras. And you know he'll punish us. No one is allowed to bring you pain besides us. And that fucking collar is our fathers' creation."

I scowled, not wanting to think about anything but Dev's mouth giving me pleasure and Levi's hands caressing my throat.

Dev released my nipples, and I silently growled. He dropped to his knees and leaned back so his gaze was even with the top of the slit on my dress. He glanced up at me, and his eyes were almost feral. "Are you nude beneath this dress, Seraphina?"

Levi chuckled. "Of course she is, our little slut." His grip on my throat tightened, cutting off the breathy moan I was so close to releasing. "Tell me what she tastes like, brother."

Dev wasted no time sliding his hands up my thighs and shoving the dress over my hips to widen the slit and give him an unobstructed view of my drenched pussy. Because, yeah, Mina was fucking salivating for these two.

"Fucking gorgeous," Dev purred, instantly slicking his fingers in my arousal. He pulled them away, and the digits glistened.

Dev brought his fingers to his mouth and licked slowly.

The sight had me close to moaning again, but Levi squeezed my throat again, keeping me silent.

"The most exquisite pussy I've ever tasted," Dev groaned. "And I'm ready to feast. Get her on the table."

Levi apparently didn't need to be told twice. He pulled me roughly by my throat until my ass hit the edge of the table. He grabbed my waist and set me on the edge. His rough hand holding my throat slowly lowered me to the wooden tabletop. I stared into his navy eyes, and my thighs clenched at the beast staring back at me.

Well, they would've clenched if Dev wasn't already there, prying my legs apart. He shoved his face between my legs, and I was ready to scream when his tongue licked a path from my ass to my clit. The only thing keeping me from another electric shock was Levi's hand squeezing my throat tight.

Dev groaned as his tongue speared me. His fingers dug into my thighs as he feasted on my pussy, and fucking hell, it felt divine. Images of that first time I had this delicious man between my thighs flitted through my mind. It seemed like yesterday and years ago all at once.

My blood began to tingle, and I squirmed in the arms of my men as they brought me to the edge over and over. Levi pinched my nipples hard then licked the hurt away. The dueling sensations paired with Dev's wicked tongue had me so fucking close.

I wheezed out a breath with the little oxygen available, and Levi chuckled. "Make her come, brother. She's desperate for it."

My mouth opened to scream, but Levi quickly clamped his

Resurrection

hand hard over my lips and winked, his blue eyes dark with lust.

I writhed beneath them, and the sounds were so fucking difficult to keep down. Dev's mouth clamped down on my clit just as he slipped two fingers inside me. He twisted and turned his fingers and fucked my pussy relentlessly with his hand. My back arched off the table, and Levi's hands stayed tightly wrapped around my throat and my mouth. I began to see spots as my vision darkened from the lack of oxygen. All of my senses fled south as Dev's teeth grazed my clit and the orgasm blasted through my body.

His fingers moved languidly, teasing my sensitive flesh while he lapped up the arousal leaking out of me.

Levi leaned over me with a smirk. "I'm going to fuck that pretty pussy now, *mi diosa*. And you're not going to make a sound. Not with Dev's dick down your throat."

He eased his grip on my throat and removed his hand from my mouth. I sucked in slow breaths, even though I desperately wanted to scream and shout and moan for these men. I nodded, my body already tingling with anticipation for what they would do next.

The way these Princes made me feel was unlike anything I'd ever experienced. My body responded to their touches, their dark stares, and their filthy words. I gripped Dev's hair and squeezed, silently begging him to fuck me.

Dev lifted his head and his mouth glistened. He licked his lips, and my pussy fucking throbbed as his eyes dilated, taking me in. "Let's smear a bit of that lipstick somewhere else, hmm?"

I nodded eagerly and opened my mouth. Dev groaned and brushed his thumb over my still-sensitive clit. "I love how eager you are for us. All ours."

It was so fucking true. I was theirs. And they were mine.

Dev stood from the chair and moved around Levi to stand near my head. Levi stood between my legs. Both men slowly unclasped their belts and unzipped their pants, almost in unison. It was so fucking hot.

I didn't know where to look first. Dev started to palm his hard dick through his red briefs, staring down at my body on display. Levi's hand slid up my thigh, and I turned back to him, tilting my head to see his thick cock staring back at me. I started to pant as he squeezed his dick, gently rubbing the head over my swollen clit. A bead of pre-cum oozed out of the head, and fuck, I wanted to tell him how much I loved this view.

Levi chuckled and his voice was rough with desire. "I know, *diabla*. You fucking love this cock, don't you?"

I nodded, and he grinned like the devil, his navy eyes lit with a fire only I could coax out of him. Maybe I couldn't talk, but I could make them just as desperate as I felt. I slipped one hand down my stomach, and the other wrapped around my breast. I squeezed and teased my nipple. My other hand I slid between my legs, and I used my fingers to spread my pussy lips wide for Levi.

He sucked in a sharp breath. "Fucking hell. Just look at that pretty pink cunt. You're soaked." Levi gripped my waist and gave Dev a dark smile. "Keep her quiet, brother."

Dev's hand slammed down over my mouth a second before Levi thrust his thick cock inside me. He didn't wait for my body to adjust, and he didn't need to. My body was made for them. My pussy clamped tightly around his dick as he fucked me relentlessly.

Dev's fingers squeezed my cheeks, and I gazed up at him. "Don't make a sound, *mera dil*." Desire laced his whispered words, and I nodded.

Levi slowed his pace and brought his thumb over my clit, rubbing slow, teasing circles as he watched us.

Dev's cock sprang from his boxers, and I started to fucking drool. His cock was longer than Levi's, and curved up just slightly. How did I miss this dick so much?

I opened my mouth, and he instantly pressed the head to my tongue. I swirled my tongue around the tip and sucked, pulling him further into my mouth. Dev cursed, and his hand snapped out to squeeze my throat. His other hand went to the back of my head, threading in my hair and holding tight. Dev pumped his cock into my mouth at a steady pace. I couldn't move. His hands locked me in place and controlled the movements completely.

Levi's fast and hard pace returned with a growl. They had me at their mercy, and my blood began to sing with pleasure. Power beat steadily somewhere inside me, responding to my euphoria. I sucked in a breath, and Dev squeezed my throat before I could moan out loud.

"You take this dick so fucking good, *diabla*," Levi grunted, his thumb moving over my clit faster. "Your body was made for me. Made for us."

Dev groaned as I sucked him in deeper, the tip of his cock hitting the back of my throat. "Yes. Fuck. Take me all the way in, *mera dil*."

"She likes that new pet name," Levi groaned. "Her little

cunt squeezed me so tight when you said it."

Dev grinned, and my eyes watered when his dick throbbed and thickened in my throat. His dilated pupils nearly blacked out the pretty green color. His movements turned choppy, and his grip on my throat and my hair tightened painfully. It felt fucking divine.

The whispered threats of the things they would do to me. The things that would happen when the five of us could finally be together. Just the thought of fucking all four of them at once was enough to send me over the edge. A scream bubbled up in my throat, but Dev tightened his grip, forcing the sound away before it could leave my body. He fucked my face with abandon as Levi destroyed my pussy with his wild pace.

My orgasm came in waves, cresting once just as Dev's hot cum shot down my throat. And then a second wave of pleasure knifed through me when Levi slammed his cock to the hilt and filled me.

He pumped slowly as my pussy throbbed and squeezed him tight. "Such a little cum slut, *diabla*. I can't wait to see you covered with all four of us."

I wanted to groan. His words had me squirming and ready for another round.

Dev's rough hands released me, and he brought his face down to mine. "Absolutely stunning." He kissed me gently, brushing his fingers along my neck soothingly.

I gasped into Dev's mouth, suddenly feeling Levi's tongue between my legs. Dev and I both turned in shock.

Levi looked up, his own cum and my arousal coating his mouth. "What? I was hungry."

Resurrection

I smiled and held back a laugh, propping myself on my elbows to watch Levi lick up the mess between my legs. Gods, I fucking loved him.

Holy shit.

My eyes widened at the thought that crossed my mind so suddenly. Did I love him? Even thinking it again made my insides feel all warm, and oh my gods, I did. I was in love with him.

Could you love four people at once? I didn't see why not. My heart was blasted into pieces anyway, surely there were enough for each of them.

After Levi got his fill, he and Dev were extra gentle helping me redress. My lipstick was a mess, and I likely had freshly fucked frizz in my wavy hair, but whatever.

We made our way out of the rooms, after they expertly reattached the very wrinkly skirts to my dress. Levi led us back out to the party. The night was officially in full swing with maybe two hundred people mingling and dancing. Dev snagged us a couple glasses of champagne. My throat was sore, but not as sore as it would be if I had been screaming their names. Score one single point for the fucking shock collar.

The air buzzed with a strange energy when we returned to the party, instantly making the hairs on the back of my neck stand on end. I caught whispers of someone locked up and on display, a man being punished for his crimes against The Obscuritas. Dread began to build in me just as Andras pushed through the crowds toward us.

"I found your sister. She's…alright." His gaze caught mine, and I frowned at the worry I saw there. "But you're not going to like this."

Levi gripped my waist, refusing to let me go. "I've got you, Seraphina. We're all here, no matter what comes."

I did not fucking like this somber mood chasing away all the happy endorphins one bit. All the hairs on my body stood as nerves wracked through my body. Something was wrong. We walked along the edges of the dance floor to the far side of the room. As we approached the corner, the crowds lessened and I caught a glimpse of Michaela's golden hair. I was instantly relieved to see she was unharmed, but that relief was quickly chased away by the stupid King next to her. She was standing before a large iron cage with Samuel Delano at her side. He smiled, looking entirely too pleased as he watched her face. Something was definitely wrong.

Levi squeezed my arm as we approached, and I sucked in a shocked breath at what I saw. Or rather, who I saw, in that cage. Joseph Bronwen. Our father. He was chained to a St. Andrews Cross, wearing only a pair of boxers. Bruises and blood marred his skin. His face was a mess of the same. Michaela turned to me, and tears streaked down her face. I raged in silence.

I had noted our father's absence at the many meals and wondered. I knew he was here. I saw him that first day, and then he vanished. Neither me nor the Princes could figure out where he was being held. Wherever he had been, it wasn't good. One of his ankles looked broken, and his fingernails were all missing. He was tortured, and from the lack of fresh blood, I'd guess most of it happened at least a couple days ago.

My body shook with so much rage, and I couldn't even scream. Samuel turned and locked eyes with me, but before he could speak, Levi stepped between us.

"If you say a fucking word to her, I will strangle you right fucking here." Levi's words were low and filled with venom. I rarely heard him sound so deadly and couldn't deny how fucking sexy it was.

Samuel shrugged and walked away without a word. I squeezed my sister's arm as she gazed at our father. His eyes flicked open and scanned the room until they landed on us.

He smiled, and it almost broke me. "My girls. Together again."

We stepped closer to the bars in front of the cage so he wouldn't have to turn his head to see us. This was the worst fucking thing ever. How many years had it been? Nearly a decade since I saw him in person, and this was our first chance to speak to each other. I knew the fucking Kings planned this. Of course they fucking did.

Everything about their plans was meant to cause maximum pain, physical and mental. Gods, they needed to fucking die.

"She's here too," our father whispered, so quiet we almost missed it. "My Lailah. She's coming too. My girls. All together again."

Michaela and I shared a look of confusion. Maybe the injuries were bad enough he didn't know what he was saying. Maybe he was seeing things?

"I did it, my love." He spoke again, and it seemed to take all the light from his eyes. "Not for the world. For you."

His eyes closed, and his breaths grew shallow. His head slumped, and Michaela let out a silent scream.

"He's not dead," Andras whispered gently. "Only passed out, I think. He's in a lot of pain."

I pulled Michaela away from the cage. We couldn't stand here all night. Not with everyone staring. My Princes guided us toward a bar in the opposite corner of the room, close to the wall of windows and glass doors leading out to the courtyard.

Typhon clasped his arm around Dev's shoulder. "Brother, I need your pickpocketing skills." Ty grinned and winked at me.

I raised an eyebrow, staring at them in confusion. When was Dev sneaking into pockets, and why did he need this skill right now?

Ty squeezed the back of Dev's neck, and Dev rolled his eyes, trying to shrug my monster man off of him. But Ty was a beast and wouldn't let go. He dragged Dev away, and I turned my confused stare to Andras.

Andras rolled his eyes. "A story for another time, *belle femme*. Let's get you both a drink."

CHAPTER TWENTY-FIVE
Devon

Typhon pulled me away from our girl, and I didn't stop him, only because I knew exactly what he needed from me and it was going to help her. The taste of her decadent cunt still coated my tongue, and my dick was about half-hard again. She was the most beautiful woman I'd ever met, and until now, I hadn't realized how truly fucking hot it was to share her with them. My anger and muddled mind blinded me before. Seeing her come undone like that and hearing the filthy things Levi said while we filled her was easily one of the sexiest experiences of my life.

Going from a high like that to seeing the life leave her eyes as she beheld her father was like a suckerpunch to my chest. I wanted to burn this world to the ground if only to never see that look of devastation in her eyes again.

"I'm going to take a guess and say Samuel has the keys to the cage," Ty whispered low enough for only me to hear. "That cross is my father's, and I know they swap torture devices."

I nodded. "And Laszlo will have the key to the collars. He'd want that control."

Ty snarled at my words, and I felt the same.

"Levi can handle his father," Ty asserted.

"I've got Laszlo." I spat the words through my teeth. It would be a small pleasure at least to lift the key from the supposed most powerful Obscuritas King.

When we were younger, the four of us were constantly sneaking around and getting into trouble. I was the smallest, not hitting my growth spurt until a few years after they did. Since I was the most unassuming, it was always my job to steal things for us. Car keys for joy rides, keys to the cellar for stealing the fancy booze, and once even keys to the cells. That last one ended badly. It was after the ritual that killed Seraphina's mother and sister.

Our fathers were in a rage that it was unsuccessful. They had power, but not what was promised. No beings came to give them what they truly wanted. Immortality. Our fathers wanted to shed their humanity completely and become daemons themselves.

Not like what we had now, with the relics and limited abilities. It would be a complete transformation. Supposedly. Why a powerful daemon would offer that to humans, I wasn't sure.

When it didn't go as planned, our fathers tortured countless members of The Obscuritas to find out what happened.

We snuck into the dungeon one night, curious enough to go and too stupid to realize what we would see.

The cells were completely filled with prisoners. And even more were chained to the walls in the damp room below the cells. Some were dead, left to rot, their decaying forms stinking up the rooms enough to make us vomit. I had never seen a dead body before then. Seraphina's mother's and sister's bodies were gone when we woke up from the failed rituals. I never knew what happened to them.

"There's Laszlo." Ty's voice pulled me from my thoughts. "I'm off to go annoy the fucker."

I snorted a laugh as Ty set his sights on Andras's father. He was chatting with a few members, one of them a famous rap star. Not anyone I liked; he was horrible to women and everyone knew it.

Ty barged into their little group, stumbling and slurring his words. I slipped quietly behind them, moving between the people behind Laszlo who were being drawn in by the commotion. Ty "fell" into Laszlo, and I jumped into action.

My face was equal parts annoyed and embarrassed as I grasped at Ty. "Sorry. Too many shots, I think."

I flicked my eyes to another player on our team, James. He was Ty's number two man, outside of the four of us. He was Ty's gym manager and one of our most trusted recruiters of the Umbra Noctis.

After that night with all the bodies filling the dungeon, we made a pact to change our fates. And destroy our fathers. We created the Umbra Noctis, a secret order of Obscuritas defectors. My brows pinched at the memories. I hadn't thought about those times in years. When things started getting rough between my father and I, after my sister died, I distanced myself from them too.

James started to fuss with Ty, and my dramatic brother started flailing and shouting even more, bringing my mind back to the task at hand.

Laszlo's eyes raged, staring hard at Ty. This was my moment. I slipped my arm between where Ty leaned against Laszlo and easily fingered the collar keys. Laszlo's arms jerked up, suddenly pushing Ty away, and I jumped back, letting the key slide up my sleeve.

"Did someone say shots?" Ty barked, slurring his words for added effect. "To the bar!"

I turned away quickly to hide the laughter on my face. Ty winked at me, and we bolted for the opposite side of the room.

CHAPTER TWENTY-SIX
Seraphina

Andras and Levi guided us out to the courtyard, and I sucked in gulps of the wintry air. The sky was cloudy and smelled like snow. The full moon shone down on us between the clouds. Two figures moved out of the shadows, and I turned quickly, needing an outlet for my rage. Andras grabbed my arms before I could attack.

"*Sois douce, belle femme,*" he whispered, his voice deep and soothing. "It's only Morax And Xavier."

Xavier stepped out of the darkness with a confident swagger and that pretty smile I remembered from my visit to the firehouse. He winked at me, and because I enjoyed teasing my Princes, I winked back.

Levi growled. He grabbed my face and stepped in front of me, blocking Xavier's view of me. "Do you need to be reminded whose cum is leaking out of your sweet cunt, *diabla*?"

I licked my lips, and Levi pushed his thumb inside my mouth, forcing it open. Andras stepped in closer and grabbed the base of my hair tightly, turning my head his way while Levi pressed his thumb down on my tongue.

Andras spit in my mouth, and my pussy throbbed. "Ours, sweetheart. You belong to us. If you wink at Xavier again, I'll be forced to let Levi pluck his eyes out. And then his little gang will come after us. Let's not start a war when we already have one up our asses, hmm?"

When I said nothing, the hot bastard smirked at me. "Good girl. Now swallow."

Levi released my bottom lip, and I swallowed dramatically. My Princes grinned, satisfaction and dark lust swirling in their gazes. We turned together as the second figure emerged from the shadows.

As soon as she saw Morax, Kaela ran to him, throwing her body into his arms. The daemon wrapped her up with a predatory growl. His horns appeared, and his eyes glowed a golden yellow as he searched her face.

"Why do you cry, *mae domina*?" Morax murmured, brushing her cheek with his large clawed hand. The daemon was massive, his presence dwarfing my five-foot-six sister.

My sister buried her head against his neck, and I stepped toward them with Andras at my side.

"They cannot speak," Andras responded. "The sparkling necklaces are shock collars."

Morax snarled, and lesser men would piss themselves at the fierceness of that sound. "I'll rip it off."

"No," Andras interrupted. "My father will know. Just a few moments and we will have the keys."

Morax nodded, his face softening as he stared into my sister's eyes. "It will be over soon."

The words left his lips, and the doors to the ballroom opened. We turned collectively, and relief washed through me at the sight of Ty and Dev pouring out onto the patio. As soon as they were away from prying eyes, Ty's drunken stumble disappeared and his feral eyes found me in the darkness.

He stalked toward me, picking me up and crushing his lips to mine. I melted into his arms, needing his strength.

Dev followed closely behind him. "Turn her around, Ty. Let's get this shit off."

Ty gripped my hips and turned us around. There was very little light out here, the cloudy skies blocking out the moonlight. Morax walked toward us with my sister at his side. He lifted his free hand, and a glowing orb of fire appeared.

My eyes widened. *That's fucking cool. Can all daemons do that? Can we learn to do that?* I needed this collar off immediately. Not being able to speak was driving me nuts.

Morax held the fire aloft, and Dev slipped the keys out of his sleeve. He stood behind me, brushing his hand down my back and making me shiver.

"Say please," Dev whispered, and I could hear the smile in his playful tone.

I turned my head and winked at him. This Dev, the one who was sweet and spicy, he was my favorite. I pulled my hair off my neck and gave him access to the stupid collar. He quickly pressed the magnetic key to the engraving on the back. As soon as I felt the lock release, I tore the thing off and snarled.

"Fucking hell that was annoying," I practically shouted. "I'm putting one of those things on Laszlo the next fucking chance I get."

Ty chuckled and wrapped his arms around my waist. "I missed your filthy mouth."

He leaned in for a kiss, and I bit down on his lip. Ty snarled at me, and I smiled, licking away the hurt. I broke away long enough to see Dev unlock the collar from my sister's neck. She whispered her thanks to him before turning back to her daemon mate.

"I'm surprised there aren't more guards out here," Michaela cocked her head, looking around the massive patio that lead to the expansive gardens beyond.

Morax huffed. "There were. Some are dead. Some are unconscious and wishing they were dead. Xavier helped me dispatch them. He's quite efficient for a human."

Xavier smiled, clearly pleased to be complimented by the daemon. "I'm more than happy to join the fray if it involves the destruction of The Obscuritas. They're bad for business."

Michaela smirked. "Good riddance."

I grinned at her with pride. "Wow, little sister. I didn't know you were so villainous."

She crossed her arms and shrugged. "They all deserve it. For what they did to our mother and Lailah. For what they're doing to our father. And for what they did to us."

I walked toward her and pulled her into a hug. I didn't know why. I wasn't overly affectionate when it came to serious feelings. But in that moment, I needed to hug my sister. Her slim arms wrapped around me, and she squeezed tight.

"For all of them," I whispered into her ear. "And for us."

"Little vixen…" Ty purred, and the devil in his voice made me shiver.

I let my sister go, and Morax immediately moved in to steal her attention away as I stalked over to my monster man.

"Yes?"

Ty's hand snapped out, and his fingers wrapped around

my throat. He pulled me in close. "Give us a song, pet. Now that you've got your voice back, why don't you use it to upset the masses?"

Levi laughed, coming up beside Ty. His navy eyes were a mix of lust and rage. "Yes, *diabla*. Show them who the fuck they're messing with."

Ty's grip tightened around my throat, and I moaned. Dev and Andras stepped up behind me, closing in. I was surrounded by my Princes. My thighs clenched, and I wanted nothing more than to get this orgy started right here.

Morax let out a dark laugh. "*Mae domina*, perhaps we should leave before your sister and her men start fucking right here on the patio."

"Ew. Sara, at least wait until I'm not here to watch," Michaela whined.

I let out a laugh, as much of a laugh as I could with Ty's fingers squeezing my throat.

He leaned in. "Soon, pet."

I nodded, completely in agreement.

"I have something for you both." Morax interrupted again, and this time I pulled away from Ty to turn to the daemon.

My Princes stayed close. Morax pulled out two small boxes, offering one to me and one to my sister.

"I almost forgot about these," Michaela whispered, tracing the M on her velvet jewelry box.

I traced the S on mine before slowly opening the box. Inside was a delicate chain necklace with a beautiful dark stone attached. I picked it up, and the stone pulsed. I felt the power of it down to my toes. It was beautiful, and I couldn't take my eyes off of it.

Andras peered over my shoulder at the necklace and raised an eyebrow. "What is it? I can feel…something."

"Me too." Dev was equally mesmerized.

"The stone you hold is called tenebrite," Morax responded, his voice low and reverent. "It carries the essence of a daemon. I am not sure who, though."

"And mine is called luxenite. It possesses the soul of a lumen." Michaela held up her necklace, and the opalescent stone twinkled in the moonlight.

Morax nodded at her words. "A daemon or lumen can choose to sacrifice their place among the stars in order to give their power to the stone. It can only be used once. And depending on how powerful the creature was, the power unleashed could be devastating."

"So, can we just drop the little stone into the ballroom and wipe all those fuckers out now?" I huffed, because hell yeah to that plan.

Morax shook his head, though, and I pouted. "No. The ritual needs to happen. But I have a feeling whatever comes after, we may need the power of at least one of those stones."

I nodded, closing the powerful trinket in my fist.

"One more thing." Morax produced a vial and presented it to us. "Each of you must drink a single drop of this potion."

"Unlikely," Andras scoffed. "What is it?"

Morax growled in irritation. "The witch didn't say, only that you'd need it. I trust her."

Drinking mysterious potions, as a rule, was a no-no. But this daemon proved himself, and I was going to trust him. Before

Andras could protest, I took the vial and dripped a single drop onto my tongue. Nothing cool happened. *What a letdown.* The princes followed my actions, each taking a drop from the vial.

When it was done, I turned my eyes to Morax. "Take Michaela and get out of here. She doesn't need to be here for this."

Morax turned to my sister, his expression torn. "I should stay, for my brother."

Michaela shook her head and glared at me. "I am *not* leaving you. Or our father."

I ignored her and forced Morax to hear me. "If you say your brother is important and this has to be done, so be it. I will do the fucking ritual, and we will be here to help him do whatever needs to be done. But take her. Now."

"Time is running out, party people," Levi murmured. "Guards headed this way."

We'd been out here too long. The Kings had probably noticed. I stared at the daemon, begging him to take my sister away from this. If it went to hell, I didn't want her here. I honestly wasn't sure I could save our father. Morax gave a single nod.

Michaela's eyes widened, catching the small movement. She backed away in anger.

His eyes turned golden, and he sighed. "We will meet you at Vespertine Hall."

"No, Sara. Morax. Don't do this—"

My sister's words were cut off when Morax snatched her waist and leapt into the sky. His wings snapped out, and in a matter of seconds, they were gone. My shoulders slumped.

Strong hands wrapped around my waist and pawed at my flesh. The mix of gentle and rough touches from my Princes fed my dark soul.

"We will be here, no matter what comes next." Andras spoke first, his voice strong and sure.

"I know." I sighed, eyeing each of them and taking strength from their confidence. "I just wanted her to be somewhere safe, in case it doesn't work out."

Levi's fingers gripped my chip, pinching hard and making me cry out. "Don't say that. We are all walking away from this."

I took the pain he offered, and the assurances. As long as I had them with me, I wouldn't be afraid. But my feelings were so wrapped up in them now, and I didn't want to die; didn't want them to die. And I would do whatever it took to keep them alive.

"If you die, we die, pet," Ty growled, sensing my thoughts somehow. "I told you once before. There is only us. All or none."

Dev nodded in agreement. "Only us."

My heart grew two sizes like I was the fucking Grinch at Dev finally accepting this crazy thing we had together.

"Alright. Only us," I conceded.

Ty grinned, and the devil was in his gaze. "Now give us a song, little vixen. And make the Kings wish they were dead."

CHAPTER TWENTY-SEVEN
Seraphina

My Princes kept the Kings occupied while I snuck up to the stage, contemplating which song I should sing. A few good options for the occasion came to mind, but the likelihood of me having time to sing more than one before the stupid Kings ripped me off the stage was slim.

My insides were buzzing with energy. Somehow, I knew it was almost time. The latent power hiding somewhere in my blood was pulsing, eager for whatever was coming next. The tenebrite stone on my wrist seemed to respond to my power in kind, a steady thrum of energy growing within. I couldn't wear it on my neck and have Laszlo rip it off when he noticed the missing collar, so I wrapped the slim chain around my wrist like a bracelet instead.

The band members eyed me suspiciously when I walked on stage, heading straight for the lead guitarist.

"Hey. Laszlo Blackbyrn has requested I sing a song before, the uh, ritual stuff."

I was prepared to give a speech, or fight, but the guy just shrugged.

"If you say so. What'll it be then?"

The guitarist's British accent sent a pang of need for my best friend to my chest. I whispered the song to him, and he and the others got into position. A microphone waited for me, and I stepped up to it, looking out at the crowd. I could see my father's cage from here, his beaten body dangling from that fucking cross. I closed my eyes, centering my mind, my heart. We were at the precipice. Everything I aimed to do for nearly a decade was coming to a head. This was an ending and a beginning. A new path was opening, but what would be on the other side, I wasn't sure.

The music began, and I opened my eyes, ready to sing. Dozens and dozens of creepy cult people stared up at me. They were so gross. I searched the crowd for my Princes and found them instantly. They stood together, and heat flooded my body at the sexiness of that foursome. I smirked. Oh yeah. A fuckfest was coming.

Ty's grin turned wicked, and he whispered something to Levi, who also grinned. My men were being filthy. Even the stoics, Dev and Andras, turned heated gazes my way. My body shivered, and I gripped the mic, preparing to sing.

"This one goes out to our fearless leaders, The Obscuritas Kings," I murmured the words, dropping my voice low and humming with the music.

I sang out the first words of the song. Tonight's performance was for them. And for me. I chose "I am the Fire" by Halestrom. As I sang out the defiant lyrics, my blood heated and my skin tingled with power. The necklace wrapped around my wrist pulsed in response to the magic waking within me. It was coming. My reckoning. My resurrection. I would claw my way out of this hell, one way or another, and this stupid cult would see its fucking end.

Resurrection

The gazes of several angry pricks peppered my skin as I swept my own across the crowd. My eyes locked with Laszlo's furious ones. I smirked, singing out the chorus once more. His lips set in a hard line. My eyes searched the crowd for my Princes, feeling their hungry gazes watching every sway of my hips. The endgame was the same, revenge to all who wronged my family, but now I had several someone's to live for, dying in the name of that goal was less appealing.

The final words of the song rang out to a symphony of whistles and thunderous applause. That latent power in me continued to pulse, and I knew it was time for the ritual. My guess was on point, as per fucking usual, and dozens of guards entered the ballroom, blocking all the exits.

My Princes were forcefully escorted to the center of the room, but it was Laszlo Blackbyrn's casual gait I tracked. He walked up to the stage, and I glared down at him.

He offered me four slow claps. "What a lovely performance. I see your voice is as enchanting as your mother's. Did you know she could sing?"

Angry tears threatened to fall when memories of my mother flashed in my mind. I did know she could sing. She would sing us to sleep nearly every night. Her voice was soft and delicate where mine was lower and rough around the edges. I used to imagine us singing together when I grew up, but Laszlo took that dream from me, like so many others.

He smirked at the turmoil written on my face. "It is time for you to meet your end. The infernal pain in my side that you are will be no more. And your essence shall be mine."

I wrinkled my nose. "Don't say essence. It sounds perverted.

Although, you are in fact a fucking pervert, so I guess that makes sense."

"Bring her to the circle," Laszlo snarled and turned away.

Several sets of hands latched onto my arms, and I resisted the urge to commit murders. Blood would get all over the band members, and they were cool, so that would be rude.

I caught a glimpse of my father being pulled from the cage and frowned. What did they have planned for him?

Morax seemed to think we'd have several minutes to get the fuck out of here once the ritual was in full swing, and we would know when to make our move by the arrival of his brother. I was mildly curious about this daemon prince, Phenex. Hopefully he wouldn't be as dull as his brother. No offense to my sister's taste in monsters, but I preferred mine a little wild.

The party guests were ushered into positions around the room, leaving a large circle at the center. Several cloaked figures poured ash from containers, creating a five-pointed star on the tiled floor. The guards pushed me to the center of it. A set of chains attached to a bar on the floor were quickly snapped around my wrists.

"Kinky." I smirked.

Ty chuckled behind me, and I turned to my monster man. His laugh was casual, but the darkness in his eyes was anything but. I winked at him, attempting to ease his stress.

Levi was next to him, placed at the next point of the star. Andras and Dev came next, forced to stand at two of the other points of the star. Chains were pulled from the floor and locked around their wrists, like my own. Four cloaked figures came forward and placed the Princes' relics in front of them, within the star. Laszlo and Samuel stepped out of the crowd, gazing at the five of us. *Well, shit. Here we fuckin' go.*

"Tonight," Laszlo's voice boomed throughout the ballroom. "The events of that unholy night will be complete. The power we were meant to have shall be unleashed. All who kneel before us shall be rewarded. *Ego Sum Tenebris.*"

"*Servimus Tenebris!*" Voices chanted all at once, and I nearly jumped out of my skin.

I rolled my eyes. "You guys are all so fucking lame."

"Silence!" Laszlo snapped, his face furious.

I smiled, because it was honestly my favorite thing to piss him off.

Samuel smiled back at me, and that was actually scary. He was so fucking creepy, and I hated that he was impossible to read.

"Bring forth the sacrifice," Samuel called out, and suddenly my father was shoved forward.

I jerked in his direction, but the chains kept me locked in place. He looked horrible, and I was glad Michaela wasn't here to see him like this. Nausea built in my stomach, and goosebumps peppered my skin. What was his part in all of this?

Laszlo nodded for my father to be brought closer, just outside the star of ash surrounding me. "To begin, a sacrifice must be made. I was hoping to have your sister for this, but she seems to have disappeared."

"What a shame," I snarled.

Laszlo smirked, and I hated that he could see me getting riled. "Your dear father will have to do. Even though he's not your biological father, surely you still care for him?"

My heart dropped into my stomach. "What the fuck did

you just say?"

Laszlo cocked his head to the side. "You didn't know? Even my son knew this. How could a creature like you possibly be born of a waste of a human like Joseph Bronwen? What your mother saw in him will always be a mystery."

I stood straight, not liking this one bit. This was not information you simply processed and moved on from. I could feel the truth of his words, though. Joseph Bronwen was always good to us, but the connection I saw he had with Michaela was always stronger than what I felt. As if some small part of me was saving space for the love of a father I didn't even know I had. And Andras knew this? How could he not tell me?

Emotions burned through me, but I forced my face to remain neutral. Laszlo wanted to see me break, and there was no way in hell I would give him that.

Two cloaked figures ushered Joseph Bronwen into the center of the star, careful not to touch any of the lines of ash. My father's eyes were bruised, and one was unable to open.

His less fucked up eye opened enough to see me ,and my stomach dropped.

"Seraphina. My fierce child." He mumbled the words, his breaths ragged. "It's okay, my girl. I'm going to see them."

"See who? What's okay?" I reached for him, holding his arms as his body shook with the effort to remain upright.

"This is my destiny. I'm sorry I did it all wrong. But we made it. And I'll be with them soon." Joseph spoke in broken sentences that made no sense.

A cloaked figure appeared behind him and held out a dagger. I recognized it immediately as the one my mother left for me.

It seemed foolish to give me a weapon. I took it, and the power within me pulsed, nearly making me moan. It rushed through me like a tidal wave, rippling inside me and filling my veins with strange magic.

"You will slit his throat, and the ritual will begin." Laszlo's command rang out in the silent room.

"No fucking way," I snapped. Hell no. I wasn't going to kill my fucking father.

"Brave girl," Joseph whispered. "You must. Set me free. I will see you in the stars."

I had no fucking clue what he was saying. My eyes burned with tears, and the room blurred. My father continued to whisper strange words that sounded almost like a prayer. And he kept saying my mother's name.

The cloaked figures around us started chanting. But I couldn't do this. I couldn't kill him.

"Seraphina." Andras's voice carried to me over the chants, and I glanced in his direction. "We're here. Always."

His words were fierce and wrapped around me like a shroud of strength. But did anyone have the strength to kill their own parent? A parent who raised them and loved them, even when I wasn't his natural born child?

"Dad." I sucked in a sob, whispering the word I hadn't said in almost a decade. "I don't want to do this."

Joseph stood straight, seemingly finding the last of his strength to stare into my tear-drenched face. "You must. Only you can set me free and save them all."

I shook my head. "I can't. Michaela, she'll hate me. I'll hate me."

Joseph attempted to smile, his lips busted and bloody. "She will understand. Do this for us. For your mother. For Lailah. For me."

The tears completely blurred my vision now as the chanting grew louder. A point of no return was coming. My father knelt before me and bowed his head, that strange prayer on his lips. I had to do this, I couldn't see a way out. Not if I was going to save everyone else. I wiped the tears from my face and brushed my fingers through my father's dark hair.

"I love you." I whispered the words and placed the knife at the back of his neck. Being an assassin meant I had knowledge of the quickest ways to kill my targets. A knife between the first and second vertebrae would end a human life almost instantly. I used all my strength to stab my father, hoping he died too quickly to feel it.

His body slumped to the floor, and his blood coated my arms. I screamed in pure rage, my voice going hoarse as I shouted over the chanting fools around the room.

The power within me grew, the weight of it coursing through my body. I glared at the Kings. Laszlo's smile was disgusting. Samuel even had a hint of glee in his dead eyes. Four cloaked figures appeared beside each of the Princes and quickly sliced their wrists. I cried out but could do nothing.

My men roared in fury, but chained as they were, remained in place. Their blood dripped to the floor. When the crimson liquid pooled on the tile, it suddenly moved away from their bodies, spiraling until a circle of blood surrounded us and the star of ash. The blood caught fire, and the ash followed next. The heat of the flames licked at my flesh. The chanting of the

Kings and their followers grew to a deafening roar as smoke filled the circle and clouded my eyes.

The Princes were shouting, calling my name, but I couldn't see them between the smoke and flames. My father's body caught fire, and I cried as he burned. A fog built around me, and I choked on the smoke as flames crept up my dress. I pulled at my chains, but I was stuck here, helpless. How was I meant to survive this?

A voice started to whisper in my mind as I dropped to my knees, unable to stand as the fire engulfed me. I was going to burn. I thought of Lo Rigby and her sister, the first innocent victims on my fiery path of vengeance. It was fitting that fire would be my end.

"Smash the stone, Seraphina!" a voice in my head shouted at me.

I ripped the tenebrite from my wrist and immediately smashed it with the hilt of my mother's dagger.

The powerful stone burst into a cloud of black smoke that swirled around me like an infernal tornado. The darkness seeped into my nose, my mouth, and my fucking ears. It filled me until I slumped forward and darkness overtook senses.

"Seraphina."

Where was I?

"You're between worlds, my darling girl."

"Who are you?" *I tried to squint into the endless night but couldn't see a thing.*

"Your creator."

"My what?" *I whirled around in the darkness.*

A voice chuckled as a dim light edged closer and closer to me. "I am Belfegor. Your father."

"My father?" My thoughts were a jumbled mess. "Were you in the stone?"

"So clever." The voice sounded proud, and the light pulsed like a heartbeat. "Yes. I wanted to be here, to see you one last time."

I remembered vaguely what Morax said about the stone. "Where will you go now? Your soul…"

"I will be at peace, daughter."

If I had the ability, I would have been crying, slumped on the floor of this deepest darkness. I was losing two fathers in one night. The light grew, a beacon in the dark, beating to a slow and steady rhythm.

"You cannot be broken by these weak creatures, Seraphina. They do not control you. They do not own you. You chose this path. You gave yourself willingly. And they cannot take from you what has been freely given."

His words were an enigma and clear all at once.

"But I don't know how to save them all. I keep failing. I'm not the hero."

The light circled around me, and its warmth was a caress. I leaned into it, needing to feel something.

"No, my darling, you are not."

I let out a whimper at his words.

"You are a queen. A queen who chooses to kneel when she is needed. And a queen who will rise again when the time comes."

The light suddenly burst into a million stars, twinkling in the darkness and filling me with hope.

"The time has come, daughter. Rise. This is your resurrection."

CHAPTER TWENTY-EIGHT
Seraphina

I felt the heat of the flames again, but they didn't burn. I was becoming the flame, crawling from the ashes of my destruction to rise above my enemies in their time of power. But it was not to be their moment, it was mine.

The starlight in that other place filled me with strength. My father's strength. Somehow, I knew he was gone but still here for one final act. Words I never uttered before in my life flowed from my lips, and the flames grew around me. My dress was gone, turned to ash along with my former self. I stood, naked and coated in fire. There was an intense burning at my back, like some *thing* was just beneath my skin and desperate to be unleashed. The world around me was nothing but a soft noise buzzing in the back of my mind. I continued to chant, feeling the pull of a new creature.

Hello, my queen. I'm coming for you.

A deep voice whispered in the flames and caressed my mind like a lover's touch. I shivered. The feel of it made my heart race. I wanted this creature to come for me.

I saw him in my mind first. He was fucking gorgeous. His dark hair was long and wild, brushing against his shoulders. Charcoal-gray horns spiraled out near the crown of his head. A pair of ash-colored wings burst from his back. The tips of the feathers glittered like shards of silver. His tanned skin glistened with a silvery glow that matched the color of his eyes. They were strange and beautiful, and I couldn't keep my gaze away from him.

His chest was bare and chiseled. His jaw was strong and clean-shaven, perfectly accenting his high cheekbones and sensual mouth. A smirk played along those teasing lips.

"Hello, my beautiful mate. I've been waiting for you."

I sucked in a breath at his words, but I couldn't refute them. I could feel the pull of this creature in my soul. We were connected on some level I didn't fully understand.

"Phenex?" I whispered the name.

He grinned, and the devilish mouth did things to my body. "Of course. But we don't have time for all that now, my sweet. We need to get the fuck out of here. You ready?"

My mouth dropped open. "Ready for what? I can't do anything."

He cocked his head, his shining eyes roaming my body and reminding me I was naked. "There is nothing you cannot do, my queen. I will teach you. But later. Now, we have to kill things and run."

Before I could respond, the daemon slammed into the tiled floor of the ballroom, now fully in the flesh. He was fucking massive. I stared up at him, licking my lips. His eyes zeroed in on my mouth. His hand snapped out and pinched my lips together.

"No, sexy lip licking. I have to save us first," Phenex crooned.

My head cocked to the side, and I was not entirely sure what to make of this creature. He turned from me, and the flames danced away from him. I could hear The Obscuritas members chanting again, but it was broken and mixed with screams. What was happening outside the flames?

Phenex turned to the wall of windows and whispered a few words. Seconds passed, and then the glass shattered.

He turned back and scooped me up into his arms. "Time to go, tiny creature."

"Wait!" I held up my hands, realizing I still held my mother's dagger. "The Princes. We need to get them too."

Phenex rolled his eyes. "You don't need them."

I snarled at him with all the strength I could muster. "They are mine, and I won't leave without them."

He huffed but nodded, silver eyes twinkling. "Very well. You're going to be such a pain in the ass, aren't you, my queen?"

I shrugged, because probably. Phenex turned with me in his arms and spoke a few words, forcing the flames back and revealing my Princes. Their eyes went wide at the sight of me in the daemon's arms. Phenex waved his hand, and the chains on their wrists snapped off.

"Your relics!" Phenex shouted at them. "Grab them, and let's go!"

To their credit, my men didn't waste time asking questions. They each grabbed their relic and ran toward us, their wings snapping out. Phenex held me tight and leapt into the sky. The flames flashed out around us, forcing the cloaked figures to flee. I couldn't see the Kings, but I didn't care. The power that pulsed within me was fading, my strength was fading. And as Phenex took to the sky with me wrapped in his arms, I closed my eyes and sunk into the darkness, searching for my father's voice. But he was gone. They both were.

PART TWO

CHAPTER TWENTY-NINE
Andras

I flew through the sky with my brothers beside me. This new daemon was fast as hell and clearly more adept in the sky than we were. But I was fast, and there was no way in hell I'd let him get far enough away from us that I'd lose sight of Seraphina in his arms. She passed out, her hair blowing in the wind, and clung to him in her sleep. I snarled, unable to leash my daemon at the sight of her cradled in the arms of a stranger.

Everything happened so fast, I was barely able to process it. When Seraphina became engulfed in the flames, my heart stopped. I thought she was truly dead, burned to death before us. But we could feel her. The ritual connected us. There was a new thread, a bond, connecting her to me, and to the others. Even now, I could feel her. It was faint but still pulsing. As if the power of it was asleep, waiting for something. What, I didn't know.

As the flames grew higher we could hear her talking to someone in the fire. I didn't see another being, but she was clearly having a conversation with someone as the flames incinerated her clothing. The shadows of wings appeared for the shortest of moments; I almost missed them. But they were there. Her wings looked similar to the tattoos on her back, almost as if she knew they were coming. I would've scoffed at the absurdity, but knowing what I did about this world of magic we were embroiled in, anything was possible.

Seraphina stood in the flames, a living goddess. Her clothes were gone, and her hair had returned to its natural red color. She was born anew in that fire. Resurrected into what, exactly, was still up for debate.

When the new daemon arrived, I knew our fathers had not planned for it. Laszlo looked positively livid. Samuel was frowning, his eyebrows practically becoming one as he gazed at the daemon. Then all hell broke loose.

Daemons and lumens appeared around us, using their various powers to blast the cloaked Obscuritas away. Laszlo and Samuel were protected, their own guards taking the brunt of the power. Several daemons and lumens under my father's command stepped forward to fight back. It was chaos. I saw members of the Umbra Noctis, our people, join the fray. But there was no time for us to fight. With Seraphina so vulnerable, we had to leave. Levi grabbed Joseph Bronwen's burnt body, and we took to the skies with our relics, leaving everything else behind.

We had been flying for hours, and my adrenaline was fading. Did this crazy asshole think we would fly all the way to Boston? I sped up to catch him, flying at his side.

"Do you know where you're going?"

He nodded. "Of course."

The asshole suddenly dove toward the earth. We followed, soaring through the clouds until the glittering lights of a city lit up beneath us. I looked around, trying to place our whereabouts. Based on the mountains surrounding the area, it looks like we were in Roanoke, Virginia. We descended swiftly. Phenex landed on the roof of the tallest building, and we followed him.

"Is she alright?" Dev asked first, his face filled with concern. He quickly took off his suit coat and tucked it around Seraphina's naked body.

Phenex growled possessively but stopped when Seraphina sighed contentedly in his arms. He smirked at us, his dark hair blowing in the breeze and his silver eyes glowing in the darkness. It was unnerving.

"She's just a little exhausted from all the power rapidly filling her veins. She can handle it."

Typhon snarled, stalking toward the daemon. "How would you fucking know? Give her to me."

He stood tall and massive before the daemon, but Phenex towered over him by a few inches.

The daemon growled, the sound deep and commanding. His fangs descended and his skin glowed with a silver hue. "She is my mate. The only reason I haven't blasted you to the stars is because of her. She requested your presence. But don't fucking test me."

"What are we doing here, Phenex?" I snapped, stepping between the two monsters before blood was spilled.

Phenex continued to narrow his eyes at Typhon. "Waiting for Mor. I can't transport you all. Not after the amount of energy it took to come to this world."

I was about to ask what the fuck he was talking about when Morax snapped into existence. One moment there were shadows, and the next he was standing beside his brother.

He nodded to each of us. "Gentlemen." Morax squeezed

his brother's arm, relief in his golden eyes. "Good to see you, brother."

Phenex grinned, cradling Seraphina in his arms as if she weighed no more than a feather. "You too. Things were getting dicey in Caligo."

Morax frowned. "Father?"

Phenex shook his head. "Father is in a magical coma, locked down by witches. But Belial..."

"Fuck." Morax ran a hand through his dark hair.

Phenex nodded. "Indeed. Bel is coming here. He may be here already. He found me just before I said the words to accept her summons. I could feel him. But I think I was able to send him away. How far, I don't know."

Morax nodded. "Good. Let's go then, before he tries to sense us." The daemon turned to us. "Grasp hands and form a circle."

I glanced at the others, giving a curt nod, and we did as he asked. I stood next to Morax, and Ty growled low as he gripped Phenex's shoulder, since he refused to let go of our girl.

Morax and Phenex closed their eyes, whispering a few words in unison. The air tightened around our bodies. It felt like my lungs were being squeezed together. My body jerked, and I nearly let go of the daemon's hand, but he held tight. My heels slammed into the earth a few moments later, and I opened my eyes, seeing Vespertine Hall before us.

Without speaking, several came forward and took Joseph Bronwen's body from Levi. They walked solemnly around the back of the mansion. We didn't follow, waiting before the front doors with Morax.

"No one else can transpose through the barrier," Morax

stated, as if we knew what he meant.

I glanced around, squinting in the darkness. I wasn't sure, but there seemed to be something surrounding the manor. It was barely distinguishable to the naked eye, more of a feeling.

Morax turned and walked to the front doors, Phenex close behind with Seraphina still asleep in his arms. My brothers and I followed the daemons.

We were no longer tethered to our fathers, I realized, grasping the relic in my hand. Walking into the manor felt like the start of something, a new life, perhaps. A new beginning had arrived for us all. The uncertainty of it bothered me, but I held my head high, watching the woman I loved and knowing I would walk through any unknowns as long as she was beside me.

Chapter Thirty
Phenex

My power was practically vibrating out of my body with her so close to me. The mate bond sang with desire and need. I wanted to take her now, feel her body mold to mine as I claimed her in front of all of them. Especially the Princes. Those dirty blooded assholes were getting on my damn nerves. And Mor was so pleasant to them. *Hello, kiss-ass much?* I was his damn brother.

The beautiful creature in my arms stirred, and I held back a groan as my dick throbbed for her. She was everything and more. So much fucking more. I only saw a glimpse of her as a young girl, from her dying father. Even then she was fierce, and I couldn't wait to see the perfect creature she would become. And now I had her in my arms, I would never let her go—not for anyone. We would rule this world and all the others together. After the war, of course. And we killed all the bad guys. And maybe the wannabe princes. Once she understood our connection, she would let me kill them. I was mostly sure of that. We would be the greatest couple to ever exist. *Ugh. Yes.* It was all going so well.

I followed Morax into the dark manor lit mostly by candlelight. His scent was different, mixed almost completely with his new mate. They hadn't sealed the bond yet, though. Silly

Mor, why did he wait? How did he resist for so long? I had my perfect other half in my sights for a few hours, and the wait was agony. I needed to take her sweet pussy and seal our bond immediately.

Just the thought of her made my mouth salivate. She probably tasted like candy. And ice cream. And chocolate.

"Fucking hell," I murmured.

Morax chuckled. "Easy, brother."

He could sense my changing mood. I could let him into my mind, but for now, I wanted all the delicious thoughts of my mate's supple curves to myself.

We walked further until arriving at a small room, outfitted like a study, not unlike those in our own home. Morax and I kept a smaller manor together, away from our father's castle. It was around the same size as this one.

I stalked into the room, and Seraphina's eyes fluttered open. Her pink lips parted, and she looked up at me, her body pressed tightly to my own. The suit coat of the dumb Prince was still draped around her, and I ripped it off. She sucked in a breath, and I growled as her nipples hardened at the onslaught of cool air. Her eyes were still locked with mine.

My arms shook with the need to take her, but I wanted her to want it too. Fuck, I needed her to tell me she wanted it.

Her eyes dilated slightly, and that was it. I couldn't handle it. I shot across the room, pinning her to the wall. I flicked my fingers, and my pants dropped to my ankles, my dick springing free and bobbing against her perfect abs. She was so fucking stunning.

Seraphina sucked in a breath once more, taking in the

changing of our positions. I wrapped her legs around my waist, and her wet cunt pressed against my dick.

"WHAT THE FUCK!" one of the Princes roared at my back. I think it was the big growly one. I could feel them coming toward us.

I snapped my head around and unleashed several sets of vines, anchoring them to the floor. The Princes snarled and roared. I smirked and turned back to my mate.

"Hello, little creature." I pressed my nose to her neck, burrowing in her wavy red hair. It was the color of fire, and I wanted to melt into her sweet and spicy scent. "You're just as stunning as I knew you would be."

She moaned as I leaned into her, my dick pulsing as the shaft pressed against her wetness. She was soaked for me, her body ready for me even now.

I leaned down and nibbled her neck, moving lower to flick my tongue over her peaked nipples. "Fuck, I need to see these perfect tits covered in my seed. I'm going to mark every inch of you."

She whimpered, and I adored the sound even as the stupid males behind us raged.

"I can't wait," I snapped, pinning her to the wall with my power. A vine snaked out wrapped around her throat just as my wings snapped out.

Her hands held tight to my biceps, and her nails dug into my skin, near enough to draw blood. I groaned.

"Yes, *mini monstra*, mark me. Make me yours." I bucked my hips, coating my dick in her wetness.

Her eyes snapped open, feral and filled with desire. "No.

Not fucking you like this."

It was my turn to whimper. "Your body says otherwise." I slowed my movements, letting the head of my cock press against her clit.

She moaned, her nails digging into my arms more. "No."

I snarled. She was being ridiculous. I picked up my pace, my dick throbbing and needing release.

"As you wish. But I'm coming all over this pretty cunt."

I didn't give her another chance to speak, leaning in and crushing my lips to hers. I forced her mouth open and dominated her with my own. She moaned, pulling me close. I bucked my hips faster, slicking in her sweet heat.

"Fuck, your scent is intoxicating. Your sweet cunt smells like sin, and I'm going to drown in it for eternity." Just the feel of her pressed against me was enough to send me over the edge.

Hot cum spurted out, marking her body. I jerked against her, the last of my orgasm fading. My dick was still half-hard, and I could easily do that a hundred more times. If she felt this good like this, I couldn't imagine how mind-blowing it would feel to fuck her properly.

I bit her bottom lip, making sure not to break the skin with my fangs. "Soon, *mini monstra*."

Unspent desire filled Seraphina's eyes, and I smirked down at her. This was her own fault. Now she'd be all hot and needy for me.

I released the vine from her throat and scooped her into my arms once more, turning back to the angry dogs behind us.

"Where is her room? She needs to get cleaned up." I arched an eyebrow and smiled.

Morax chuckled. "Careful, brother. They are enamored with her."

"I don't blame them." I shrugged then wrinkled my nose. "I can smell her all over them. Who's the one with the bit of smoldering embers?" My gaze snapped to the navy-eyed Prince. "You, I think. You fucked my mate recently?"

Levi snarled at me. "She is ours."

I snarled back, hugging her tightly to my chest. "She's mine! And you can—"

"Stop it!" Seraphina stirred in my arms, her energy fading again and her eyes glazing over. "Stop fighting. Please."

My snarl softened, and I squeezed her limp body close to mine, unable to cause her a moment of harm. We would deal with this problem later.

"Yes, my queen," I murmured, kissing her forehead.

Her eyes closed and she snuggled into my arms, a satisfied purr rumbling in my chest.

"Will you put your fucking dick away?" the bright green-eyed Prince snapped.

I chuckled. "Show me to her rooms, and I will get dressed. Didn't realize we had prudes amongst us."

The big, wolf-like one smirked but smothered it before anyone noticed, and I grinned.

"Ty and Levi, show him the way," the final Prince commanded, and I could see this one thought he was in charge here. "Dev and I will go speak with Morax and ensure the manor is properly guarded. We will join you soon."

Morax shoved off the wall and followed the dark Prince and the prude out of the room. The pretty boy stalked closer, his dark-blue eyes flitting between mine and Seraphina. "I'm Levi. This is Ty."

I nodded, deciding to play nice for her sake. "You can call me Phen."

Ty crossed his arms, the tattoos dancing as his biceps bulged. He was pretty too, in a dark and sinful way. His scent was like a bite of poison. I could see why my *mini monstra* was drawn to them. Maybe I could let her keep them for playtime. My insides didn't completely recoil at the thought. How strange, since the mate bond generally kicked all thoughts of others from one's mind.

A flash of memory crossed my mind. Her father. He said something, so softly I almost missed it. And so strange I almost ignored it. *Her mates.*

I tugged on the thread of power connecting me to Seraphina. It wasn't as strong as it should be. Something felt like it was missing. Perhaps once we properly fucked and claimed each other, it would settle. Yes, that was definitely it.

The two Princes led us through a maze of hallways until we arrived at a large suite. There was a massive bed draped in sheer fabrics and covered in pillows at the center. Levi removed some of the pillows and pulled back the blankets. I laid our queen on the bed, tucking her in. She probably needed a shower, but I preferred her covered in my cum so these idiots didn't forget who Seraphina belonged to. Levi immediately lay down beside her. A decisively possessive growl built in my chest, but I decided not to kill him.

There was some tiny part of me that enjoyed the pretty Prince. I was no stranger to the delights of males. Over the centuries, I explored pleasure with a variety of men and women. The eyes of a predator were glued to my back. Ty. He was watching me while I watched Levi. There was tension, and I had an inkling these two may have been more than friends. How delicious. Visions of us playing together with Seraphina had my dick hardening once more. I grunted, leaving them to attend to her and searching for the shower. Dick in hand, I stroked myself until I came twice more in the shower, thinking of all the sinful things I was going to do to my mate, and maybe even her little toy princes.

CHAPTER THIRTY-ONE
Seraphina

My senses returned slowly. Everything felt the same and different all at once. The latent power flowing through me was stronger, just at the edge, so close I could taste it. The feeling was intoxicating. I wanted it, needed it to bend to my will.

I stirred, waking from the vivid dreams of worlds burning. Dreaming of fire wasn't new for me, but this was different. Dream me thrived in the fire, dancing with the flames and feeding them. The warmth of another body against my back brought me out of the fiery dreams. I tried to process what happened last night. Was it last night? I honestly didn't know. I was so exhausted.

The only moment of clarity was that sexy-as-fuck daemon wanting to fuck me. I said no, because I'm crazy, apparently. Mina, my horny-as-fuck pussy, must have been sleeping. She would never turn down dick like that.

Images of the daemon thrusting his cock between my pussy lips had my thighs clenching. Fuck. But my Princes were there too. They were screaming angrily as the daemon used my flesh and covered me in his cum. My cheeks flushed with shame. How could I let this stranger do that to me? They must hate me right now.

"Awake, *mera dil*?" Dev's rough voice brushed against my ear.

I nodded. "Barely." I was naked under the blankets. How I got here was still a bit fuzzy.

"What can I do? What do you need?" Dev's arms circled my body, tucking me in close.

"How long have I been sleeping?" I murmured.

Dev squeezed my body tightly. "About two days."

"Fuck." I turned in his arms, my gaze finding his. "Where is everyone? Where's my sister?"

He smiled, his eyes peppering my skin with tingling glances, making me shiver. "She is safe. For now, we are all safe. We are at Vespertine Hall."

I nodded, relieved to know we made it out alive. Well, not all of us. I choked out a sob. "My father."

Dev's smile dropped instantly, and his forehead pressed to mine. "I am so sorry, Seraphina."

I closed my eyes, tears threatening to spill over. Michaela must have been devastated. I needed to go to her. I pushed out of his arms, and Dev let me go.

"I need a shower and to see my sister," I demanded, crawling out of the bed and going to the ensuite. I shut the door, needing to be alone.

Joseph Bronwen was dead. He was dead and it was my fault. Did she know? Would she hate me? Both of our parents were dead now, but this time, I was the one who took his life.

I slumped in the shower, the hot water pouring over me.

"Seraphina, may I—" Dev's voice was cut short on the other side of the door.

Suddenly, a massive daemon was there, jumping into the

shower and pulling me into his arms. "I am here, my sweet."

I was too tired to move, to force this stranger away. But he also didn't feel like a stranger. Phenex, I remembered. His body was warm and comforting. His chest was bare, but he wore jeans, which were now soaked as he cradled me against his chest. My princes surged into the room.

"Seraphina! What happened?" Levi shouted, jumping into the shower, his clothes instantly soaked as he brushed his fingers against my cheek.

"Back off," Phenex snarled, squeezing me.

"Fuck you, daemon dick," Ty snarled, stepping forward.

This shower was becoming seriously crowded, and I had had enough. I shoved out of Phen's arms and stood before them all. "STOP IT. I will kick you all out if you don't fucking stop it."

I glared at every one of them, including Dev and Andras, who were leaning against the vanities. I turned to Phenex last. His eyes were on my face, their color brilliant like starlight. It was nearly impossible to look away. And maybe at another moment, I'd get lost in those eyes, but I was too sad and too angry.

"I don't know you. You're new. And maybe you're cool, but right now, you're at the bottom of the list, buddy," I snapped, and Phen frowned.

"How can you say this? Don't you feel our bond?" He looked at me with puppy dog eyes, like I just revealed Santa Claus wasn't real.

My arms went to my hips, and I didn't care about my naked body on display. "I don't know what I feel. But I do know these men here"—I gestured to the Princes—"they're mine. And I am theirs. That hasn't changed just because we have some kind of weird bond."

Phenex growled and stood, towering over me, but I wasn't afraid and glared back at him.

Levi chuckled. "We are, as always, yours to command, *diabla*."

The tension broke, and Phenex smirked. "Fuck, she's feisty."

Andras scoffed. "You have no idea."

I rolled my eyes. "Now get the fuck out so I can actually shower. I need to speak with my sister."

Ty's rough hands grazed my throat. "As you wish, little vixen. We will escort you when you're ready."

Phenex pushed Ty toward the shower door. "Yes *we* will."

The five hot-as-fuck creatures, three of them sopping wet, exited the bathroom, and I sighed, leaning my forehead against the tile. This was a shitshow. My pussy throbbed, and I smirked to myself. A shitshow I was maybe a little bit interested in diving head first into.

Walking through the halls to find Michaela was pure torture. I was anxious as fuck to see her, and also terrified she would never speak to me again. The Princes and Phenex walked beside me, offering me strength. Phenex was a prince too, I suppose, so now I had five royals under my thumb. If only I could hide behind them and not deal with this. Some all-powerful creature I was. I smoothed my hands against my leggings. Now that we were no longer in captivity, I could dress how I liked. It was comfy clothes all day long for me. My feet needed a break from the heels.

Phen could communicate with his brother and said we'd find him and Michaela in the smaller dining hall having lunch. It was nearly midday, but the cloudy skies of the northeast offered little light. Winter was in full swing in Massachusetts.

I squared my shoulders and walked into the dining hall, Levi holding the door and the others pausing to let me lead. He winked at me, offering a reassuring smile.

My sister was sitting next to Morax, nibbling on her lunch, her eyes staring into the distance as if she were lost in thought. I cleared my throat, and her head snapped up.

Michaela shot out of her chair and ran at me. I braced my feet, ready to take a punch in the face if she so desired. But she didn't hit me or scream at me. My little sister wrapped her arms around me, hugging tightly. My arms instantly did the same.

"I'm so sorry," I whispered, the words catching in my throat.

"Me too," she murmured back.

I pulled her away, staring into her beautiful blue and brown eyes filled with tears. "Why in the hell are you sorry?"

She frowned. "This wasn't your fault. And I'm sorry you had to do what you did."

I shook my head. "Kaela. Please don't. I failed you. I killed him."

She nodded, squeezing my hands. "I know." She glanced at the Princes at my back. "They told me everything. I made them tell me."

I scoffed. "Do you mean your daemon made them?"

She smiled softly, but it didn't reach her eyes. "Hey. I'm

tough too."

I squeezed her hands. "I know you are. More than me, I think." Everything Michaela had been through, and everything coming at us, she could handle it. I could see that. She was strong as hell.

Michaela shook her head. "No way. I don't know if I could have done what you did, even if it meant saving everyone. And that would have been wrong."

I nodded, unable to stop the tears. "He said…he said it was okay. He said he was going to them, to mom and Lailah."

Michaela's own tears flowed down her cheeks. Morax came up behind her, his massive frame offering comfort.

She leaned into him, keeping hold of my hands. "I hope he is. I hope they are all together."

"Me too." I swallowed, letting go of her to wipe away the salty tears rushing out of me. I wasn't really the crying type, but if there was a time, this was it.

"This is not over," Morax added, joining our conversation. His eyes scanned the others as he spoke. "Belial is here, on Earth. He has imprisoned our father, and we believe he's using him as a conduit to boost his own strength. What his plans are, I cannot say."

Phenex nodded in agreement. "Our brother is cruel and hungry for power. He doesn't care about anyone but himself. I thought our father was cruel, but it seems Belial is finally unleashing his darker side."

"So what do we do?" My gaze slid to Phenex. His silver eyes were more gray now, his power dimmed. They were still beautiful, and it was difficult to look away.

He smirked at me, as if he knew, and I narrowed my eyes at him. The stupid daemon was undeterred. "We get you at full strength. You are the daughters of Aurora Valdis and… well your father was Belfegor. The power in your veins is likely exceptional. Belfegor was from a different breed of daemons. He was not from Caligo."

"What does that mean?" I frowned, confused as hell.

"It means we don't really know what you are capable of, *mini monstra*," Phenex murmured, and I couldn't help glancing at his lush lips.

I clapped my hands together. "Well, let's get this shit going then."

A door opened on the far side of the room, and I peaked around Morax to see who it was. My breath caught in my throat, and this time it was my turn to run across the room. Tibby's eyes widened as I ran at her. She flinched, and I stopped short of wrapping her in my arms.

There were two imposing figures at her back. A woman with dark bronzed skin and curling hair. Her eyes glittered with the fierce look of a predator. The other creature was the daemon who saved Tibby. His horns were out, spiraling out of his long blond hair, and his skin glowed with a green hue.

They both stared at me, watching and waiting. For what, I wasn't sure.

Tibby's bright-blonde pixie cut was on display, no wigs or eccentric outfits. Her makeup was minimal, and she wore an oversize sweatshirt and dark jeans. Her face was shy, and her bright-brown eyes searched mine.

"Tibby." I whispered her name, remembering the last time I

saw her, being tortured by that prick of a King. "Are you okay?"

She sighed. "No. But I will be."

The daemon behind her brushed his hand down her arm, and she shivered. The woman smiled.

I had no clue what was going on, but I was glad she was here. She was safe. I turned my gaze to the daemon. "Thank you for saving her."

He nodded. "I wish I'd been able to do it sooner."

Tibby smiled at him, and her cheeks flushed. We needed some girl time soon. I was dying to know what this throuple vibe was all about.

"Gremory, you little shit. Out here saving humans?" Phenex laughed, coming up behind me and clapping the daemon on the shoulder. His eyes turned to the woman. "And who's the witch?"

My eyebrows shot up. She was a witch?

The woman rolled her eyes. "My name is Delphine. And don't forget it. Lest you find poison in your food."

Phenex grinned, his eyes glittering at the challenge, but Gremory spoke before he could retort. "She's my mate, Phen. Touch her and I'll cut your dick off. Or rather, I'll let her do it."

I laughed. "My money is on the witch. She looks intimidating as hell."

Delphine smirked. "You're not wrong. Nice to officially meet you, Seraphina. It is you who saved Tabitha first, you know."

I cocked my head, unsure of her meaning. "How's that?"

Tibby held up her hand, the scar on her palm that mirrored mine visible. It was the only scar I had. The only wound that left a mark.

"She should never have survived the mental torture those scum inflicted on her mind. But you vowed to protect Tabitha when you made a blood oath with her. Without it, she would have gone insane from the assault on her psyche. Because of you, I was able to coax her mind back to health." Delphine's eyes flicked to Tibby, and a soft smile played around her lips.

She cared for my friend, saved her again when I couldn't. Although it felt loads better knowing something I did, even unintentionally, kept my only friend from losing her mind.

I smiled at Tibby. "What are friends for, right?"

She smiled back at me.

I leaned forward then hesitated. "Can I hug you?"

Tibby's smile grew, and she nodded. I wrapped my arms around her tiny frame and almost started crying again when she hugged me back.

Gods. So many emotions were coming out of me today. But I was relieved as fuck to have her and my sister here safely. This feeling was long fucking overdue.

Chapter Thirty-Two
Morax

Seeing Michaela hug her sister, feeling the happiness radiating from her, meant more to me than words could convey. The sadness within her beat a steady pace beneath the surface, but I could feel it ebbing away with their reunion. Her happiness was everything to me.

She had been furious when I, essentially, kidnapped her and left the others to complete the ritual with The Obscuritas trash, but I wasn't sorry. I was desperate to get her away from there, and with Seraphina's approval, I didn't hesitate. She raged at me, throwing her delicate fists against my chest.

Tears flowed from her eyes as she screamed at me to take her back. I dropped to my knees and held her close as she cried and we waited. When my brother crossed between our worlds, I felt his mind the moment his clawed feet reached the ground. Michaela was soothed then, remaining calm as long as I updated her on their progress.

I didn't want to leave her even to help bring them all back to Vespertine Hall, but knowing her sister's safety was everything to her, I left her with multiple guards, including Gremory and his witch.

That woman was deadly enough to keep my mate safe for a few moments, at least.

Seeing her with Grem and Tabitha was curious. Their scents were mingled. Not in the sense they were sexual, but something was brewing. Seeing Seraphina with her harem, I was willing to believe anything at this point. Relationships, I was quickly discovering, were not so black and white.

Well, except for mine. Michaela was *mine*. Ours was just that. Ours, and no one else would join this party. My soul was completely and utterly hers. The idea of her fucking anyone else made me physically ill.

I felt my mate's gaze before I looked up. Her bright-blue and golden-brown eyes searched mine. What was she looking for? A rush of power flowed between us, and her pink lips parted. My nostrils flared and noted the change in her scent. Fuck.

"*Mae domina*. We need to go." I kissed her hand and scooped her into my arms. The thread of our mate bond pulsed as our skin connected, and I nearly groaned.

"What's happening?" she murmured, her voice laced with power as she trembled in my arms. "I feel strange."

I stalked out of the room to the sound of my brother's quiet laughter. *Bed her well, brother.*

Fuck off. I slammed the doors of my mind shut. I didn't want my brother anywhere near my mate right now. I feared for his life, and anyone else's at this point.

"Morax," Michaela moaned, and my dick throbbed at her husky tone.

"Yes, mate." I lowered my head, nipping at her neck as I practically ran to our bedchambers. "I've got you. It's the mate bond. It's settling. Calling us to solidify the union of our souls."

She laughed, and the sound was music to my ears. "What?"

I grinned, the devil showing in my eyes. "I'm going to fuck you, little doe. Over and over. Until our scents are one and you cannot tell where my soul ends and yours begins."

Her breath hitched, and I stopped, setting her on her feet. I gripped her face in my hands, my claws extending and my daemon form coming out at the scent of my mate's arousal. "Run, little doe."

Michaela pupils dilated. She smirked at me then took off down the hall. I counted to ten, giving her a head start. It didn't matter. I would catch my prey. There was nothing and no one who could stop me in this.

I took off down the hall, chasing her scent. Her arousal grew. My dirty little mate enjoyed being hunted. I couldn't see her, but I could feel her ahead of me, running through the halls and toward our room.

I'm coming for you. I murmured down the bond. It was growing stronger by the second. Soon we would be able to share all our thoughts, our feelings. We would be one in every way that mattered.

"Come and get me then," Michaela whispered, but I heard her. I was attuned to every sound she made.

I snarled, my wings snapping out, almost too wide for the halls. I flew through the air toward the doors of our room. I flicked my hand, and the doors flung themselves open. I folded my wings behind my back and stalked into the room. I smiled seconds before Michaela pounced from the spot she was hiding in.

"Got you!" She laughed and then gasped when I took her in my arms and tossed her onto the bed.

I wasted no time peeling the leggings down her legs. I smirked like the devil, noticing the wet spot on her pink cotton thong. "My little doe. You're already wet for me. Did you enjoy being hunted?"

She licked her lips, and I was instantly jealous of her tongue. "By you, always."

I chuckled, tearing her sweater in half to reveal more of her perfect pale flesh. "Good girl."

"Less clothing. I want to feel you," she moaned, her hands reaching for me.

Michaela was every dream I ever wished for, and I could deny her nothing. I ripped my clothes off, tearing the fabric in the process. My claws snapped out, and I tore her bra. She yelped, and I loved the sound. My claws tore at her thong next, baring her silky flesh completely for me.

I stood back, stroking my cock and taking her in. "Open your pretty legs. Let me see you."

Michael's legs snapped wide, and I growled in satisfaction at her eagerness. My tongue snaked across my lips at the sight of her pretty cunt.

"Exquisite. Now use your fingers. Open for me, little lumen."

Her face flushed with desire, and I growled, stalking closer to her. I pulled her ankles to the edge of the bed and dropped to my knees. I needed to taste her. My mate spread her pretty pussy with her fingers, and I licked up her center, groaning at the delicious taste of her.

"Fuck. You're the most delectable creature I've ever tasted." My tongue pressed inside her, and Michaela moaned, the sound both seductive and sweet. I ravished her, feasted on her until she screamed for me.

Her breaths came in short gasps, and her perky little tits heaved.

"This is only the beginning, mate." I stood, stroking myself and watching her squirm.

"Morax," she panted, her voice whining. "I want you."

"Tell me what you want, little lumen." I urged her. "Beg me."

She whimpered, reaching for me, her voice laced with desire. "I want you to fuck me. Please. I need you inside me."

I groaned, and my cock throbbed almost painfully. "Yes, my perfect mate. You beg so prettily for me."

She sat up, her eyes locked on my dick. "Can I taste?"

The mix of innocence and lust on her face was enough to drive me insane. I nodded, unable to speak. She crawled toward me, reaching for my cock. Her soft hands gripped my shaft and stroked slowly. My mate leaned in, and the tip of her tongue flicked at the head of my cock. I sucked in a breath as she took me in further, her tongue circling, exploring, tasting.

I gripped her golden hair in my hand. "I need to fuck your mouth, little lumen."

She nodded, looking up at me with her mouth open and ready. It was the most beautiful sight. I eased my cock in further, and she hallowed out her cheeks. She knew exactly what I needed, sensing my every reaction. The bond between us thrummed with power. The head of my cock reached the back of her throat, and her eyes watered as I fucked her pretty mouth.

"Yes, little lumen. You take my cock so well. I was made for you. And you for me." I grunted, thrusting deeper. "I'm going to fill each of your tight little holes. Going to mark every inch of your body with my seed."

Michaela moaned, and her throat hummed against my cock. I nearly came in her mouth but held off by sheer force of will. The first time would be deep inside her sweet pussy. And I needed her now.

"I need you, *mae domina*. My mate. My love. I need to feel you now." I was practically begging, pulling out of her mouth and laying her back on the bed.

Her blonde hair fanned around her head like a halo. Her eyes were lit with lust and shining with power. I would never get enough of her.

I positioned myself between her legs, stroking my length in her wet cunt. She squirmed, and I grinned, a purr building in my chest.

"It may hurt a little, *mae domina*," I murmured. The idea of causing her pain sent a spike of fear through my heart.

She reached out, her delicate fingers squeezing my forearm. "I trust you, Morax. I was made for you, remember?"

I smiled, and the purr grew as my love for her practically choked the oxygen from the room. "Yes, you were."

I pressed the head of my cock to her entrance, easing in slowly. Her tight pussy squeezed my cock.

"Breathe, little lumen. Let me in."

Her eyes shut tightly, and her mouth dropped open into a silent *oh* as I eased myself deeper inside her perfect wet pussy. She moaned, and her back arched slightly as she took my cock.

My sweet mate's pussy sucked me in greedily, and I chuckled. "So needy for me. You're doing so well, little lumen. The sight of your pretty cunt taking my cock is everything. I'll never get enough of this perfect pussy, my princess."

"More. More. More." She begged, and I moved my hips slowly.

I leaned over her, capturing her lips with mine. She opened for me eagerly, and I kissed her with a growl in my throat. I began to thrust at a steady pace, kissing and praising her. Her pussy felt divine. My body thrummed with power, and my wings snapped back out. She reached out and ran her fingers along the edge of one, forcing a full body shudder out of me. The touch of my mate's soft hand against my wings was enough to make me feral.

"You're going to have me coming sooner if you keep doing that, little lumen," I growled, unable to keep my daemon leashed. The feeling of her fingers stroking my wings was euphoric.

"Come for me then," she teased, smirking up at me.

I bared my fangs at her and let my eyes glow with power. "You first."

There was no holding back now. I wrapped her legs around my waist and angled myself to fill her more deeply. Pressing my thumb to her clit, I circled slowly as my thrusts increased. Her eyes closed and I snarled. "Eyes on me, little lumen. I want to see your face when I fill you up."

Her eyes snapped open, and I fucked my mate harder. Her pussy squeezed me tighter, and her screams grew louder. I was close, and so was she. Our mate bond hummed with power as the joining of our souls reached its peak. I pulled her up, needing her close, holding her in my lap. Knowing exactly what I needed without speaking, she ground her hips down on me and her peaked nipples brushed against my chest as she impaled herself on my cock.

"That's it, little lumen. Ride me. Take what you need from me. Fuck, you feel so good. My perfect mate," I praised her, nibbling the flushed skin of her collarbone. "I'm going to mark this flesh. The world will know you're mine."

"Yes, yours. Morax," Michaela moaned, her voice barely above a whisper. "I love you."

Her eyes glowed the brightest blue and warmest cognac with her lumen power as she spoke the words and her pussy squeezed even tighter. She screamed my name again and again as she came for me. My power buzzed, filling the room. Unable to hold back any longer, I bit down on her neck just as my seed filled her. Our moans mingled as the taste of her blood filled my mouth. Her arms wrapped tightly around my neck, pulling me close as I marked her in the ways of our kind. Power zipped through my body. The magic rushing through her blood was astounding.

"Morax!" Michaela shouted, and the alarm in her tone had my head snapping up.

What I saw then, it was magnificent. "Your wings."

Michaela's eyes were wide, still glowing brighter than the sun and sky above. "Wings? I have wings. How did this happen?"

I smiled, my face alight with wonder for this perfect creature. "The joining of our souls must have set something off inside you. Your powers are manifesting." I stared in wonder at the bright-white feathered wings at her back. I reached out and stroked them gently. Her eyes closed slowly, and she shivered.

I could feel her energy levels dropping, her body coming

down from our joining. "To send them back, just wish it, or will them to go."

She nodded, her eyes still closed, and after a few moments, her wings disappeared. I lowered her to the bed with me, my cock still inside her. The wound on her neck was already closing, leaving behind a small raised tattoo of my teeth. I licked it and she shivered.

"I love you, Michaela Valdis."

CHAPTER THIRTY-THREE
Leviathan

We received word this morning that the witch could help us with our relics. We thought they would be destroyed in the ritual, but they weren't. We gathered outside after breakfast, my brothers and I, Seraphina, and the unfortunate tagalong, Phenex.

The witch, Delphine, joined us in the courtyard behind the manor shortly after we arrived. The other daemon, who I happened to like, Gremory, was with her. Tibby as well. My face softened as I glanced at Seraphina's friend. She had been through so much at the hands of our fathers, and I wasn't sure how to talk to her. My father scrambled her brain, and Andras's father broke her spirit. And yet, she was here, reserved and skittish, but here. And that alone showed so much courage.

Gremory snapped a chair into existence for Tibby, and she flushed, thanking him. Delphine marched toward us. She was a striking woman but entirely too serious for my tastes. It was obvious she was powerful too, hopefully enough to rid us of these damn leashes.

Seraphina crossed her arms, eyeing the witch, and I smirked. I could see she was sizing up the other woman. That was a cat fight I'd gladly watch. Seraphina's hair was still strange to see. It was a fiery red, her natural color. She looked sexy as hell, but

I almost missed the silvery blue locks. The unique color suited her just as much. She wore dark-green leggings and a black cropped sweater. I was tempted to steal her away and strip her of the clothes to reveal the delicious flesh beneath. We were all a bit sexually frustrated. Phenex refused to leave us alone with her, and she refused to fuck with him around. The last few days were tortuous, to say the least.

"Alright." Delphine cut through my sexually charged thoughts. "I believe the relics are tied to the daemon blood your creepy-as-shit fathers forced into you a decade ago. If we expel the blood from your bodies, Phenex here can cast some hellfire and destroy the relics when they are vulnerable."

"Will we lose our powers then?" Andras crossed his arms. Our fearless leader was dressed almost casual in slacks and a fitted crewneck sweater. He looked like a GQ model, of course.

"Yes and no." Delphine frowned. "Did you all know your mothers?"

I cocked my head to the side. "That's a strange question."

She shook her head. "Not really. You see, humans cannot accept daemon or lumen blood into their bodies and gain power the way you did. It's essentially poison. I have a theory they were lumens. Or that you had lumen grandparents. Phenex and Gremory confirmed it. We thought your scents were just mingled with others, but I think it's your blood that brought the powers forth."

"Intriguing," Andras murmured. "A fact I am certain our fathers knew, and they forced the issue."

"Like they chose our mothers and forced them to have kids?" Dev cut in, his voice shaking with anger.

"Yes," Ty snarled, arms crossed and looking dangerous as hell.

"When we expel the bad blood, we're going to replace it with another." The witch cut in.

"Whose?" I asked, fairly certain I knew.

"Mine, of course." Seraphina grinned. "Right?"

The witch nodded. "Yours or Phenex's. And I don't think he's interested."

Phenex growled. "I fucking hate this plan. I don't want my mate's blood flowing in their stupid veins. And they sure as fuck can't have mine."

Seraphina rolled her eyes. "Lucky for us all, you're not in charge. I am. And I say they can have as much of my blood as they fucking want."

Phenex snarled, stomping away.

"Why you want this many irrational men, I'll never know." Delphine smirked.

Seraphina shrugged, her own smirk devilish. "They're delicious?"

The witch laughed, and I liked her a little bit more. "Fair point. They are easy on the eyes."

"I can hear you, love," Gremory shouted from his position next to Tibby. "Shall I remind you who *your* mate is?"

Delphine turned to Gremory with a wink. "Perhaps later, when I have you on your knees."

The daemon chuckled, his eyes glowing. "As you wish."

"He's so well trained." Seraphina laughed, and the sound was music to my ears. "Perhaps you can teach me your ways."

I stalked toward her and dropped to the ground, my knees hitting the dewy grass. "You think I'm afraid to bow before you, *mi diosa*?"

Seraphina reached out, stroking her hand through my hair. A deep growl built in my chest at the feel of her nails scraping against my scalp.

Phenex was suddenly there, kneeling beside me. "Me too. I will kneel for my queen at her command."

Delphine laughed. "It doesn't seem like you're having any trouble."

Seraphina grinned, her tongue darting out to lick her lush lips. "I suppose not."

"When are we going to do this? With our relics?" Dev cut in, ruining the moment.

"In three days. At the new moon," she responded with certainty.

Andras nodded. "Right then. Seraphina, sweetheart, shall we continue to practice with your power?"

She huffed dramatically. I stood slowly and wrapped my arms around her curvy waist. "I believe in you, *mi diosa*. You can do this."

Phenex stood as well, shoving me aside and grabbing her face. "I believe in you too, *mini monstra*."

Seraphina rolled her eyes and shoved away from us both. I sighed. The crazy asshole was actually growing on me. If he weren't a daemon attempting to steal our girl, he'd fit right in with the crew. He was obviously hot as hell, and even Seraphina was attracted to him, though she tried to deny it. Phenex was charming and funny, and just as growly as Ty, which she fucking loved.

If we didn't figure this shit out soon, I was certain it would end badly. Our group was fracturing at a time when we needed to come together most. Andras and I stayed up late into the night discussing the disconnect. And we had the feeling if Phenex wasn't accepted by us and Seraphina, we would never be whole again.

CHAPTER THIRTY-FOUR
Tabitha

The cool air made me shiver, but I was enjoying the morning surrounded by people I trusted. It still felt strange to have my own mind back. Flashes of the terrible things Laszlo forced me to do, the lies he made me tell, all swirled in the back of my mind like a fucked up carousel of nightmares.

"Are you cold, love?" Gremory murmured, leaning down from his position standing behind me.

The fact that I didn't even flinch at his close proximity almost made me cry. I didn't think I would ever be unafraid again, but Grem and Delphine brought me back to life.

I shivered again, but this time not from the cold. Grem was so fucking sexy, even when he wasn't trying to be. His attentiveness made him doubly attractive. I turned my head up to meet his eyes, something else I never thought I would be able to do again. Laszlo wouldn't let me look anyone in the face.

I smiled softly. "I'm a little chilly, but it's nice."

Grem smiled back at me, his bright-blond hair blowing gently in the wind. His silvery blue eyes searched my face. "I can make it a little nicer." He whispered a few words, and within moments, created a pit before us filled with firewood.

"*Lustro*," Delphine whispered, waving her hand casually at the wood pile and it immediately came to life with roaring flames.

Grem growled at her, but it wasn't malicious. "Show-off."

Delphine arched an eyebrow at him, and the fire in her gaze was enough to make goosebumps pebble my skin. The heat between Gremory and Delphine was palpable. Anyone could see the bond between them. A very small piece of my heart ached to feel that with someone. And if I was being completely honest, I wanted it to be with them. From the moment I met Grem, a connection formed, a bond of friendship unlike anything I'd ever felt, besides my connection with Seraphina.

Speaking of my devilish best friend. I grinned when she approached us. "Hey, Nova."

"Hey, Zenith." Seraphina leaned in as if to hug me but stopped.

I nodded, realizing she was waiting for me. She hugged me tightly, and I returned her embrace, letting out a heavy breath. I missed her so fucking much, and I was so fucking sorry for everything I did that led to this.

"Sara…" I started, but she cut me off.

"Don't even fucking think about apologizing to me." Her voice was soft and hard all at once, as if she was afraid to be forceful with me but needed me to understand her words. Seraphina's blue-green eyes blazed with emotion as she stared into my face. "We are in this together, Tibby. And nothing you did was your own choice. I will fucking kill him for what he did to you."

"Get in line," Grem growled at my back, his fingers brushing gently against my shoulders.

Blood rushed from my head to my core at his innocent touch, and my cheeks flushed.

I cleared my throat, forcing my body to remain calm and focus on my friend. "I know it wasn't me. And I'm trying not to take the blame for the shitshow we are in now. But some part of me was still in there, watching it all happen, even if I couldn't stop it. Maybe if I had power like you, I could've been stronger."

Seraphina crossed her arms, shaking her head. "No. I supposedly have big, bad power thrumming in my veins, and I haven't been able to end the fucking Kings. We weren't ready to fight them before, but we will be soon."

I nodded, feeling that fire in her eyes mirrored in my own. She was right.

"Go kick some ass then, Nova."

"I like seeing this fire in you, love," Grem whispered, brushing his fingers against my neck.

Heat pooled in my center at his touch, and I wanted badly to lean into it, but my body remained still. A strong part of me was still trapped in that cycle of abuse, and even though I knew with every fiber of my being Grem was good, my body needed time.

But he was right. The fire was building within me. "I wish I had the power to fight like you all do."

Grem stepped in front of my chair and knelt before me. His blond hair fluttered around his shoulders, and his light-blue eyes captured my own boring brown gaze. His jaw ticked with mild irritation, as if he could read my mind, but I knew he would never. Not after Laszlo.

"Tabitha Marsden," Grem growled, his voice low. "You are one of the strongest people I have ever met. You have strength of heart and mind like I have never seen."

My cheeks flushed, and I dropped his gaze, looking down at my hands and fidgeting. Grem's rough fingers reached out slowly and lifted my chin, forcing me to meet his gaze once more.

"Your part in this is not over. I believe there is more to come for you, love. If you can take any of my words with you, believe that."

My skin heated where his hand still connected with my face. A rush of emotions flooded my insides at his words. If anyone was going to bring me to life and give me the strength to continue this path, it was him.

Chapter Thirty-Five
Michaela

I was literally on cloud nine. All those movies with people being giddy and weird after sex, they weren't kidding. It was more than that, though. We were bonded in ways no movie could know about, and all I wanted to do was feel him inside me again. And we did. Like, ten more times. Not before Morax took me into the bath and forced my body to rest and heal.

He wasn't wrong about the pain. The first time he entered me, there was a little pain. And a little blood, although I didn't notice that until after. Considering he drank from me when we had sex that first time, the blood between my legs didn't bother him at all. He wasted no time scooping me up and into the bathtub. I was exhausted, and he gently massaged my body, whispering sweet things while I recovered.

And then we had sex over and over. Morax wasn't lying when he said we were going to fuck for days. My body healed quickly, my lumen blood keeping it strong. And my libido was nearly high enough to match his. The feral look in his eyes when his cock entered me was the sexiest thing I'd ever seen. And oh holy shit, his cock. When I first saw it all those months ago, I imagined what those ribbed rings along the shaft would feel like. It was magical. The added ridges caressed my body and filled me like nothing I could ever describe. I had no concept of time when he was fucking me. The world could've ended, and we'd never know it.

Alas, it didn't end. And my power was getting restless. My wings came out several more times, and I was eager to try them out. Morax understood. Our bond was so strong, we could feel each other's emotions. I'd never been so connected to someone in my life. And I would never get enough of it.

Morax chuckled at my side. "Will you stop thinking about fucking? You're driving me insane, and it was your idea to leave the bedroom."

I smirked, my cheeks flushing, and his eyes glowed as he tracked the color rising up my face.

"I can't help it. I do want to fly and try out my power. But I also want…"

Morax stopped, and his hands snapped out, gripping my waist and pressing me into the wall. "I know what you want, little lumen."

My breaths grew shallow, and my body hummed with desire for my mate.

"My mate," I whispered.

Morax growled, crushing his lips to mine and holding me tight against the wall. He pulled away, leaving me wanting more. "Yes, your mate. And I will be more than happy to satisfy all of your filthy desires, little doe."

I flushed at the nickname. I loved it, loved when he hunted me and claimed his prize. "Once I learn to fly, this hunting thing will be on a whole other level."

Morax grinned, a growl building in his chest. "I look forward to it, little doe."

Morax learned from Phenex that my sister was outside the manor training. They were testing her power, but she was apparently having trouble controlling it.

As we walked toward them, a fireball shot in our direction. I screamed, but Morax easily deflected it.

He snarled at my sister. "I am not afraid to kill you, little psycho, if you hurt my mate."

Seraphina rolled her eyes, hands on her hips, red hair flying in the wind like some kind of superhero. "I knew you'd protect her. See? She's fine."

I skipped over to my sister, my angry daemon stomping several paces behind. "How's it going?" I looked between her and Morax's brother Phenex, sensing tension.

She sighed, running her hand through her wavy hair. "Poorly."

Phenex laughed, his tattooed arms crossed and his gray eyes twinkling with mischief. "Joining us so soon? I thought my brother was made of stronger stuff. Perhaps he's not satisfying you?"

A massive rock appeared in Morax's hand, and he chucked it at his brother's head. Phenex dodged it easily enough, laughing as he ran and Morax gave chase.

"How did he do that?" Seraphina huffed pointing at my mate. "Why can't I do that?"

I squeezed her arm and leaned in, unable to keep my secret any longer. "Want to see something cool?"

She nodded, and I called my wings forth. They snapped

out, and the rush of power zipped through my body like a drug. Her eyes went wide, and I beamed with pride.

"Holy fuck, Michaela! You have wings! They are so fucking pretty!" Seraphina smiled wide, and I grinned back at her, so ridiculously proud.

I squealed like a child, but I didn't care. "Right? I love them so much. They came out when…" I dropped my voice to a whisper. "When we had sex."

Seraphina snorted a laugh. "Oh my gods. My baby sister got her wings because of a great orgasm?!"

My face flushed, and my eyes snapped to Morax as several people chuckled. There were too many people with super-hearing around here.

He was at my side instantly. "Anyone says a single word, I will cut out their tongues."

Phenex laughed, pretending to zip his lips shut.

Morax stroked my cheek with his rough hand. "You didn't get it from sex, *mae domina*. It was unleashed with our mate bond. I have a theory about that. Your power may be tied to it."

"What?" Seraphina and I said in unison.

He nodded, his voice certain, golden eyes watching me. "We've gone over the details of that first ritual. And the spells you've told me about, the words your mother would whisper when your power dimmed. I think she was protecting you. Making sure you could hide more easily until we could find each other."

"How would she know Michaela would find her mate?" Seraphina crossed her arms, raising an eyebrow.

Phenex responded first. "She was the most gifted seer our

people had ever known. Even more than the witches," he added, winking at Delphine rolling her eyes several feet away.

Seraphina sighed. "So my powers are on the fritz because I don't have a fucking mate?"

I shrugged, unsure what to say. Which didn't seem to matter, because Phenex was suddenly scooping her up with a snarl. Several grumpy Princes prowled closer to them.

"You do have a mate, you just refuse to acknowledge him." His voice was deep and predatory.

But with my heightened senses, I detected a hint of hurt. My sister's rejection was hurting him. She shoved out of his arms, and I pulled her aside.

"Are you so sure?" I whispered to my sister. I looked at Morax and suddenly a bubble of warmth surrounded us. "They can't hear us. Now answer truthfully. Do you honestly feel nothing between you and Phenex?"

Seraphina sighed. "I don't know. No? But my feelings for the Princes haven't changed. I could never leave them behind for a *mate* I barely know." She added air quotes to the word like it was crazy to even think of such things.

But having found my own, and knowing instantly there was something between us, it didn't seem crazy at all. In fact, I was starting to think my wild and tough-as-nails older sister may find herself with multiple mates.

I quirked a brow and grinned at her. "Who says you can't have more than one?"

She smirked, crossing her arms, her bright aquamarine eyes twinkling at the idea. "Wouldn't that be something?"

I shrugged. "We live in a world with magic and daemons

and lumens and who knows what else. Having more than one mate doesn't seem all that crazy to me."

Seraphina's brows furrowed, and she narrowed her eyes at me. "And since when did you become so wise?"

I smiled smugly. The bubble of silence around us suddenly dissipated, and we turned to see Phenex tackling his brother to the ground. I laughed, watching them wrestle. I could feel Morax's joy, and it made my heart soar to see him happy. We all needed this. And I had an idea how to help my sister to find her happiness too.

"Does this place have a basement?" I asked without preamble.

Seraphina arched a brow at me curiously. "Uh, yeah. Why?"

"Let's throw a party. A rave. We deserve it. One night with no rules or uncertain futures or stupid cults. Just some fun."

My sister grinned. "Hell yeah. It's not exactly set up for that."

"We can help with that!" Phenex called from his position pinned beneath Morax.

I grinned back at her. This was going to be epic.

CHAPTER THIRTY-SIX
Gremory

We walked back to our rooms after the afternoon of training. Well, there wasn't much training. Seraphina had no control over her power. It was there, any daemon or lumen could sense the ocean of magic in her blood, but for whatever reason, she couldn't access it, except for bits and pieces when she was particularly emotional. Which was often, considering the annoying pest of a daemon prince hovering at her back.

Phenex was a wounded puppy with the rage of a lion, but she seemed capable of handling his moods.

"Your thoughts are loud and busy, Grem." Delphine quirked a brow, side-eyeing me.

I winked at her, but she could see through my casual demeanor. Delphine Bellinor was my mate, and we were bonded to our very bones. Every emotion barreling through me, she understood it, sometimes before I did. Which was also why the petite woman walking between us was here. I glanced down at Tabitha, sniffing the air around her to sense her emotions. I refused to probe her mind in any way. She had enough assholes digging into her mind already, and I would never be another.

After I stole her away from the Blackbyrn Manor, I brought her straight to Delphine. If there was one person on this Earth

Resurrection

who could help Tabitha, it was her. The moment I landed back at Vespertine Hall with the unconscious and mortally wounded woman, my mate jumped into action.

We healed Tabitha's flesh wounds easily enough, but it was her mind that was a fucking mess. It took hours for Delphine to pull the damaged girl from her own hiding place inside her head. Only with our combined power could we do so, and it soothed the rage in me to bring her back to life.

Tabitha slept for the next twelve hours or so after she was healed. I stayed by her side, not wanting her to be left alone and wake up scared. My witch, my perfect master and mate, encouraged me to do so.

She had a sly smile about her when she checked in on us, but when I asked her what she was keeping from me, she merely winked and walked away. She was infuriating like that, and I loved her for it.

Delphine was the perfect creature for me. She was dominant, clever, and gorgeous as hell. We met in New Orleans, roughly six years ago. I knew instantly she was to be mine but found out quickly not only was I to be hers, I would become her submissive.

I wasn't exactly the soft and whimpering type, but Delphine quickly scolding me for assuming submissives were weak, as they were anything but. I'd never been in a relationship with a woman who took the dominant role, but with her, it was fucking thrilling. She reeled me in, and before I knew what was happening, I was begging for her to leash me. I smirked at the depraved memories.

When Tabitha first woke up after she was healed, we were

both in the room. The tiny human's eyes locked with mine, and I felt the beginnings of our bond form instantly. I nearly ran from the room, but my mate reached out and squeezed my hand, reassuring me this bond was real. She knew, of course, that this was coming. My mate was not the great seer Aurora Valdis had been, but her magical talents were powerful, and she could sense bonds before they were even formed.

I'd never heard of such a thing, having a mate bond for more than one creature. And to think she was human! How the hell that was even possible was a question I didn't have answers for. Tabitha still didn't know we were mated, and Delphine said we would tell her when the time was right. I trusted her and agreed to keep the knowledge a secret for now. It may overwhelm her, anyway.

In the short time since her near death at that manor, Tabitha flourished. She was still scared and her nightmares were hell, but she was so damn strong.

"My ladies." I bowed, opening the door to our rooms and allowing them to enter first.

Tabitha smiled, small and tentative. Her caramel-brown eyes darted away from mine before I could drown in them.

"So, are we going to the party tonight?" I asked, flopping down onto the couch tucked in the corner of the room.

Tabitha crawled onto the bed and tucked her legs beneath her. She chewed on a fingernail. Delphine pulled her dainty fingers away from her mouth.

"Do you want to go, sweet girl?" Delphine asked, brushing her fingers against Tabitha's cheek.

Tabitha's skin flushed, and she looked at me. My dick

throbbed at the heat I found buried in her gaze. Her eyes turned up to Delphine's before she responded.

"Maybe." Tabitha's voice was soft and tinkling like that of the fae. "Will you go with me?"

I swear she had a fae ancestor for how pixie-like she appeared. And I said as much to my mate, but she only responded in her usual cryptic manner.

Delphine smiled. "Of course."

I grinned. "As if we would let you go without us."

Tabitha grinned. "It will be nice to do something other than mope around. I might mope myself right into the floor if I don't do something fun soon."

I chuckled, standing from the couch and stalking toward my little human. Delphine's eyes watched me with a smirk.

"Are we boring you, love? If so, I will do whatever I can to…stimulate you."

Tabitha giggled, but then her eyes snapped up to my witch and back to mine and her smile faded. "I'm sure you guys are ready to get back to…your life, or whatever. I think I can find a room on my own. And I am very grateful for how much you've helped me. I'll never be able to repay you for saving my life."

Her words sent a spike of pain to my gut. I dropped to my knees before her, before them both. "There is nothing to repay, love. You deserved to be saved. You deserve to be happy. Loved."

Delphine brushed her long fingers through Tabitha's short blonde hair. "Do you want your own room, darling girl? If you say you want to leave, you are free to, of course. But if you want our thoughts, we would prefer you to stay."

Tabitha's heart picked up, pattering like a hummingbird in

her chest. "Why? Aren't you like mates, or whatever?"

I glanced up at my witch. Her love for me pulsed through our mate bond, and I purred at the feel of it. She smiled, and it took my breath away each time. She nodded, and I dropped my gaze back to the sweet human sitting before us.

"We are, love." I reached out and took Tabitha's hand. She shivered as I rubbed circles against the fast pulse at her wrist. "And in my centuries of life, I never knew a daemon to take more than one mate. But we are in a new age. It is only natural for creatures to evolve."

Her eyes were wide as she absorbed my words, and I continued.

"The first time I saw you, the smallest spark of light burst into my heart and never left. I think I was meant to find you, Tabitha. *We* were meant to find you. Can you feel it?"

Her breath hitched, and she licked her pink lips. I tracked the movement.

"I think so. I'm just…" Her voice was soft, barely above a whisper.

Delphine turned Tabitha's chin gently, commanding her attention. "Never be afraid to share your feelings with us, darling girl. There will be no other creatures in this world or the next who will care for you the way we do. No matter what you want or don't want from us."

My heart burst with love and pride at my mate's words. She was always so strong and fierce, but my lioness was a softie at heart. She held more love inside her than any creature I'd ever met.

"I'm scared." Tabitha's soft voice cut the silence. "I'm scared to have feelings, to care. To trust. It's never worked out for me."

Delphine nodded. "And we will do whatever you need to earn your trust. Isn't that right, Grem?"

"Absolutely. I am your servant, love. As much as I belong to Delphine, I belong to you, in whatever way you would have me."

Tabitha's pretty eyes filled with tears, and she nodded. My mate and I moved at the same moment, each wiping a tear from her cheek. The bonds between the three of us hummed with power, becoming more solid with our declarations. A new beginning had arrived for us, and I was eager to see what would come next.

CHAPTER THIRTY-SEVEN
Seraphina

I stomped through the stupid mansion after the unsuccessful training session. The power inside me wouldn't follow any of my commands. I could feel it there, buzzing in my veins and desperate to get out, but no matter what words I said or how calm I tried to be, the magic just wouldn't come out. Not magic, Vis-el. That's what the daemons and lumens called their power. Magic was different, something the witches claimed. Witches were attuned to the elements in a different way. Daemons and lumens were born with an affinity to certain elements, but able to manipulate them all to a certain extent. There was so much fucking information about all this shit, my head was going to explode.

It was exhausting. My body felt weary, and my mind buzzed with a million questions and dark intrusive thoughts over my failures. I missed having Tibby in my ear, laughing and keeping me occupied. Seeing her free from the influence of the fucking Kings soothed my heart a little, but gods damn if it wasn't cracking apart with all the bullshit we'd been hit with.

Dev's sister was still with the Kings. In the mayhem following the ritual, he couldn't find her, and I knew part of him was still stuck in North Carolina with her. I knew that pain, considering I only just reunited with my own sister. Audrey Kingston was dead. Andras tried to deliver the news gently, but fuck if I wasn't furious. She was a pawn in a game of devils and never stood a chance. Just another innocent person I failed to save. That moment of strength and clarity from my birth father faded into nothing as my failures threatened to gobble me up.

I ran, my arms and legs pumping as I picked up speed, fleeing the others and just needing to get away. It was a big ass mansion, and without Tibby in my ear telling where to go next, I quickly got lost in the maze of hallways. My breathing turned ragged, and I slowed, having sprinted two flights of stairs and officially run out of oxygen. The halls were dimly lit, with very little daylight getting through. Most of the windows were cloaked in heavy velvet curtains, letting only slivers of the sun's rays through. It was eerie as hell, but I kind of liked it.

I paused at a doorway when I heard a machine humming with power and opened it further. It was some kind of control room, about the size of a bedroom. One entire wall was covered in television screens. There were computers and all kinds of tech gadgets filling shelves along the walls. It was organized chaos. I walked along the wall of screens. They were clearly camera feeds, but not just for the manner. The feeds were connected to cameras at The Towne House, Ty's gym, even Dev's bar. A commanding presence charged the air in the room, and I knew who it was without looking.

"This wasn't here last time I was at Vespertine Hall," I mused, turning toward my dark Prince.

He leaned against the doorframe, looking elegant-as-fuck in gray slacks and a white button-down shirt. The sleeves were rolled up, his version of casual.

"Do you mean when you were here spying on us and blowing up cars?" Andras smirked, arching a brow at me.

I grinned and put on my best innocent smile. "Who says I did that?"

Andras shoved off the walk and walked toward me. He reached out a hand, brushing his thumb across my bottom lip. "Only you would be brave enough to go against my father like that."

His compliment made my insides melt, but I wasn't in the mood for those. My recent failings were still too sharp in my mind, and I turned from him, looking at the screens.

"Tibby should see this, she'd be salivating over all this tech. Bet she'd start flickin' the bean immediately." I internally rolled my eyes at myself. *Seraphina, you're a dumbass.*

Andras sighed. "Gods, you have a filthy mouth, sweetheart."

I skipped over that comment too. "Have you ever seen the movie *The Dark Knight*?"

"No."

"This totally reminds me—" I stopped short, registering his words. "Wait, what? Are you serious?"

Andras's mouth thinned into a flat line. "Do I look serious?"

I looked him over. "You mostly look frumpy."

He closed his eyes and pinched the bridge of his nose. "Sweetheart. I'm going to punish you soon if you keep insulting me."

I shrugged my shoulders and continued to taunt the devil. "I'm stating facts. Anyway, this setup is like a scene from that movie. Is there also a button we can press and it all goes boom?"

Andras smirked. "I highly doubt it."

"Then we get Tibby to make one. Never know when we might need it." I grinned.

His lips turned down, and his eyes looked pityingly at me. "She isn't well, Seraphina. Not yet."

I put my hands on my hips. "Maybe it will help. She loves this stuff, it's familiar. Something she was good at before I dragged her into all this bullshit."

Andras reached out and squeezed my shoulders, his strong grip kneading my muscles expertly. "None of this is your fault."

I wasn't in the mood to hear that shit. I shrugged out of his arms and pushed past him to leave.

"Whatever."

His hand snapped out, catching me by the back of the neck and forcing me to stop. Andras's hot breath fanned against my ear. "Did you just shrug me off? That was the last straw, sweetheart."

Andras moved quickly, shoving me against the wall and expertly pulling my arms behind my back to keep me still. I could probably get out of this, but right now, I didn't want to. I needed an escape. Something or someone to take control and quiet the anxiety building inside me.

"Repeat after me." Andras spoke quietly, his voice no less commanding. "This is not my fault."

I grunted, refusing to say it. His hand smacked across my ass so forcefully, I was certain there'd be a handprint, even with my leggings on.

Another Prince suddenly appeared in my peripheral. "And what's going on here?" Ty's deep voice purred.

Andras tightened his hold. "Our girl is being disobedient.

She's getting lost in her negative thoughts and needs to be reminded of who she is."

I shivered at his words, and the threat behind them. This fucker was going to force me to say nice things about myself. Well, he could try.

"With pleasure. I do love punishing my little vixen," Ty growled, coming closer. He pulled out a pocket knife and flicked it open, the sharp blade gleaming in the light. "Where shall we start?"

Andras pulled me away from the wall and into his chest. "Get her leggings off."

Mina immediately perked up, my horny-as-hell pussy throbbing with need at his words. Ty moved quickly, peeling the soft fabric down my legs. He left my thong on, but when the leggings were tossed aside, he returned with his knife and cut the lace away from my body. He flipped the blade and slipped the handle between my legs, teasing my clit with the hilt, and I moaned.

Ty chuckled. "She's soaked for us."

"Leave her wet cunt for now. No pleasure for you, sweetheart," Andras purred, his voice like silk.

"Asshole," I mumbled, and his grip tightened to the point of pain around my neck.

Andras forced me to my knees. "Repeat after me. This is not my fault."

I mashed my lips together, refusing to say it. He looked at Ty and nodded. Without a word, Ty dropped his gym shorts to the floor, and his very hard dick stared me in the face. My mouth watered, and I licked my lips. His piercing glinted in the low lights, and I really really wanted to lick it.

"If you can't obey, you suck," Andras quipped.

"Ready to obey, pet?" Ty grinned wickedly, his hand stroking his cock.

I was not saying the damn words, so I opened my mouth and glared up at Ty. His eyes heated, and he stepped forward, shoving his dick down my throat without warning. I gagged, breathing through my nose and trying not to choke. He pulled out and thrust back in again, giving me no time to breathe. He fucked my mouth so forcefully tears pricked at my eyes. Blood rushed to my clit, my body alight with desire for this monster before me.

"Fuck, you look so good with my dick in your mouth, pet," Ty growled.

I moaned at his words, loving the feel of him, and my pussy pulsed with need. Ty pulled out, and I gasped, feeling empty.

"Say the words, sweetheart," Andras demanded.

"You're going to have to try harder than that, boys," I murmured, grinning up at them.

Andras snarled, his temper rising. He pulled me up and bent me in half, so my face was once again level with Ty's delicious dick. "Fuck her face until the tears leak from her pretty eyes."

"Did you hear that, pet?" Ty rumbled, threading his hand in my hair. "I'm going to make you cry."

His rough hands tightened in my hair, and then his cock was down my throat again. I moaned, sucking and licking, tasting the pre-cum leaking from the tip and loving every fucking bit of it.

Andras moved behind me, his hand on my ass. He pulled

away and smacked hard on my left cheek, three quick slaps. I moaned with Ty's cock filling my mouth and sucked harder.

Ty chuckled. "Fuck do that again, brother. She liked it."

Andras smacked my ass again, three more slaps on the same cheek. The sting of it burned so fucking good. Andras slipped his hand between my legs, his fingers teasing my pussy and flicking my clit. I whimpered at the light touches, and my mind emptied of thoughts as these two devil princes took control of my body.

He moved away, and I would've screamed at him if it weren't for the dick in my mouth. Ty thrust further, faster, and I took it all. I hallowed out my cheeks, and tears began to fall from my eyes. His grip in my hair tightened, and I moaned as his cock throbbed.

"Yes, pet. Give me your tears. Give me your pain." Ty's growl turned into a groan just before his hot cum spilled down my throat. "Fuck. Yes, such a good slut, taking my cock."

Ty pulled out slowly and rubbed the tip of his cock across my lips, smearing his cum on my face. He grinned. "Who do you belong to, pet?"

"You, monster man," I mumbled the words, my pussy throbbing with so much need.

"Typhon. On the floor," Andras commanded, forcing us into new positions.

Ty obeyed, my big scary Prince following commands like a good boy. I loved to see it. Andras gripped my neck once more and walked me over to Ty so that I was standing with his head between my legs. He stared up at my body with hungry eyes.

"What a fucking gorgeous view. Come here, pet. Sit on my

face," Ty snarled, gripping my calves.

I looked up at Andras, and he smirked, heat flooding his gaze as I waited for his commands. He reached down between my legs and used his fingers to spread my pussy open, giving Ty a show. "He wants this cunt, sweetheart."

I nodded, licking my lips.

"Do you want to feel his mouth here?" Andras purred, his fingers teasing me, probing.

I nodded again.

He smiled, and his expression was pure sin. "Then say the fucking words."

I whined, but I couldn't hold out any longer. I needed the release. "It wasn't my fucking fault."

Andras slipped one finger inside me and pressed his thumb to my clit. "Again."

My eyes closed, and I moaned at his expert touches. "It wasn't my fault."

"Good girl. Now sit on Ty's face and let us give you what you need."

I dropped to the floor instantly. Ty gripped my thighs, and his tongue was on me immediately. He sucked my pussy into his mouth like he was starved. The sounds coming out of me were slutty as hell, but I couldn't keep them in. Not with these sexy-as-fuck men wringing pleasure from my body over and over again.

Andras stepped in front of me, slowly undoing his belt and pants. His dick sprang forth, and fuck, it was sexy as hell. Who knew dicks could be sexy? I sure as fuck didn't, but it was true. I opened my mouth and stared into the eyes of the devil.

Andras smirked, his beautiful face a mix of pleasure and sin. "Aren't you the obedient slut for us?"

Ty used that moment to slip his tongue inside me, and I moaned just as Andras pressed his cock to my lips. I flicked my tongue against the tip and leaned forward to take him in fully. He groaned, murmuring praises as he fucked my mouth slowly.

Andras continued his slow movements, controlling my body with his hands in my fiery hair while Ty teased my clit with his tongue. I rolled my hips, moaning and needing more.

"That's it, angel. Ride his face while you take my cock. Take what you need from him while I fuck your pretty throat." Andras's voice was deep and filled with desire.

Ty's hands pulled me in closer, and I moved my hips, riding his tongue. His hand cupped my ass and spread my cheeks, teasing the tight hole with his fingers.

I moaned louder, loving the feel of both my Princes at once. My mind was blissfully blank as we shared pleasure in this moment.

"Fuck, angel. Your mouth is exquisite," Andras murmured. "Ty, brother. Make her come while I fill her up with mine."

His filthy words and Ty's dark chuckle were near enough to send me over the edge. Ty's finger pressed into my ass, teasing my hole while his tongue lapped at my clit with reckless abandon. Andras's movements grew jerky, and he praised me over and over as he fucked my mouth. I felt his dick swell just before the cum spilled down my throat. I moaned around him when my own orgasm washed through my body like a tidal wave. I shivered and jerked against the men holding my body hostage.

Andras pulled out and followed Ty, smearing his cum on

my lips. "Say it again."

"It wasn't my fault." I whispered the words immediately, the fight having left my body when the orgasm crashed through me.

Andras pulled me up, and my legs shook slightly. "It wasn't your fault. And I will continue to make you say those words until you believe them." He brushed the hair from my face, and I nodded.

Because if I believed anything, it was that.

Chapter Thirty-Eight
Phenex

I was trying very hard not to murder the Princes. The big one, Typhon, was going on and on about how delicious my mate tasted when she rode his fucking face the other day. I knew he was doing it to piss me off, and it was fucking working. If I wasn't so distracted dealing with the others and making sure we were fully prepared for an attack by my evil brother, I would've found them and ripped their dicks off before they got anywhere near her.

Of course, I wouldn't actually do that. I wanted Seraphina to love me. And she wouldn't love me if I hurt them. How was I meant to make her love me and accept me as her mate when she was so smitten with them? It was infuriating.

At night, I played out the last moments of her father's life in my head. Seraphina's father died in my arms. She didn't know that yet, and I had no fucking clue how to tell her. But I would, eventually.

I flew through the halls of the Valdis Palace, bodies littering the floors. Aurora had escaped our world, but there was someone here I needed to speak with. Someone who sent me a most intriguing note.

I came to the bedroom of Aurora and her mate. I heard of her marriage to the outlaw daemon. Caligo was in uproar, my father in particular. He wanted Aurora, and she refused him, marrying a truxen daemon instead.

That daemon was now sprawled out on the floor, clutching a precious stone to his chest. He was bleeding from several wounds that would instantly kill a mortal. There were dozens of dead soldiers loyal to my father around him. The daemon gazed up at me.

"I've been waiting for you." His words were filled with pain.

I dropped to my knees beside him, curious more than anything. "What do you know of my mate?"

The note he sent burned into my brain long after I destroyed it. He knew who my mate was.

It was a secret desire of mine to find my mate. The creature who would be my other half, my equal. My everything. I wanted more than I cared to admit.

"She is going to be your queen. She will be the best of us. The most powerful creature our world has seen in a millenia."

My pride soared for this creature. I had to have her. "Tell me who it is."

The daemon smiled, his eyes sad and filled with pain. "My daughter. She will be yours. But there will be more—" He coughed savagely, and blood trickled from his lips.

I frowned. "Why aren't you healing?"

The daemon opened his closed hand, and I stared at the glowing tenebrite stone. "Send this to Aurora for our daughter. For Seraphina. Her mates."

My eyes widened. He was dying because he'd already gifted his soul to the stone. His life ebbed away on this plane, and would become a gift. And his words were confusing. Mates?

She will be yours. He said those words. But the rest confused me. Did he know about these Princes? Were these human hybrids supposed to be hers too? It was unheard of…one woman for us all to share and bond with. I frowned, mulling over this information with the evidence before me.

Michaela's laughter pulled me from my thoughts. She and Morax were decorating for the party, and being absurdly in love. The stench was fucking cloying.

"I'm going out for a bit," I growled, leaving them to it.

I didn't really know where I was going, but I made my way outside, stomping around and pouting like a child.

The sound of someone grunting with exertion caught my heightened senses, and I circled around the mansion toward the dense woods behind it. Devon was close to the edge of the protective shields we placed around the grounds. He was digging, or rather filling, a hole.

He frowned when he saw me. "Do you need something?"

I crossed my arms. "What are you doing?"

He stopped for a moment and turned his bright-green eyes to me. "Burying Joseph Bronwen. I wanted Seraphina and Michaela to have a place to mourn him. Don't have a headstone, but at least we can surround it with flowers or something."

"A stone?" I cocked my head to the side, curious.

He arched his brow. "Yeah. A headstone. We bury our dead in cemeteries with a stone stating their name."

I frowned. "I can help with that. What should it say?"

Devon stared at me like I was crazy. "Uh, his name. And maybe…beloved husband and devoted father."

I nodded and closed my eyes. I pictured the stone in my

Resurrection

mind, imagining the words Devon spoke. I whispered a few words, coaxing the earth to follow my commands. The stone formed beneath the surface and slowly shoved its way out at my command, just at the edge of the freshly dug grave. When I opened my eyes, the headstone was there just as I envisioned.

Devon's mouth was open, and he stared at me. "Can you teach me how to do that?"

I shrugged. "Probably. Why?"

Devon's gaze dropped to the stone. "I'd like to make a few myself. For those we've lost."

I shoved my hands in my jeans. "Alright. I can help you."

The young Prince looked back at me with a half-smile. I returned his smile with one of my own. This was mildly pleasant.

"Why were you stomping out here?" Devon asked, leaning on the shovel. His muscular arms filled out the T-shirt he wore impeccably well.

But the reminder of my previous mood had me snarling again. I was about to rage, but something stopped me. A tug at a bond, barely noticeable, but it was there. "I am struggling to understand Seraphina. And what her needs are."

Devon's small smile turned into a grin. "Good luck with that. She's practically a sphinx. And unless she wants you to know what she's thinking, you won't."

Devon's quiet laughter turned into a louder chuckle, and I shrugged, rolling my eyes.

"Of course. The stars blessed me with a mate who causes more chaos than I do."

The Prince nodded, smiling. "Best to enjoy the ride, my friend. From someone who was in a similar place, and then in the damn doghouse, just trust her. If you trust her, you'll figure it out."

I pursed my lips and crossed my arms, pondering his words. "Thank you."

Devon nodded, offering his hand, and I reached out and shook it. A bond hummed between us, and we stared at each other, feeling the strange connection stirring. I left without another word. I didn't know what to make of the bonds forming between me and others. Well, that wasn't entirely true. I was beginning to think something was happening between myself and these Princes. And Devon's words wrang out in my head. Trust her. I always loved an adventure, so might as well dive head first into this one.

CHAPTER THIRTY-NINE
Typhon

Taunting the daemon prince was my new favorite pastime. Well, second favorite, right behind devouring Seraphina's sexy-as-fuck pussy. And fucking her mouth. And her ass. Okay, it was my favorite right after every inch of Seraphina's sweet and sinful body.

He and Devon were currently chatting and working together to set up the bar for the event tonight. I watched them curiously. They were being oddly friendly. Levi walked up beside me, his gaze following mine.

"Since when are they friendly?" Levi smirked, crossing his arms. His tattooed biceps bulged, the flames enhancing his muscles.

I shrugged, pretending I didn't care when it was obvious I cared too much. "Since a few hours ago, it looks like. Perhaps the daemon is changing tactics to get closer to our girl."

"As if he could if she didn't want him to," he quipped, and I grunted in agreement.

"True. Perhaps she does want him to, though. Would you be good with it?" I glanced at him, watching his face for the truth.

Levi was more easygoing and willing to make friends when I wasn't. "Don't you feel it? When our bonds snapped into place with Seraphina during that ritual, something else did too. Someone else, I think."

I mulled over his words. I did feel it. When she was engulfed in those flames, some chain unlinked itself from my soul and wound its way to her, binding me to her more fully. And to my brothers as well; but it was strange, almost as if a link was missing. Was it this daemon prince? This fucker was going to complete our group?

"He's hot," Levi said with a chuckle.

I snarled, jealousy rearing up inside me. Levi turned to me with a knowing smile, and I wanted to punch him in his pretty fucking mouth.

He sensed my warring emotions down our bond and laughed. "Learn to share, Ty. Could be fun."

Levi grinned, his face wicked and tempting. He always knew how to rile me up.

My cock twitched, and his eyes flicked down to my gym shorts. Levi licked his lips, and I stepped closer to him, our chests brushing against each other. I was feeling extra predatory at the thought of sharing Levi with anyone else. Seraphina, yes, but the daemon? Why did that make me equally horny and filled with rage?

"We'll see." The words left my mouth in a deadly purr.

The party was slowly getting started when Dev and his new daemon bestie called us out to the woods near the edge of the boundary. Michaela and Morax were asked to come as well. Seraphina walked at my side, and I wrapped my arm around her waist, pulling her close. She smelled divine. Since that ritual, my senses had been heightened even further. Hints of musky amber and black currant rolled off her in waves. She was the perfect blend of sweet and smoky. I wanted to drown in her scent.

"Your thoughts are in the gutter, monster man." Seraphina snickered, elbowing me in the ribs. "I might not be able to read them exactly, but the testosterone in the air is cloying."

"Don't pretend you're not down in this gutter of sin with me, little vixen." As if she wasn't equally depraved. My pet's soul was just as black as mine.

She scoffed but leaned into my arms. I could feel Phenex's eyes on us. Seraphina pointedly ignored him.

The sun had set hours ago, but Morax and Phenex created orbs of light for us to see. And when we came close to the woods beyond, Seraphina gasped. There were several headstones before us. A small graveyard with one newly dug grave and similar headstones covered the area. I could make out a few of them. Seraphina could as well, by the sudden rigidity of her body against mine.

Michaela walked over to us, Morax following close behind. Seraphina left my arms and hugged her sister close.

"I came out here the other day to think," Dev started, breaking the silence. "I was thinking of my father, and how there was so much left unsaid between us. My mother, who was killed when I was too young to save her. And my sister, who I thought was dead and now lives with my worst enemies. I just wanted somewhere to go to talk to them and remember. I took the liberty of burying your father here, so that you might have a place to go and talk to him. We added the others, your mother, sister, and a few friends and family my brothers and I have lost on this journey."

"We?" Seraphina cut in, her eyes shining.

Dev turned to Phenex. "Phen created the headstones, he wanted to help, and added a few of his own lost souls as well."

Seraphina walked toward a headstone with her biological father's name on it. "Thank you. I wish I had known him."

Phenex moved closer to her, and I resisted the urge to step between them. His face was solemn and serious, something I hadn't seen from the flippant daemon since his arrival. "I didn't know him well, but I was there when he died."

Seraphina's eyes snapped to his, her mouth open in shock. "What? Did you kill him?"

Phenex brought his hands up in surrender immediately. "No! It was Belial and my mother's soldiers who cut him down. They didn't kill him. He was incredibly strong, and when I found him, the room was littered with bodies. His wounds would've healed eventually, perhaps a few scars from the stellatium blades. Belfegor's death was his choice. He gave his soul to the stone you used in the ritual. To bring us together."

"My father died just to bring you here? Are you fucking kidding me?" Seraphina snarled, her voice laced with pain and irritation.

Phenex stumbled back, unsure.

It was Morax who spoke next. "My brother may be impulsive and impish at times, but he is not a liar. And to those who mean something to him, he is loyal and kind. He revealed none of this, even to me, to protect you and your family."

Phenex looked sheepishly at his brother. "He told me I would find my true mate. His daughter. Said he had seen it and was proud of you. Of what you would become."

"Well, fuck him for dying that way and not being here to tell me himself. What I would become? I've become a massive disappointment." Seraphina's face was flushed with emotions. "This isn't about being nice. This is more bullshit about mates. I make my own choices. And I choose who I give myself to. I have chosen these men!" Seraphina shouted her declarations, pointing at us.

The hurt on Phenex's face was almost enough to make me feel for the daemon. Dev clearly did. He tried to talk to our girl, but she wasn't having it. Seraphina stalked off, and Michaela ran after her.

Morax sighed and followed them, unable to keep any amount of distance between himself and his own mate.

Andras stuffed his hands in his pockets and frowned, watching the daemon prince. "I believe you."

We turned to Andras, his quiet words drawing our attention.

Phenex's eyebrows shot up in surprise. "You do?"

Andras nodded. "I do. I cannot ignore the bonds forming between us. We all feel them. Seraphina does as well, but she is afraid. Our fierce woman is only afraid of one thing, herself."

"When her father told me she was my mate," Phenex murmured quietly. "He said something else. He was nearly gone, but he said there were more. She would have more. I think he saw you all as well."

Levi nodded. "It feels right, for whatever that's worth. I think our girl will come around. We need to show her that we're all in. Brothers?"

Phenex smirked. "Can't say I ever wished for more brothers. The ones I have are pain in the ass. But perhaps this will be something new. Kinky brothers." He wiggled his eyebrows and winked at Devon.

Levi laughed. "Oh man, you are so getting fucked in the ass, Dev."

"Fuck off, Levi!" Dev shouted, his cheeks flushing in the dim light.

Levi's grin was infectious, and I couldn't help but smile. "Alright. I'm in."

"As am I," Andras murmured, offering the smallest of smiles, the reserved prick.

"You know I am. Let's shower our sexy-as-sin queen with so much pleasure she'll never know what hit her." Levi elbowed me in the ribs, and I shoved him playfully.

The beat of music emanating from the mansion grew, and the noise intensified as the rave kicked off in the basement. I closed my eyes, searching for the spark of darkness that was Seraphina's soul. She wasn't in the basement yet. I sensed her upstairs in her rooms, likely with her sister.

"Let us join the fray," Andras spoke, back to his usually commanding presence. "Seraphina will join at her sister's insistence, I am certain."

I nodded in agreement, and we walked back to Vespertine Hall. The chains linking me to my brothers felt more solid, stronger. Our bond was nearly unbreakable. I had a feeling Seraphina was the key to our binding. And once that happened, we'd be fucking unstoppable.

CHAPTER FORTY
Seraphina

I was so fucking annoyed with that daemon prince. He went and did something ridiculously sweet, and I was seconds away from crying, but then he went and made it about himself. He was so fucking obsessed with this mate thing.

Michaela followed me, saying nothing, just holding my hand. I instantly felt like a jackass for ruining the moment, but that was Phenex's fault too. We got to my rooms, and I flopped face down on my bed. The weight of Michaela's body next to mine eased some of my unhappiness. I was still so fucking relieved she was here with me.

"You're really hard on that guy." Michaela laughed.

"He's annoying," I snapped back, my voice muffled in the blankets.

She scoffed. "So are you."

I turned my head to her, mouth open. "What the hell!"

She grinned at me. "Well, you are. You've got five sexy-as-hell monsters vying for your attention, ready to worship you."

"I can hear you, mate," Morax hissed from outside the room. He'd followed us back but closed the door to give us some alone time.

Michaela giggled. "It's fun to rile him up."

I rolled my eyes. "I don't want the dirty details, little sister."

She grinned again, lying back on the bed. We lay there, eye to eye.

"As I was saying, what are you so afraid of? Go get those men and make them bow to you."

I sighed. That sounded unbelievably appealing. And I couldn't figure out exactly why it was so hard for me to accept.

"I guess I'm scared. We've lost so many people. I nearly lost them. And now I'm meant to be something big, or whatever Belfegor said. And add another person to my life I could lose. I don't think I could stand it."

Michaela propped her hand against her blonde hair. "We haven't had it easy, that's for damn sure. But what I've gained, where we are right now, I can't say it hasn't been worth it. If I never met Morax, I think my life would've always been a shadow of what it could be."

I flopped over on my back. It was almost annoying how smart and enlightening Kaela was. "I've built so many walls around myself. It's hard to take them down."

Michaela poked me and grinned like the devil was on her shoulder. "Well, that's why you have five muscular, hot men with big—"

"*MICHAELA*, do not finish that sentence," Morax snarled as he ripped open the door.

She rolled her eyes. "With big *hearts* ready to break those walls down. Gosh, Mor, you're so sensitive."

I laughed out loud, watching the daemon before us glowing with unfiltered jealousy. The predatory gaze he now had aimed at my sister was hot as fuck, and I could totally see why she enjoyed taunting the guy.

Resurrection

Morax stalked over to the bed with a snarl and flipped my sister over his shoulder. "Excuse me. My mate needs to be taught a lesson."

He turned around, and Michaela's face was flushed with wicked glee. "Now get ready, because we will be going down to the party in like twenty minutes. And you're going to sing!"

Morax spanked her ass, and she yelped. He murmured something I couldn't hear, but the flush of my sister's face told me I really didn't want to know. I highly doubted they'd be ready in twenty minutes.

An hour or so later, I skipped through the halls with my sister and her grumpy daemon mate. Amidst the preparations for the party, Michaela snagged us a bunch of clothing options too. She was wearing a neon-blue leather bodycon dress and white platform sneakers. Her blonde hair hung straight down her back, and glitter paint covered her skin. Morax couldn't keep his eyes off her, and it made me smile. I was so fucking happy for her.

I went with something a bit more risque, because I too enjoyed taunting devils. I wore a neon-pink bikini with a mesh mini dress over it. The dress was white, and the mesh design stretched over my skin, leaving very little to the imagination. I paired it with white chunky platform heels. My red hair was a kinky, wavy mess brushing over my shoulders. And my skin was coated in glitter, just like Michaela's. I added a pair of hot-pink devil horns to my ensemble as well, because, obviously.

When we arrived, several daemons were waiting by the doors to the basement. They passed out glow bracelets and necklaces, and a few had body paint. I got a wicked idea.

"You two go on in, I'll be right behind you," I said to Michaela with an evil grin.

She laughed, watching me hike my dress up and roll the bikini down. I whispered the details of my design to the girl with the paint brushes, and she winked at me. Yes, this was going to be fun. I waited a few minutes for the paint to dry and mulled over what song I wanted to sing tonight. More than anything did I want to just get lost in the crowds and feel the music, but when Michaela suggested I sing for everyone, the idea thrilled me too.

Tonight I would sing for a crowd of people loyal to my sister and I. People who fought like hell to get here and came together to say a collective fuck you to The Obscuritas. But I also needed to sing something for my Princes. And Phenex. Which, I guess he was one of my Princes too. If I said so. I couldn't deny the pull of my soul to his. There was something connecting us. But I refused to leave the others just for him and our strange connection. If he couldn't fucking figure that out, we'd never move forward.

The basement was completely transformed for the party. There were still prisoner cells along the one wall, but otherwise the space was completely opened up for a massive dance floor. The ceilings were high for a basement, and disco balls hung from open rafters. The only light came from the stage, where a DJ was mixing, keeping the growing crowd entertained. I searched the sea of glowing and glittered bodies, but didn't see any of my Princes. I recognized several faces, though, including James, Ty's gym manager, and Xavier, the firefighter from Levi's station. Jade, a boxer I met at Ty's gym, was also in the crowd, her dark skin glowing with neon paint as she danced with another female I didn't know. My girls Josie and Lottie were dancing on a smaller stage with shining poles in sexy-as-hell corsets. Andras informed me they were here, along with so many others. The Umbra Noctis had been gathering people to our side over the last few years, and even in the last few weeks when we were held captive.

The lumen friend of my sister, Nuri, was here too. She and Lo were chatting near the bar. Their outfits were a little more conservative, but I could see the inked flesh through slits of fabric down the left side of Lo's body. They were meant to cover her scars from the fire I caused. But all I could see was the pain I made her endure. And her sister. Her innocent sister, who lost her life because of me.

My chest started to burn, and my throat closed up. How could she be here? Be on my side? If I were her, I would never forgive the person who killed my sister. Fuck, I'd kill that motherfucker myself. But here she was, helping us, helping me. It wasn't right. I didn't deserve her help.

"Nova," Tibby called out. Her voice pulled me from the coming panic attack.

I turned away from Lo and searched for my friend. She came through a small group of people, a bright-pink pixie in a sea of glowing monsters. She wore a hot-pink bodysuit that clung to her like a second skin. She also had platform heels like mine, only hers were hot pink to match her outfit. She wasn't wearing a wig, but rocking her bright-blonde hair in a messy pixie cut. Her makeup was bright and brought out the fairy vibes of her delicate features.

"Tibby!" I ran to her, stopping short of giving her a hug. "You look amazing, Zenith." I smiled.

She smiled back, and I registered the big bad bodyguards behind her. Gremory was dressed in jeans and a shiny purple shirt. His blond hair was down around his shoulders and glittering with sparkly hairspray. Delphine wore a leopard print bodysuit and her dark curly hair was piled on top of her head. The blood-red lipstick stood out against her dark skin beautifully. Her hazel eyes assessed me, and I stared her down in return. She dropped her eyes first, and I smirked triumphantly before closing in on my best friend.

"How are you?" I asked tentatively. She looked so much better, even the light was returning to her eyes.

Tibby smiled. "Better. A lot better. Feeling more myself every hour, it seems like."

I grinned back at her. "I'm so fucking happy about that."

Tibby stepped forward and hugged me, and I wrapped her in my arms. I was close to crying as I hugged my oldest and only friend.

"You good with these two?" I whispered into her ear.

Gremory raised an eyebrow, obviously hearing my question with his heightened senses.

But she was mine first, and I could give two fucks about what he heard me say. "Do I need to hurt them?"

Tibby giggled and pulled away. Her face was flushed, and there was something more in her reserved gaze. "No. I think

I'll keep them around for now."

Delphine chuckled. "Come, little one. Let's go dance." Her voice was a soft purr.

I registered the note of command, and Tibby instantly turned to the striking woman. She waved goodbye as Gremory wrapped an arm around her waist. I was so fucking happy to see her getting the love and attention she deserved. Maybe the seriously powerful and dominant witch wasn't my first choice, but if she was making my only friend happy, I could accept that.

My Princes were still nowhere in sight, so I headed for the stage, ready to sing my first song of the night. I was going with something loud and in defiance of our predicament with the fucking Kings. I would shout these lyrics to the world and fucking hope they could hear me. That my voice would shake the foundation of that wretched manor and they would know Seraphina Valdis was coming for them.

The song was "Black Sheep" by Dorothy, a fellow take-no-shit female with a ridiculously good voice. I hoped to do her song justice. The DJ passed me a mic as soon as I walked on stage. I looked out at the crowd as the music quieted. Dozens and dozens of eyes turned my way. Some were glowing, pulses of power emanating from the daemons and lumens mixed into the crowd.

"Well. I'm not one for speeches. And I'm not good at feelings." I shrugged, walking the stage before this fierce group. "But I am grateful you're here. Those who fought to get us out of Blackbyrn Manor, thank you. Those who joined us since, thank you. I have a feeling the shit hasn't actually hit the fan yet, so when it does, just know I will give every fucking thing

I have to kill those fucking bastards."

The people roared a defiant sound, shaking the walls, and I grinned. I nodded to the DJ to start the song and closed my eyes, feeling the music in my bones. This was a reckoning. My mission to avenge my family and exact my deadly revenge on The Obscuritas was so much more now. I would destroy the entire fucking cult. Every last one of those sick fucks would feel my wrath. And we would have our vengeance for all we had lost.

When the final notes of the song bellowed out of me, the raucous crowd erupted into applause. My blood began to sing with power, and I stared down at my arms, feeling the glow of it desperate to break free. And in that moment, I felt them. My eyes didn't need to scan the crowd. I turned my head, and they were there at the edge of the stage. My fucking Princes, all five of them. Fuck, they looked hot. Mina whined, and I clenched my thighs in an attempt to quiet her. Ty's nostrils flared, and he whispered something too low for me to hear. The others heard, and their grins turned dark and feral.

But I wasn't afraid. Not of them, never of them. And I was ready to take the next step into the unknown. To allow them in. To break that final wall around my dark heart and give it to them. Would they break it? Could I survive this?

Everything in me screamed to run, but not from them. My body was begging me to leap into their arms, and for once, my mind, body, and soul were in agreement.

I nodded to the DJ for my next song, and the first instrumental notes of Rihanna's "Love on the Brain" echoed into the basement. I slowed it down, taking my time to sing out the lyrics, focusing all my attention on the five monsters standing before me. Their devilish gazes tracked my every movement across the stage, and I reveled in their attention. The bonds linking me to each of these creatures hummed with a heady power so strong, it should have scared me. But I refused to cower to my fears. I would dive into this fire head first and relish the pain and pleasure my Princes had to offer. And I would give them every piece of my broken, fucked up heart.

As soon as the song ended and the deafening applause rang out once more, Ty leapt onto the stage. He knocked the mic out of my hand, grabbed my face, and crushed his lips to mine. Whistles and more applause sounded throughout the party as this monster laid his claim on my soul. I opened for him, eager for the taste of him, but he pulled away too soon.

His hazel eyes were almost glowing. "You are the most stunning, infuriating creature. Now come dance with us. I'm tired of all these males drooling over you."

I grinned up at him. "What males? I only saw five Princes eye-fucking me in the crowd."

Ty chuckled and spanked my ass. "More to come, pet." He picked me up, and before I knew what was happening, I was flying through the air.

I screamed, the sound whooshing out of me as strong arms caught me easily. I looked into the eyes of my new daemon prince. His irises were glowing a silver so bright they looked like starlight. His lips twitched, hiding a smile as he watched me.

"The others weren't kidding when they said you could sing. I've never heard such a beautiful voice." His praises had my insides melting and my pussy soaking.

I blushed, my skin heating as his eyes traveled downward.

Phenex growled as he took in the scraps of clothing barely covering my body. My pussy pulsed, and his nostrils flared. I wiggled, attempting to get out of his arms, but he held me firmly against his chest.

"And where do you think you're going, now that I've got you in my arms?" Phenex mused, his silver eyes twinkling. His horns spiraled out of his head, and his tongue flicked out. It was forked and pierced.

I immediately needed to know what it would feel like between my legs. I bit my lip and squirmed, the heat building in my core almost too much. Mina was going fucking nuts with horny rage. "Shall we dance?"

Phenex smirked, scenting my arousal. "Hope you don't mind if it turns into an orgy."

I smiled my own devilish smile. "As long as I'm the main attraction."

Andras suddenly appeared at my side and gripped my chin, forcing my head to the side. "No orgies on the dance floor. I won't be sharing your screams of pleasure with every asshole in here."

I rolled my eyes and smacked Phenex on the shoulder. "Put me down, daemon."

His eyes crinkled when he smiled, and he set me on my feet, his hands still resting lightly on my hips. He was still over a foot taller than me, and I had four-inch heels on. His hair was wavy and unkempt, brushing against his shoulders. He had a jawline straight from the gods, and the colorful tattoos dancing down his arms were full of stories I wanted to ask about.

The DJ was back to mixing, and a steady beat played out,

almost as rapid as my heartbeat. The Princes surrounded me, blocking any view others might have had, and I smirked at them, turning in slow circles and moving my hips side to side. I brushed my fingertips across their chests as I moved.

Ty wore all black, as usual, but managed to get a bit of paint on his arms, and it glowed against his biceps. Levi brought his arm up and dragged his fingers through his hair, watching me with the eyes of a predator. He wore a white sleeveless shirt, and I laughed out loud at the glowing words on it. The shirt had an arrow pointing up and down, with the words *Two Seater* in-between.

"You're ridiculous." I laughed again, moving my body against his and wrapping my arms around his neck. "It's my favorite."

Levi grinned, his navy eyes like liquid pools of darkness in the dim lights. "You're my favorite."

He leaned in and kissed me, his tongue running along the seam of my lips. I nipped at it, needing more. A body pressed against me from behind, and I leaned back slightly another of my Princes. I scented whiskey and felt the scratch of a five-day shadow against my neck. Devon.

"You look good enough to eat, my queen," Dev murmured into my neck, trailing kisses down my skin even as Levi continued his teasing kisses against my lips.

I wrapped an arm around Dev's head, threading my hands in his lush black hair, and pulled him closer. The heat of bodies pressed in on us, and I knew all my Princes surrounded me. More hands teased and touched my body as I lost myself to the music and danced for them. My blood was a million degrees as their rough hands pawed at me, slipping along the fabric of my bikini. Someone pushed the fabric aside and warm air assaulted my nipples. I moaned as someone rolled the tender bud between their fingers.

I opened my eyes, and stared into the predatory gaze of my dark Prince.

"I have an idea. Time to go." Andras was as controlling as ever. And I not-so-secretly fucking loved it.

I pouted up at him. "But we're just getting started."

Andras dragged his thumb across my bottom lip. "Yes, sweetheart, we are."

Devon arranged my bikini top to cover my nips, and I winked at him. Such a gentleman. He held out his arm for me, and I took it, following Andras. Levi came up and took my other arm, and I glanced back to see Ty and Phenex walking behind us.

The rave was in full swing, with partygoers in various stages of undress. Things were taking a wilder turn, and part of me wanted to stay and enjoy the show. But the five men prowling around me were clearly on a mission, and I was too curious to see how this would go. Power hummed in my veins, and I started to truly feel their emotions. Lust. Hunger. Desire. Pain and pleasure. The feel of them under my skin caused a whimper to escape my lips.

"Feeling a little needy, *diabla*?" Levi teased, and I pinched his arm.

"Yeah. Needy and empty. Who's going to fill me up first?" I purred, and several low growls sounded around me, making me laugh.

Andras turned his head slightly as he walked in front of us.

"That's for us to know, and you to feel."

"Curiouser and curiouser," I whispered.

Another surge of desire coursed through my body, and I moaned. This was new, whatever this feeling was. It was more than just desire and a need to be fucked. It was something deeper. An abyss was opening within me, and deep in my bones, I knew these men would tip me over the edge.

CHAPTER FORTY-ONE
Phenex

Seraphina was driving me insane. Her scent was changing, and I could feel the mating bond between us pulsing with need. We were being called together, and it was taking all my self-control not to rip her from their arms and fuck her senseless. And yet, another part of me didn't want that. I could feel the bonds between these Princes snapping into place, the power growing between us. Despite all the ways of our kind claiming a mate was a one-on-one situation, I knew now it wasn't always so.

We made our way through the mansion to Seraphina's rooms. The Princes had reconstructed several rooms to interconnect to keep each other close. I was staying in a room near my brother, but I hoped after tonight, that would change. Fuck, did I need that to change. Every moment spent separated from her was utter torture.

When Seraphina began to sing, it was indeed a siren's call. I'd never heard a voice as beautiful as hers. Maybe I was biased, but whatever. My dick had been rock hard ever since. And now my sexy-as-fuck mate was feeling the pull too, and if she refused me now, I'd go completely insane.

We walked into the rooms, and I couldn't hold back. I snatched her by the waist and shoved her against the wall. Her feet dangled in the air; the little monster was trapped.

I stared into her ocean eyes and groaned when her tongue flicked out to lick her lips. "Seraphina. Can I kiss you?"

Her eyes bored into mine, searching. I hoped she found what she needed to let me in.

Her hands circled my neck, and her fingers played with my hair, making me shiver. "Yes."

I was on her in seconds, bruising her lips with the force of my need for her. She tasted of starlight and hellfire all at once. Her tongue danced with mine, and I growled, digging my fingers into her hips and claiming her for myself. My wings snapped out, and I could feel my power glowing just beneath the surface of my skin.

We pulled apart, our breaths mingling.

"That should've been the first. And it most definitely won't be the last."

I dropped her to the floor, and she wobbled slightly on her heels, which amused me. I smirked, and before I could move, she punched me right in the gut. It was a good fucking punch too, and I doubled over for a moment.

"What was that for?" I growled, ready to spank the fuck out of her.

She shrugged. "I felt like it."

Ty chuckled. "You'll learn quickly that our little vixen is vicious when the mood strikes her."

I prowled toward her, circling her hungrily. My mate didn't look scared, no hint of fear about her. I inhaled, and a deadly purr built in my chest. "You want to be subdued. To be claimed."

She smirked at me, slowly bringing her arms up to pull the

scrap of a dress over her head. Her body was mouthwatering. Her curves were like a decadent dessert that needed to be savored. I was going to lick every inch of her skin.

"Tonight, we're going to feast, my brothers," Andras spoke, his voice deep and commanding. "And Seraphina, our dark angel, will be blindfolded."

"I will?" Seraphina laughed, pulling the strings of her bikini achingly slow.

My mouth watered, and I could feel the hunger of my brothers reaching its peak. Andras circled closer and snatched her wrists. Seraphina smiled coyly.

"You will." Andras pulled her arms tightly behind her back with one hand and wrapped the other around her throat. "And your pretty cunt will weep for us, over and over, until your mind is quiet, and all that's left is us. Your mates."

Seraphina's chest heaved with heavy breaths. "My mates?"

Dev stepped forward and pulled her bikini strings apart. The neon fabric fell to the floor, and I groaned at the sight of her naked flesh on display. She was perfect in every way. A loud laugh escaped my throat when I noticed the paint. Scribbled across the soft mound of flesh above her perfect pussy were the words *Property of the Fucking Princes*.

The other Princes chuckled. Levi responded first. "Seraphina. *Diabla*. Did you let someone write that on your body?"

Seraphina grinned like the daemon she most certainly was. "Perhaps."

"Give me a name," Ty growled low, and the sound was sexy enough to make my dick twitch.

The devil girl simply licked her lips and slowly ran her

fingers down her body, tracing the words. "If you don't like it, I could go find someone who would."

The snarl ripped from my throat before I could stop it. "No." My skin grew hot and the temperature rose within the room at the thought of another seeing her like this. "Only us."

Her smirk turned smug. "Only us."

Seraphina's words had five daemons growling with possessive intentions. Dev stalked closer, brushing his fingers down her throat.

"I know you feel it, *mera dil*," Dev's voice was low and desperate. "The bonds between us. Let us in, my queen."

She whimpered between them as Dev teased her peaked nipples. "I'm trying. You're going to have to help me."

I watched as Dev's hand slipped between her thighs and she moaned loudly for him. I wanted to bottle that sound and keep it as a souvenir. My dick ached for attention, and I began to undress.

The pretty one was watching me, and my gaze slid to his as I pulled my cock free of my pants and started to stroke. His eyes heated.

"I need to fuck someone soon, or I'll go insane," I growled.

Seraphina's breath hitched. "Who did you have in mind?"

I stroked my cock slowly, enjoying her attention and Levi's. "You, of course. I'm going to take each of your holes and brand them with my scent. I'd enjoy this one too, if it's allowed." I nodded at Levi.

The big one snarled, stepping in front of Levi, and I grinned. I knew that fucker had a thing for Levi. I saw the bond between them instantly. Their souls called to each other so audibly.

Levi laughed, and the sound was filthy. He was enjoying this. And by the scent of our mate, so was she. I turned back to her. "Would you like that, *mini monstra*? Want to watch your mates fuck each other, and you, all at once?"

She nodded eagerly. "It's about fucking time."

Before I could respond, Andras took control once more. "Devon. Undress. And get on your knees."

Dev's cheeks flushed, and I could feel his curiosity and desire warring with his fears.

Levi shoved off the wall and came to his aid, squeezing Dev's bicep. "You knew your punishment was coming. And you said you'd do anything for her." Levi grinned. "Don't worry. I'll join you, brother."

I had the feeling Dev was going to suck his first dick, and this was highly amusing. Mostly because daemons had zero boundaries. Lumens were nearly as fluid as daemons. The stipulations and repressive rules of humans relating to sex were absurd.

"Don't worry, sweet Dev. I'll be gentle." I smirked, feeling my eyes glow with power.

Ty stepped next to me, almost as tall as I was and equally as broad in the chest. He unzipped his jeans and freed his cock, and I eyed it hungrily.

Ty winked at me. "Like what you see?"

I grinned. "Yes. I've always wanted to pierce my dick. Was waiting for my mate, though."

"Oh my god, stop talking and start sucking for fuck's sake," Seraphina snapped, stomping her foot and glaring at us. "I'm feeling left out now."

Andras laughed, pulling Seraphina against his body. "You won't be left out, angel." He pulled her to the bed and sat her on the edge, spreading her legs wide and dropping between them. "You're soaked, sweetheart. And I'm ravenous."

He began kissing her fair skin, from her knees and down her inner thighs, teasing her. I watched, mesmerized, barely registering the now naked Dev and Levi kneeling before Ty and me. I pulled my gaze away from our mate and looked down at the sexy-as-fuck men before us. My dick throbbed, and Dev licked his lips, his mouth level with my cock.

"Taste," I commanded.

Dev's eyes darted to Levi just as he leaned in and licked a path up the shaft of Ty's cock. Ty groaned, and Levi grinned, taking the pierced head of Ty's cock into his mouth. Dev turned back to me, his eyes locking with mine as he opened his mouth, and I pressed forward. I rested the head of my cock on his tongue and waited for him to make a move. His movements were uncertain, but I could taste the desire coming off him in waves.

Seraphina groaned, and I glanced up to see her watching us. Andras was feasting on her sweet cunt, but her moans were for us. "Fuck, that's so fucking hot."

Her words spurred Dev on, and he wrapped his lips around my cock, making me groan. His mouth was warm, and I filled it further, thrusting to the back of his throat.

"You look fucking good gagging on my dick, Dev," I growled, threading my hands in his hair. "I'm going to fuck your face now."

Ty chuckled beside me, his hands going into Levi's hair.

"You too, pretty boy." He thrust his hips forward, and Levi moaned as the Prince used his face for his own pleasure.

I snarled, needing more from my own Prince, and tightened my hold on his hair. His arms shot up, his hands resting on my thighs and his fingers digging in as I fucked his mouth. He gagged and moaned, and I could see his own cock, hard and throbbing, between his legs. Dev was definitely enjoying this. The fact that mine was the first to enter his mouth pleased me greatly.

Our groans of pleasure mixed with Seraphina's as her own grew louder. Andras teased and licked her while she watched us. It was hot as fuck, and if I wasn't so eager to fuck her too, I'd fill this man's belly with my cum.

The bond that pulsed with life between Dev and I suddenly snapped into full power, and he gasped. I pulled back, and he stared up at me.

"What the hell was that?" His eyes were glowing a brilliant sea-foam green.

I stared back at him in shock. "It was a mate bond. I thought it was your connection to Seraphina that drew me to you and the others, but it's more than that."

Seraphina screamed, the orgasm Andras gave her causing all of us to turn and witness the ecstasy on her face. Her eyes opened, and her shocked stare darted between us. "You have a mate bond with Devon?"

I nodded slowly. "It's unheard of to bond like this with more than one creature. But it's true. I can feel it humming with life between us."

Seraphina smiled, and the light on her face was glorious.

"That's fucking awesome."

Andras stood, a smirk on his face and Seraphina's arousal glistening on his lips. "I had a suspicion this was true. The threads connecting us after that ritual, I do not think it was my father's intention, but it linked us. And now that you're here, I can see that it was meant to be this way all along."

I shook my head, running my hand through my hair. "You are more clever than me, because while I felt a connection, I assumed it was only for her, and her feelings for you."

Seraphina flopped back on to the bed, her legs spread wide and giving us a view of her perfect, pink cunt. I snarled, stalking toward her, but Andras stopped me.

"Ty, blindfold her," he commanded. "Before this night is over, our bonds will be sealed, and nothing the Kings do will be able to take that away from us."

The others murmured agreement, and we watched as Ty slipped the silk blindfold over her eyes. Levi turned on music, and the sounds filled the air loud enough to hide our whispers. Seraphina was going to receive more pleasure than she could handle. And I was gaining four new mates.

CHAPTER FORTY-TWO
Seraphina

Seeing my Princes suck each other's dicks was easily the best gift I'd ever received. Levi and Ty I knew would be hot as hell, but Dev on his knees for Phenex…fuck, that was amazing. Dev's eyes were glowing, and a power emanated from him in waves. Even with the blindfold on now, I could feel him. His love, his hunger. Every sensation was heightened, and I could feel them all. I loved him, so fucking much.

And seriously, I wouldn't have said no to Phen's dick either. That daemon was sex on a stick and naked. It was a fucking crime. His cock was thick and had a slight curve I couldn't wait to feel. And maybe I was a little jealous that Dev got to taste him first.

The bed dipped, and several sets of hands reached for me at once. Someone was between my legs, another kneeling near my head. The silky flesh of a Prince's cock smacked against my cheek. I stuck out my tongue, ready to tell these fuckers off, but when I opened my mouth, it was filled with dick. I moaned, licking the head and smiling. This was Ty, he was currently the only pierced cock of the bunch.

He chuckled. "I know you know whose dick you're sucking, pet. Look at you. The perfect little fuck toy."

I moaned, and my empty pussy throbbed like a needy slut.

Resurrection

"More. More. More." The words came out muffled around Ty's cock.

"So demanding." Andras laughed, the sound soft and deadly. "Give our queen what she needs."

In the next moment, a thick cock filled me, and I moaned loudly at the feel of my Prince. It wasn't Ty or Andras, now that I knew where they were. I reached out with my hands to feel for my other Princes while Ty held my head steady, using my mouth for his pleasure. The bed dipped once more and two of my men guided my hands to their bodies. I stroked them both as the Prince between my legs pulled out and buried himself once more.

"Fuck, *mi diosa*. I missed this pretty pussy," Levi groaned, and I hummed with pleasure around Ty's cock, knowing my sexy firefighter was fucking me.

He slammed into me over and over. Hands reached for my nipples, teasing and tweaking the aching buds in equal measure. Levi's hands gripped my waist tightly as he pounded into me. Ty adjusted his position to lean over me, forcing his cock deeper into my throat. Someone reached down and circled my clit. My body was alight with arousal, and my orgasm was coming on fast. My senses were heightened twice over with the blindfold.

"Come for me, *diabla*. Milk my cock," Levi growled, and I moaned.

The fingers teasing my clit circled the swollen bud faster, and in the next moment, I screamed around Ty's cock as the pleasure washed through my body.

"Fuck yes," Levi snarled and slammed into me again and again until his cock swelled and he unleashed himself inside me.

Our mate bond burst within me, and suddenly, I could feel him everywhere. His emotions flooded my system. There was so much love within him I could fucking cry. His bond filled me with a fire hotter than Hades, and I wanted to burn in this feeling forever.

Ty pulled his cock from my mouth, and I gasped for air. I was immediately pulled off the bed, my Princes giving me no reprieve. One of them took my place, and I was positioned on top of another Prince, a delicious new dick positioned at my entrance. This one was slimmer than Levi, the head slightly larger. I smiled, leaning down and pressing my hands to my Prince's chest. I rocked my hips, slicking his cock in my arousal. He groaned, and my smile widened.

"Fuck me, Devon Parrish," I murmured.

His groans intensified as I took control and lined up his cock and then slowly lowered myself onto him. His cock wasn't as thick, but gods damn was he long and hitting that g-spot already.

"Fuck, you feel good."

I rocked my hips, fucking him slowly, until a hand wrapped around my throat and I gasped. He leaned in and kissed me, lush lips dominating my own. Andras. His kisses were pure sin.

He shoved me down toward Dev and was suddenly behind me, teasing my ass with his fingers. A slick gel against my hole made me gasp, and I shivered, ready for what came next.

Dev rocked his hips in time with mine and fucked me like it was our last night on earth.

"Dev. Open your mouth," Ty growled, and I whimpered.

"Yes, fuck. I want to see that," I whined, more than tempted to rip off this blindfold.

"No, my love," Andras murmured behind me. "You will listen, and you will feel." At his words, he lined the head of his cock with my ass, pressing in slowly. He groaned, pushing his cock deeper, until he was buried inside me. "You feel divine, Seraphina."

I moaned again, feeling so fucking full.

"Fucking hell, this is the hottest thing I've ever witnessed," Phenex exclaimed, and I could feel him close. "Open your mouth, *mini monstra*. I need to fuck it."

My body was a vessel, and the Princes were here to claim every inch of it. My thoughts were scattered to the ends of the Earth, and I could only obey their commands. I leaned over Dev, and Phenex guided my mouth to his waiting cock. I flicked my tongue over the slit and tasted the salty goodness he offered. Andras pulled out of my ass and pressed in again, over and over, building a steady pace that Dev matched beneath us. The bonds between us pulsed with power, and I was beginning to feel more of Andras. His mate bond was like an icy breeze sweeping through me. It was cold and biting, and I fucking loved it.

I moaned around Phen's cock while my Princes fucked me so thoroughly my body was in danger of imploding. With Andras and Dev's mate bonds solidified, I was filled with power and could sense my skin beginning to glow.

"Stunning," Andras murmured, his pace increasing. "And all ours."

"Yes." The word was garbled around the throbbing cock in my mouth, but I was certain he understood.

"*Je t'aime, ma reine.*" Andras began speaking in French.

His first words were a declaration, but the ones that followed were filthy. My body responded to his praise and degradation in equal measures. His pace grew jerky, and Dev groaned beneath me.

They were both close, and so was I. My third orgasm was slow and steady, building within me like the slow pressure before a dam breaks. Phenex pulled his cock from my mouth and squeezed my cheeks tightly.

"My fucking mate," he growled, the sound deep and guttural. "You look fucking delicious getting fucked like this, *mini monstra*. I can't wait to fill you up. Those perfect tits bouncing in my face."

"Fuck, yes. Please. Fuck. I'm close." I moaned their names, scrunching my eyes closed behind my blindfold and relishing every inch of their flesh pounding into mine.

Dev moaned my name and jerked up, his dick hitting my g-spot just so, and I screamed as the dam within me finally broke. He unloaded, his cock pulsing inside me. Andras grabbed my hair, pulling my head back harshly and biting down on my neck as he continued to fuck my ass. He pumped into me three more times and groaned as his hot cum filled me. But it was the bond shining with hope and love and all the things I didn't think I would ever find that had my body shaking with so much fucking pleasure.

CHAPTER FORTY-THREE
Typhon

This was abso-fucking-lutely the most turned on I'd ever been. Seraphina's perfect body was glowing, a shining power as bright as the moon oozing from her pores. And I could feel it. The bonds between my brothers and I were stronger than ever. And with each connection falling into place with our girl, my power grew too. I needed to feel her sweet cunt wrapped around my cock immediately. Or maybe her ass? Fuck, I'd take them both. All I knew was my dick was hard as fuck and ready for her.

Having Levi on his knees for me nearly sent me over the edge, but I held back. Forcing my cock down Dev's throat while he shared Seraphina with Andras was even fucking hotter. Every moment of this joining was something I'd never forget.

I pulled Seraphina's limp body from between my brothers and lifted her into my arms. I crushed my lips to hers. She tasted of sin and starlight. Sweet and smoky. She was everything I'd ever wanted in a partner. My filthy pet responded eagerly, wrapping her legs around my waist and kissing me in kind. She bit my lip, drawing blood, and I snarled into the kiss, slamming her against the bedroom wall.

The chain linking this gorgeous creature to my soul shuddered with the force of our joint power.

"I need to fuck you, pet," I growled, my dick throbbing at the sight of my blood on her lips. I ripped off the blindfold, needing to see her. Seraphina's ocean eyes were shining with that luminescent power. I wanted to drown in their depths and sink beneath the waves.

"Then fuck me, monster man," she snarled back at me, flicking her tongue out to lick the blood coating her mouth. "I'm yours for the taking."

A low growl from the daemon prince drew my attention away from the dark goddess in my arms. Phenex's gray eyes had turned to quicksilver, his own daemonic power shining through. He smiled, showing off his fangs, and I grinned back at him.

"May I join you?" the daemon prince asked, that deep growl still emanating from his soul.

He stroked his dick lazily, as if he were unaffected, but I could see the desperation in his eyes. Phenex needed Seraphina to let him in, to accept him. I turned my gaze back to her. She was watching him, her eyes filled with lust, and something more.

I leaned in and nipped at her slender neck, the soft flesh begging for my teeth. Andras's bite marks still lingered there, and I licked at the wound. She moaned for me, and it was the most beautiful sound.

"What do you say, little vixen?" I murmured, trailing kisses along her jawline. "I know you can feel him too. Don't deny it. We want him too."

She pulled away, staring into my eyes. "You do?"

I smirked and nodded. "It feels right. We all agreed. Equals."

Seraphina eyed the daemon prince. She licked her lips again and nodded. I groaned, and Phenex lurched forward, grasping the back of her neck and pulling her into a soul-sucking kiss. My cock rested against her dripping cunt, and I started rocking my hips, coating the shaft in her arousal. She whimpered into Phen's mouth.

I chuckled. "Our girl is begging to be filled. Shall we feed her hunger?"

Phen pulled away from her, and the sight of my blood on his mouth made me feral.

"I want to feel her pretty pink pussy milking my cock." Phen let out a devilish purr.

I grinned. "Looks like I'm taking your ass tonight, pet."

Seraphina's eyes turned wicked, and she reached between us and gripped my dick in her petite hand. "Then shut the fuck up and take it."

Fuck, I loved this woman. Without speaking, Phen and I knew exactly what the other wanted. He slipped between Seraphina and the wall. I gripped her ass and flipped her around to face him, and he pulled her close, his arms hooking underneath her knees. Her toned body fit perfectly between us. Phen lined his cock with her dripping pussy and slowly eased his thick cock inside her. She moaned like a perfect little slut for us, her eyes rolling back and fluttering closed.

"No," Phen demanded. "Keep them open. I want to see the pleasure in your eyes when I fuck you."

Her lips parted in ecstasy as I lined up my cock, only pressing the head into her tight little ass. "Fuck, pet. You feel so fucking good. Take a breath for me, let me in. Let us make you see stars."

She moaned again, her breaths low and slow as I eased my

dick into her ass. I pressed my body into hers, smashing her between us until every inch of her body was joined with ours. The feel of Phen's cock fucking her along side my own was the sweetest drug. We moved in tandem, slow and teasing. She writhed between us, one hand tangled in my hair and the other digging sharp nails into Phen's chest.

He groaned as she drew blood, and I increased my pace, the sight of it driving me mad.

Seraphina chuckled between pants. "My monster man is a blood slut."

Phen grinned, and the silver in his eyes pulsed. He leaned forward and sank his fangs into her shoulder before she could stop him, as if she would even try. The wound was small, but enough to bleed. The crimson liquid trailed over her tits, and I snarled, bringing my mouth down over the punctured skin to lap at the blood. My dick hardened further at the taste of her on my tongue.

"I fucking love you, Seraphina," I growled, fucking her harder, deeper, needing more. I would always need more of her.

She moaned, panting my name over and over. Phen groaned too, enjoying the ride I gave them both. I was so fucking close and could feel her body tightening around me.

"Come for me, pet," I snarled, demanding her release, and her body responded.

Seraphina screamed my name as her perfect ass squeezed my cock. I pumped into her, ungodly pleasure spilling out of me as I filled her. She'd be leaking cum for days after this. The chains that bonded me and our girl reverberated within my soul, and a sea of emotions flooded my body. I could feel everything she was feeling. All the pleasure, the fierce love. It was enough to make me hard again.

"I love you too, Typhon." Seraphina mumbled the words, and I grinned like a fucking kid on Christmas.

"I know you do. And you're stuck with me for eternity, Seraphina." I kissed her softly and pulled out of her ass, enjoying the sight of my cum leaking out of her. "Time to let that last wall down, little vixen. It's all or nothing."

Seraphina turned back to Phen, and his eyes shone with need for our girl. If she rejected the poor fucker now, I didn't think he'd ever recover. I could feel her brief hesitation, and there was a moment of complete stillness as we all waited for her response.

CHAPTER FORTY-FOUR
Phenex

My dick was buried inside Seraphina's sweet pussy, but it wasn't nearly enough. My body vibrated with desire and the urge to claim my mate. To take this perfect creature and make her mine in every possible way. Seraphina's glimmering eyes were looking directly into my soul. I held her gaze, dropping every guard I ever held around my heart and hoping she could see what she needed to accept me as hers.

For years, I dreamt of her, my mate. I had no idea what she would look like, how she would act. And when I saw her for the first time, writhing in those flames, her fierce heart defiant even then, I knew she was everything I could ever want. The Princes, who I once saw as a threat, were a surprise. But seeing her with them, how they cared for each other, and the feelings pouring out of them and through our bonds showed me what I should have known all along. This woman was ours, as equals. Her dark and fractured heart could only be pieced together by the five of us.

My lips parted, and I was ready to beg for her, when she finally spoke.

"Something…happened when you spoke to me in the flames," she whispered.

The room was silent as a graveyard as we hung on her every

word.

"I built a cage around my heart a decade ago. And in so many months, these men behind me somehow found the keys I'd tossed away."

She leaned in and her plump lips brushed against my throat. I whimpered like the whipped dick I was and felt her smile against my skin.

"But it wasn't enough." Her voice was silky and inviting. "There was one more lock. One more key to fully let me out. And when I heard your voice, somehow I knew you'd be the one to set me free."

Seraphina pulled away and caught my eyes in her siren's gaze. "How did I know that? How could it be so, unless you were my mate?"

I sucked in a breath, my heart bursting as the word escaped her lips. "I am your mate, *mini monstra*. And so are they. We are yours. Your monsters. The devils on your doorstep. Give us your commands, and the world will burn. I will lay your enemies' corpses at your feet, should you wish it. I am yours."

She smiled, a sly, sensual thing that had my dick throbbing inside her. "Then fuck me like you're mine, daemon prince." She wriggled in my arms, and I snarled.

My wings snapped out, and I hissed, my forked tongue flicking against her pretty, sinful mouth. Her eyes took in my wings and my horns, and her gaze turned wicked. She reached out and stroked the bat-like membrane, and I purred at the forbidden touch.

"As you wish, my queen," I growled. My clawed feet shoved off the floor, and I flapped my wings twice, rushing to the bed and laying her out before me.

The other Princes stood around the bed, our gazes all ensnared by the perfect creature laid out before us. I edged my way onto the bed and spread her thighs wide as I leaned down between them. I inhaled the scent of her with a deadly purr. I could smell the salty cum of our mates, and the combination of their scents was driving me mad with need. She needed my mark, to have me claim a piece of her soul for myself.

I slowly trailed my tongue from her ass to her clit and growled in satisfaction at the sounds she made for me. I slipped my tongue inside her decadent cunt and urged her on. This entire fucking manor would hear her scream for me. My claws dug into her toned thighs as I feasted on my mate. She squirmed and begged, but the Princes grabbed her arms and head to keep her still, forcing her to take the pleasure I offered.

They whispered filthy words, teasing her nipples and kneading her tender flesh. When the sounds coming out of her increased and her body began to shake, I pulled away.

"What the fuck. No!" Seraphina shouted in rage, her voice nearly hoarse.

I chuckled, enjoying how needy she was for me. "Beg me for it, mate. I've been in anguish for days, *mini monstra*. My heart near to breaking at your dismissal. I want you as desperate for me as I have been for you. Is your body aching? I can give you what you need. If you fucking beg."

The Princes surrounding her growled and snarled, their dicks growing hard again for our mate. I smiled a wicked grin at her. But she wasn't afraid. Not this creature of darkness with a power that could rattle the stars above.

She leaned up on her elbow, taking her weight on the left side, and brought her hand down between her legs. Her slim fingers slipped between the pink lips of her pussy, and she spread herself open for me. I snarled, digging my claws into her thighs, pricking the skin enough to bleed.

She moaned, her head dropping back. "I can take your pain, daemon prince. And your pleasure." Her head snapped up, and her aquamarine eyes locked with mine. "Please fuck me, mate of mine."

The pleading of her tone and the claiming in her words set my insides on fire. No force on this Earth or any other could keep me away from her now. With her fingers still spreading her pussy for me, I pushed inside her, forcing her tight little cunt to stretch for me. The feeling was magnificent. A thousand times more intense with her words ringing in my head. She called me her mate. She was mine, and I was hers.

I fucked her into oblivion, the first orgasm screaming out of her in seconds. Her pussy tightened around my cock again, but I gave her no relief, pounding into her. The feeling of her body molding perfectly to mine was fucking divine.

"You feel so fucking good, Seraphina," I murmured, calling her by her full name. I wanted her to hear me. "I will never get enough of you. You're mine now, *mini monstra*. And you are perfect."

She whimpered as I tilted her hips up and forced her to take my cock deeper. "Fuck. More."

I grinned, increasing my pace. "Say it. Tell me who you belong to." I brought my hand down to her clit and circled the overstimulated pink bud with my thumb.

She writhed, her own nails turning to claws and ripping into the sheets. The others watched in awe as she began to transform. Her skin glowed like moonlight. Silver horns spiraled out of her fiery red hair. The glint of fangs peaked out from her open mouth. Her wings were coming next, I was sure of it.

I pulled her off the bed and wrapped her legs around my hips, keeping my cock nestled inside her warmth. She panted loudly against my throat. I was so fucking close.

"Say it."

"I'm yours. I'm theirs. And you're all mine," she screamed, the orgasm bursting through her and forcing my own to follow.

I shouted her name over and over before biting down on her neck, my fangs ripping into her flesh. The power in her blood was at its peak in this moment. Our bond trembled with the weight of our joining. The gasps and curses of the others caught my ear, and I pulled my mouth away to see the magnificent wings at her back. They were purest black, like the night sky, and the feathers at the ends faded into silver and gold. I'd never seen a pair of wings so beautiful.

She opened her eyes and a silver glow ringed the blue-green irises as her power hummed with life. She turned her head to the side, her mouth open with wonder and her chest heaving. "Wings. I have wings."

"Of course you do, my love." I smiled. "Now send them away so we can get you cleaned up."

The smile on her face lit me up from the inside out. Her emotions jolted down the bond, wonder and awe, purest joy. There was no hesitation now, no fear. Seraphina's body grew heavier as her adrenaline waned. I carried her into the en suite, and the others followed. The massive shower was not quite big enough for the six of us, but we took turns caring for our mate. With our bonds fully formed, it was easy to move as one, think as one. It wasn't as in sync as it could be, but that would come with time.

Mate bonds created a symbiosis between creatures that even witch magic could not break. With practice, we would become an unstoppable force. My brother wouldn't stand a chance. I would have him on his knees before her. His followers turned to ash.

They would all bow before us. My brothers, my queen. My mates.

CHAPTER FORTY-FIVE
Seraphina

My mates and I walked through the manor and out to the yard where we'd been training. The two days following our first fuck fest, we didn't leave the room. Well, I didn't. My mates stepped out now and then for food and drinks, but they refused to let me leave. Not until we fucked a hundred more times. I had no idea my body could take so much dick. But hot damn, was I a raging slut for my Princes. My mates.

I couldn't get enough of them. It had been terrifying at first, or at least, I thought it would be. My soul was black with hate and my heart so full of revenge, I didn't think I could truly let them in. I wanted to, so fucking badly, but until that night, I didn't know I could.

The power within me pulsed with life, and I sent a zip of pleasure down the bonds, just for fun.

Ty's rough hand squeezed the back of my neck, and I grinned. "If you think I won't fuck you right here for everyone to see, you're sorely mistaken, little vixen."

"I second that." Levi laughed, adjusting his crotch. "I've been fucking half-cocked for days. One more tease from you and the next fuck fest will be a show for all the guests."

I laughed, which promptly turned into a yelp when Andras's

Resurrection

hand smacked hard against my ass. I wore leggings, but the fabric was not thick enough to protect me from his punishments.

"Behave, sweetheart," he murmured. "Or we will chain you to the bed."

I turned my head to look back at him and winked. "Promises, promises."

We stepped into the yard as one, and most of the household was waiting for us. My sister and her daemon and Nuriela and Lo stood together. Tibby perched on Gremory's shoulders like a little fairy, Delphine standing beside them and smirking up at my best friend. I smiled, so fucking happy to see her looking more like the feisty Brit I met all those years ago.

Delphine turned from them and walked toward us. "Thought I was going to have to use magic to get you assholes out of that room."

Morax chuckled. "I doubt even your magic would have worked, Malefica."

Delphine was not just a witch, but a royal with some kind of heavy ass magic. The Malefica were the leaders of the witches from their world. Phen explained all of this during one of the rare moments of the last few days when his mouth wasn't on my pussy or stuffed with cock.

I groaned, the image of him taking Ty's dick down his throat making my thighs clench. Phenex snarled, and I giggled, covering my mouth.

"Oh my god." Kaela's mouth dropped open. "Did you just giggle? Who are you and where is my snarly sister?"

I smiled at her. "Oh, she's still in here. You'd be giggling too if you saw the movie playing in my head."

Andras sighed audibly, and I caught him rolling his eyes. "Seraphina. I will gladly punish you in front of everyone."

"For fuck's sake," Delphine shouted. "Get your heads out of your asses for just a minute, will you? Or would you like to be attached to those relics forever?"

Her words instantly sobered me. I was more than ready for them to be destroyed. The Princes brought the relics forth. The cloudy sky smelled like snow, and I couldn't see the setting sun, but the air tasted like dusk. My senses were heightened when my power finally manifested. I could hear, see, and smell every tiny thing. I could taste the magic in the air around us. My back itched, my wings ready to be unleashed.

I was maybe obsessed with them, but who fucking wouldn't be? They were fucking sexy as hell. And when my mates brushed their fingers through the feathers, the feeling was akin to the most pleasurable orgasm I'd ever had.

"Seraphina," Devon groaned, rubbing his neck, his eyes blazing with desire. "Please stop thinking so loudly."

I blew him a kiss and turned back to the witch. She snapped at my mates, putting them into four corners, with Phen and I at the center. Delphine handed me the blade that I used in the ritual. The same one I killed my father with. Guilt swirled in the pit of my stomach, and Phen squeezed my hand, sending soothing thoughts down our bond. I could feel the same power brushing against my skin from the others, letting me know they were here with me.

"You will use the blade to cut into each of your palms and fill this cup." Delphine held up a shining gold goblet. "Once it is filled, I will begin. When I speak the final words, unleash hellfire on the relics."

"I've never done that." I cut in, unsure how I was supposed to figure that out now. Any time I tried to use my power before, it never did what I needed it to.

"You will be able to this time. Now that your mate bonds are settled, you should be able to control your power." She looked around at the others. "You will be able to aid each other, boost your own power by thinking as one unit."

The others nodded, and I squared my shoulders, prepared to try. The spectators took several steps back. Morax positioned his body in front of my sister, and she rolled her eyes but didn't protest. Grem was now doing the same for Tibby. She smiled at me encouragingly.

Delphine closed her eyes and began to chant. I slit my palm with the knife, shoving my fears and guilt to the far corners of my mind. I passed the dagger to Phen, and he cut into his skin immediately. She passed the goblet, and we squeezed our blood into it. She passed the cup and dagger around to the others, chanting in a foreign tongue the entire time.

As our blood gathered as one, the witch's magic pulsed through the air. A line of golden light shimmered into existence, connecting the four Princes at each corner to each other and then to us. I gasped at the weight of it. This witch was strong as hell. She passed the cup back to me, full of the blood of my mates. I brought it to my lips and drank, taking them in. Whatever magic this was, the feel of it was intoxicating.

Phenex took the cup next, drinking deeply, then passed it back to the others. Delphine chanted louder as the magic she created came to a crescendo. I closed my eyes, feeling the connection between the Princes and I reaching a new height. The power within me surged, and I beckoned forth a fire hotter than anything on this fucking Earth. As one, we unleashed our power on the relics, burning them to ash. The Princes shouted, their unbridled happiness shining down our bonds as the tethers were snapped.

The Kings could no longer control or suppress their power. One by one, their wings snapped out, their eyes glowed, and my Princes transformed into the hottest fucking monsters I'd ever seen. Ty roared, the sound sending shivers down my body. My own wings snapped out, and I shot into the sky.

CHAPTER FORTY-SIX

Devon

My wings appeared, and I took off into the sky after my mate. The others followed, Phen zipping past me with a laugh. He was such a competitive asshole, but I liked that about him. One of the many things I liked about him. The memory of his throbbing dick in my mouth flashed before my eyes, and I nearly groaned out loud. I knew Andras would make good on his promises to dole out punishments in any way he saw fit. What I didn't expect was how much I enjoyed my punishment.

Something changed between the other Princes and I when Seraphina finally accepted us. We were bound to each other in ways I never knew existed. Even now, I could feel them. Feel their elation at our new freedom, their love for our queen. Every thought they had washed through me in waves. It was hard to control that first night, but we were getting better. Too much sharing could make a person go crazy. And after self-imposed separation on my part, figuring out how to mute the chatter was imperative. And I would be telling no one how much I secretly enjoyed it, either.

I flew through the clouds, chasing after the love of my life and my brothers. She turned back and caught my eye, and I nearly fell to the earth at the beauty of her smile. It was stunning, full of unfiltered, raw happiness. She hadn't smiled like that once since I met her. And I wanted nothing more than to make her smile like that every day for the rest of our lives. Pushing my body harder, I chased her through the sky until I was close enough to reach out and take her hand. We flew side by side, smiling like idiots.

"This is the most amazing fucking thing," she shouted, her smile turning sly. "Other than seeing you taking Phen's dick down your throat."

I rolled my eyes and snatched her around the waist. She yelped, her wings disappearing, but I held her close.

"You have a filthy mouth, my queen." I smirked at her, drinking in the power glowing beneath her skin.

"And what are you going to do about it?" she purred, wrapping her body around mine like a limpet.

I brushed my thumb across her plump lips. "You'll find out soon enough."

She smirked, undeterred. "You know what else is amazing?"

"What's that, *mera dil*?" I whispered, hanging on her every word.

She leaned in, her lips brushing along my jawline until she reached my ear. "Being your mate."

Before I could respond, Seraphina leapt out of my arms, her wings reappearing as she dove back to Earth.

My heart soared at her declaration, and I sent wave after wave of love down the bond for her to know how much it meant to me. After all we had been through, all the ways I fucked things up for us, we survived. We would get through this, together, one way or another.

Resurrection

Two sets of wings rushed toward Seraphina, and I started to shout in alarm, only to realize they were friendlies. Michaela and Morax circled my girl, their excitement evident.

Seraphina reached out and took her sister's hand, and together they flew toward the sun. Michaela's wings were brightest white and glistened in the sunlight. With Seraphina's black as midnight wings at her side, they were glorious to behold.

A sharp pain pierced my heart at the sight, and I quickly turned away from them. My sister was still lost, brainwashed and controlled by Laszlo and Samuel. I hated leaving her behind that night, but in the chaos following the ritual, I couldn't find her. Until she was free, my heart could not truly be full. Leyja was my only living relative, and I needed to save her.

"Dev!" Levi tore through the sky, nearly barreling into me. "I have an idea."

"What's that?" I asked, curious.

Levi swooped beneath me so we were facing each other. "I think we should go get your sister. Now, before they've had time to get their shit together. The Kings are scrambling. We have full control of our daemons now. Let's sneak in, grab her, and run."

His words tugged at my heart, and I so desperately wanted to listen, but it was a suicide mission. I shook my head. "They've been one step ahead of us at every turn. I can't risk losing one of you."

Levi rolled his eyes. "I can't stand the pain you're in without her. And until we are all equally blissed out, we won't be as strong as we could be. Let us help you."

Andras suddenly dropped from this sky, his ink-colored

wings blotting out the sun. "I don't normally agree with Levi's crazy ideas, but I think I have a plan for this one."

We turned as one, diving to the earth below. Seraphina and Ty had landed. They were looking up at us, as if they already knew what was coming. I dropped to the earth, landing a little less gracefully than Levi and Andras.

Phenex joined us a moment later. "So, we're going hunting?" He wiggled his eyebrows.

Andras narrowed his eyes. "No. This is a subtle rescue mission. We go in, get Leyja, and get the fuck out. No fighting. No confrontations."

"Stealth mode." Ty chuckled, his eyes darkening. "I like it."

"When do we leave?" Seraphina clapped.

As one, we turned to her and said. "No."

"You will stay here," Andras commanded, his voice fierce. Anyone else would bow before his dangerous tone and sharp eyes, but not our girl.

She snarled at him, her hands on her hips and her adorable horns poking out from her windswept crimson hair. "Fuck that! We are doing this together."

"*Mi diosa.*" Levi cut in, his voice sweet and pleading. "Let us do this for Dev. Knowing you're here, safe, will make it easier for us."

"I am *not* some weak bitch who waits at home," Seraphina snapped, she stepped up to Andras, glaring at him. "You know this about me."

Phenex crept up behind her and wrapped his arms around her waist. She protested, but not enough to make him let go.

"We know, *mini monstra*," Phenex murmured against her

neck. "But this isn't about you. It's about them. Let your Princes do this thing together. And we will offer up your pretty pussy as a reward when they return."

"And someone needs to stay behind with the chaotic daemon," Andras quipped, his expression turning exasperated. "I'm already allowing Levi to go. One reckless Prince is enough."

Seraphina rolled her eyes, but her desire and amusement shuddering through the bonds made me smile. She was coming around to the idea. She leaned into Phenex as he trailed kisses down her neck. "Fine. But you all better listen to Andras. No stupid shit. Get Leyja and come back to me."

Ty smirked, his fangs elongated and his eyes glinting with dark desires. "Alright then, little vixen. I'll behave. Only if you promise to let me tie you up and taste you when I return."

"Deal." She grinned, shoving away from Phen and leaping into Ty's muscular arms. He caught her easily, growling deep in his chest and kissing her hungrily.

Andras snatched the back of her neck and forced her to look at him. "You behave too, sweetheart. Let's go, brothers."

We each took our turns kissing Seraphina goodbye. I went last, holding her in my arms for an extra moment.

She looked up at me, love and nervous energy shining in her aquamarine eyes. "Please come back to me."

I held her face, bringing my forehead down to hers. "Always."

CHAPTER FORTY-SEVEN
Leviathan

We decided to return to Blackbyrn Manor via helicopter. Phen and Morax were teaching us how to teleport, but with our powers so newly restored, it was safer this way. None of us wanted Phen to leave Seraphina either. She gave us shit for that, but we were in complete agreement that one of her mates would always be by her side.

Our plan was simple: cause a scene to draw everyone away, grab Leyja, and run like hell.

Adrenaline buzzed through my veins, setting my insides on fire. With my daemon no longer tethered to that stupid relic, my power surged through me more freely. The element of fire seemed to be the easiest one for me to summon. A blessing, and a curse, really.

I thought of all the souls lost in fires over the years. If only I had been freed sooner, I could've been a better firefighter, saved more people.

Ty's strong hand grasped my thigh and squeezed. He could feel my emotions, hear my thoughts. Unlike Dev and Andras, Ty and I rarely kept our shields up against our brothers. Dev was getting better at letting us in, and Andras...well he was Andras. No one would ever fully get inside his mind.

I supposed that wasn't entirely true. Ty and I had a bet going

Resurrection

that someday soon, Seraphina would wiggle her cute ass right past his shields and never shut up about it.

Andras sighed. "That will only happen if I let it."

I laughed. "Whatever you say, boss daddy."

Ty chuckled. "I like that one."

Dev smiled, staring out the window. I could feel his unease losing its sharp edge, and satisfaction snuggled up to my daemon. Making my brothers happy was my second favorite thing, right after making Seraphina come all over my face.

"Keep your head clear, Levi," Andras snapped, his voice stern. He was all business, wearing a sexy-as-fuck navy suit. Probably Hugo Boss or some shit.

I opted for casual, with dark jeans and a gray T-shirt that said *Fuck, Marry, Mate Me*. Seraphina laughed, and the sound of her happiness was exactly what I hoped for when I had it made. Even in the dead of winter, the fire within kept me warm. Typhon wore black jeans and a grungy looking sweater. All of his clothes were ripped to shreds, and I swear he did that shit on purpose, the sexy bastard.

Devon wore black slacks and a black button-down, more formal like Andras and just as sexy. Before we left, Seraphina's filthy thoughts had my dick twitching and I was already desperate to get back to her.

The helicopter landed at a private helipad atop an office building Andras owned in Atlanta. We planned to fly from here, and I was eager to get into the sky. I could feel the anxious energy of the others to use their wings once more as well. Flying with Seraphina after our powers were unleashed was indescribable.

Phen and Mor did some kind of magic with the Delphine

to sense their evil dick brother, and couldn't place him at the manor. There was very low energy coming from the manor at all. We weren't sure what that meant but hoped it would give us the chance to rescue Dev's sister quickly.

Andras led us into the night sky, and we sped through the clouds. Dev was at his side, and Ty and I took up positions in the back.

When the manor came into view, I wasn't surprised to see it looking impeccable once more. During the ritual, the windows had all been blown to hell and there were scorch marks on the lawn from the fire thrown during the fighting. All the evidence of that night had disappeared. We dropped to the roof of the manor, landing near one of the turrets with a small, secret door into the Conservatory. There was a guard posted, but Ty quickly knocked him out before he could alert anyone.

We crept through the house, killing or laying out anyone we came across. There were less guards than we anticipated, but we also knew this place better than anyone, even more than our fathers. As teens, we found every hidden passage, servant hallway, and secret door there was to find. Using those now helped us avoid detection.

Dev had watched his sister as often as he could after discovering she was alive. Her rooms were on the same level as our fathers, closer to Samuel. I assumed this was for him to have regular access to her mind and keep her subdued.

We knew now her mother's lumen blood was likely keeping her from going insane, but pulling her out of their control was going to be a hundred times harder than it was to bring Tibby back. I just hoped it wasn't too late.

Resurrection

We made it to their rooms, dispatching the guards posted at her doors. Ty and I took up our positions outside the room while Dev and Andras went in. I heard Leyja's muffled voice and a thud. The door opened, and Andras poked his head out.

"She's knocked out. Let's go." He stepped aside, and we crowded into the room.

Dev held his knocked-out sister in his arms. He was frowning, a feeling of unease coming off him in waves.

"What's wrong?" I asked, looking between Dev and Andras.

Andras shook his head. "This doesn't feel right. It was almost too easy."

I crossed my arms. "Maybe we are just that good? Let's get the hell out of here before our fathers figure out we're here."

In the next moment, a guard came through the door. Ty was on him instantly, covering his mouth with one hand and pressing into the man's throat with the other.

Andras walked slowly toward them, his eyes deadly calm and a painful chill coming off him in waves. His power was strongest with the element of water, ice his preferred form.

"Where is my father?" Andras spoke, his voice a sinister whisper that almost had me shivering.

Ty released the man enough for him to speak, but the guard just laughed. Ty punched him in the gut before conjuring a blade with his own power over earth. He slammed the sharp edge into the guard's shoulder. The weak human grunted in pain.

"Tell me now or you die. Where the fuck are the Kings?" Andras snarled, his patience long gone.

The guard laughed again. "Gone."

Ty roared. "This was a trap."

"Where did they go?" I twisted the blade in the fucker's arm, needing to hear him say it, even if I already knew. I punched him in the mouth, my fury growing.

He grinned, blood dripping from his mouth. "They went to take your woman."

All the blood rushed to my stomach, and I felt like I could faint. No. Fuck no.

Dev sucked in a gasp. "There's no way they would go to Vespertine on their own, not without—"

"Belial," Andras spat out the name. "He's there too. Let's go."

Ty pulled the blade from the guard's shoulder and swiped it across his neck. The man dropped to the floor, dead instantly with how deep Ty cut into his flesh.

I closed my eyes and tried to sense Phen or Seraphina, but it was as if our bonds were blocked. "We need to get the fuck out of here. There's something blocking us. I can't reach them."

Andras pulled out his cell and snarled in frustration. "No signal. Let's go."

I turned to the window and watched as Dev used his considerable control over the element of air to send a blast of wind at the glass. But it didn't break. He cursed.

"They want to keep us busy. We'll have to fight our way out." Ty growled. "Levi, you and Dev go the way we came in and get his sister out of here. Once you're in the sky, try to reach them. We will meet you at the helipad."

I shook my head. "We shouldn't split up."

Andras sighed. "Ty is right. We can't fight and protect Leyja. Go. We will see you soon."

I hated this but nodded, accepting their plan. Dev and

I moved quickly, running through the passages as fast as we could. The walls rumbled and shouting began all around us. Andras and Ty were causing as much chaos as they could so we could get out.

My body was screaming for me to help them, but I couldn't, not yet. The bond linking me to Seraphina was horrifically silent. I couldn't feel her at all. I refused to believe she was gone. Because if she left this earthly plane, then so would I. Not to die, no. I'd go to hell or heaven or wherever the fuck her soul rested and drag her back to this world. Our story was just beginning, and there was no creature alive who could keep me from my mate.

CHAPTER FORTY-EIGHT
Seraphina

Something stirred in my blood, waking me. I was wrapped up in Phen's arms. We fucked like lovers finally reunited after being separated for years before falling asleep. I missed my other Princes, but having that time alone with Phen was pretty fucking great.

He was a ball of chaotic energy, more than all my other mates combined. And so fucking powerful. Remembering how he tied me up with vines and used his power to fuck me in a thousand new positions had my damn pussy throbbing all over again.

Phen stirred, his arms wrapping tightly around me. One of his hands slipped between my legs, and he growled possessively. "Wet for me already, *mini monstra*?"

I moved my hand over his and urged his fingers to press inside me. "What? Are you too tired to play? Keep up, daemon prince."

Phen chuckled and his thick cock throbbed against my backside. He was about to speak but suddenly went rigid and silent. A moment passed, and then he swore. "Fuck. Get dressed."

Phen jumped from the bed, tossing clothes at me and dressing himself quickly. I hurriedly slipped on my leggings and sweatshirt, a weird feeling inside me bubbling over. Something was very wrong. I tugged at the bonds between me and my Princes, but I couldn't feel them. It was as if they were blocked from me.

"I can't feel the others, can you?" I asked, hoping he could sense something.

Phen shook his head. "No. And Morax is freaking out. There's commotion in the house. Fuck."

My heart seized, and I ran to him, squeezing his hand. "What is it?"

"The Kings are here. With my brother. Belial has come."

My blood ran cold at his words. The power surged within me, and I called for my sister. I sensed her close by and grabbed a few daggers before fleeing the room, Phen close behind me.

People were shouting, humans, daemons, and lumens running through the halls. From the screams, it sounded like the Kings breached our defenses. They were inside the mansion.

"What do we do? Because all I want to do is kill Laszlo and take the rest down with me," I shouted at Phen over the commotion.

He frowned, his gray eyes filled with doubt. "Belial is incredibly strong. He channels my father's power. Mor and I will try to subdue him."

Sensing his unease, I punched Phen's arm as we ran. "Hey, mate of mine. You're strong as fuck, Phen. So am I. We can do this."

Phen smirked at me, some of his cockiness coming back into his face. His power rose from within his veins, making his eyes glow silver. "I know we can, *mini monstra*. You're stronger than all of us."

I hoped that was true because if not, this might not end so well.

———◦◦◦———

We found my sister and Morax in a hallway close to the ballroom. Morax was in full daemon mode, and it was fucking awesome. My sister was holding her own against the human guards trying to steal her away while Morax fought against another daemon.

I snarled, feeling my horns coming out and my eyes glowing with power. I roared my fury, running at them with my blades out. These fuckers didn't deserve my power, so I cut them to pieces with my daggers instead.

Once the last one fell at my feet, I looked up to see my sister smiling at me.

She cocked her head at me. "Why do I feel like you enjoyed that?"

I grinned, wiping their gross blood from my face. "Maybe I did. Just a little."

We turned to see Morax holding a daemon against the far wall, and Phen rushed in, his clawed hand sinking into the daemon's chest and ripping out his heart. It was fucking glorious. The creature dropped to the floor, and Morax whipped out a tiny blade that shone in the darkness. It was made of stellatium, one of the only things on this Earth that could kill a daemon or lumen. Morax stabbed the heart, and the daemon burst into a cloud of stardust.

Resurrection

The two monsters turned to us, and I sauntered over to Phen, wrapping my hands around his neck.

"That was so fucking hot." I pushed up on my tiptoes and crushed my lips to his.

My mate growled low, gripping the back of my neck and dominating my mouth with his own. "Keep Mina on a leash, *mini monstra*. We have more enemies to kill."

I laughed and saw Kaela rolling her eyes and making a gagging motion. "Fine. But I want to fuck you covered in the blood of those enemies later."

He chuckled, and the sound sent zips of pleasure straight to my pussy. "As you wish, my queen."

Morax interrupted us. "Belial is in the courtyard behind the mansion. I can feel him there. I don't want either of you near him." His eyes locked with my sister's, and I could almost feel his fear.

"I'm not letting you go after him alone," Kaela snarled, staring him down. "And you!" She pointed at me, her face scrunching with anger.

Damn she was a firecracker. Her bravery filled me with fucking pride. I gave her my best innocent look. "What did I do?"

Kaela wagged her finger in my face. "No sending me away this time. If you're fighting, so am I."

The last thing I wanted was my sister anywhere near the Kings, but she was right. Her power was strong, and we needed every powerful creature we could get.

I nodded. "Alright. I can't reach the Princes, something is blocking us. I have a feeling it's Laszlo's doing. They wanted to separate us."

Phen snarled, his full daemon on display and looking delicious as fuck. "Then let's go kill the bastards."

The four of us ran through the mansion, hunting our enemies and cutting down any in our way. We caught up with Nuriela and Lo, but there was no time to chat. I glimpsed Lo kicking some serious ass, and a pang of guilt cut through my heart. I hated that she was involved in this, but there was nothing I could say now. She was here, fighting with us, and that's more than I could ever ask for.

I took a left down a servant's hall and cut through the kitchen. Several human guards were blocking our way through. Phen was about to rush them, but I stopped him.

"Wait, I want to try something."

I snatched a container of powdered sugar and chucked it at them. Just as it began to fall, I shot out a tiny fireball. The sugar exploded into a massive fireball, whooshing through the kitchen. Morax quickly created a shield around us, but the guards were not so lucky.

"What the fuck was that?" Morax shouted angrily, checking to make sure my sister was unharmed.

She swatted him away.

"I always wanted to try that and never had the opportunity." I shrugged, thinking of Tibby. "Fun fact Tibby told me once, and it seemed like a good time to test out the firepower of powdered sugar."

Phen smacked my ass and I yelped in surprise. "You're kind of insane, *mini monstra*. I am so fucking in love with you."

I grinned, my heart soaring at his words, but Morax was

Resurrection

in full grouch mode and shoved me forward. "Let's go, little psycho. We have bigger enemies to destroy."

We crept out of the kitchen through a servant's door and slinked along the side of the mansion, toward the courtyard. The cloudy night sky provided us cover, and Phen whispered a few words to cloak the sound of our footsteps. That one was handy; I needed to learn it.

Whispers carried on the cool night breeze, and we slowed our pace. Belial stood with the Kings, his arms crossed and looking bored. He was massive, bigger than Morax and Phen in his beast mode. He had the same dark hair, although his was short and manicured, like a fancy businessman. His black horns stood straight out from the crown of his head. His eyes glowed bright-green and his black, dragon-like wings shimmered with a dusting of the same color across the scales.

He wore dark slacks and a white V-neck shirt, fitted to show off his considerable muscle. But it was the cocky smirk on his face that made alarm bells ring in my head.

"Come out, brothers," he purred, the sound eerie as hell. "Or are you still too cowardly to face me?"

Phen and Morax shared a look, and before Kaela or I could stop them, their wings snapped out and they rushed at Belial. The three daemons crashed into each other, and the sound was like thunder. They fought, using their considerable powers to destroy the other. But the three were evenly matched, quickly blocking blades and fireballs before they could do any damage.

I sensed another presence, but it was too late. A knife wrapped around Kaela's throat and another around my own.

"Let's go, my pretties," a slimy voice cooed in my ear, and

I snarled but complied.

I couldn't do anything while Kaela had a knife to her throat. Our jailers forced us out of the shadows and toward Samuel and Laszlo. Laszlo's predatory smile made my skin crawl. His eyes slowly took in every inch of my body until they settled on my face.

"Seraphina." He purred my name, and I wanted to vomit. "Did you think I would let you get away from me so easily?"

I straightened my spine. "I wouldn't say it was easy."

In the next second, I slammed my skull into the face of the creature holding the knife to my throat. The blade cut into my skin, and I hissed, grabbing it and twisting it out of the guard's hand. Another human. I stabbed the slim blade into his eye, and he screamed as he died.

I turned to the one holding my sister, but he pressed the blade tighter to her throat, drawing a trickle of blood in the process. Morax roared, but couldn't get away from Belial.

My head snapped back to Laszlo, and I glared at him. "Let her go, you piece of shit."

Laszlo shook his head, his eyes crinkling with mirth. "I'm going to enjoy breaking you, daughter of Aurora."

Several more creatures, daemons and lumens alike, dropped from the skies. One of them had a bow and arrow. She pulled the bow taut, pointing the arrow at my sister's heart.

Laszlo walked slowly, deliberating, stopping only a few feet from me. He looked so much like Andras, except for the evil distorting his features.

His voice was barely above a whisper. "You're going to bind yourself to me, or I will kill her."

Morax roared, and I turned my eyes to the sky where they fought. Belial somehow got the upper hand and shot bolts of electric power Phenex. He fell from the sky, unconscious, and crashed to the earth with a thundering sound. A strangled cry left my throat, and Laszlo smirked.

Belial gripped Morax by the throat and dove from the sky. He slammed Morax into the earth next to his brother. Our daemons were down, and I was running out of allies.

Belial stalked over to us. "We must go. They won't be out for long."

Laszlo pulled out a dagger and used the blade to tip my chin up. "You will bind yourself to me now. Do this, and no more will die."

I stared back at the fucking monster before me, unable to think of a way out of this. I felt for my Princes, but the bonds remained quiet. My sister whimpered, and I turned to her.

"Don't do this," she whispered.

But I had to. I would do anything to save her, to save them. I squared my shoulders. "Fine. I'll do your stupid blood oath. But if you hurt anyone I love, if any of my mates or my sister are harmed, the deal is fucking off."

Laszlo's arm snapped out, and he held my throat tightly. "Fine," he growled. "But if one of our mates harms me, I get to kill them. And you will obey my every command. And you will enjoy it."

I gritted my teeth. This was going to fucking suck. "You're a fucking creep."

Laszlo grinned triumphantly. He let go of my throat and used the dagger to cut his hand and then mine. He clasped our hands together and chanted. The power of the blood oath reminded me of the moment I unknowingly performed one with Tibby. But this one felt icky. It crept under my skin like morphine, coating my veins in a nasty film. I could feel my free will being stripped away and a desire to please pulsing through my blood. He finished chanting, and I stood, my mind and body a warzone of conflicting emotions.

Laszlo brushed his fingers against my jawline. "Open your mouth."

My mouth opened before I could even think to say no. Laszlo spat on my tongue, and some twisted piece of me preened inside.

"Now swallow," he commanded, and I did, leaning into his touch. He grinned. "You're mine now."

Belial chuckled. "Very entertaining. Bring the other one and let's go."

My eyes snapped to the daemon. "No. My sister is not to be harmed."

Laszlo grabbed my face, forcing my attention back to him. "She won't be harmed, by me. You said nothing of Belial."

I started to scream, and Laszlo slapped me hard across the face. "Be quiet, slave. You will speak only when I tell you, do you understand?"

I nodded, needing to please him first even as part of me raged against it inside. My will was a wild animal locked behind an impenetrable cage.

"You will respond with *yes, master*." Laszlo wrapped his fingers around my throat and brought his face down close to mind, our lips barely brushing against each other's. "Say it."

"Yes, master." The stupid words flew from my lips, and bile

rose in my throat.

Laszlo nibbled my bottom lip, and I sighed, wanting more and hating myself all at once. He turned to Michaela. "You will do as you are told, or your mate will be killed. And I will make you watch as I fuck your sister."

Angry tears streamed down my sister's face. She was furious and afraid, her fear radiating out of her. But she was strong too, so fucking strong. "Fuck you."

Laszlo smirked and nodded to Samuel. "Keep her calm."

Samuel nodded, closing in on my sister. His voice was soothing, like a lullaby, as he spoke to her, praising her bravery and commanding her to stand down. I could see her trying to fight him off, but her emotions were too chaotic and the slimy fucker slipped into her mind.

I watched the light dim behind her sky-blue and golden-brown eyes. The creature holding her forced her toward Belial. Laszlo commanded me to follow, and as one, we joined the daemon inside a circle of ash. He began chanting instantly. Power built around us, and it felt like the oxygen was being squeezed out of me. The wind picked up around us, circling us like a tornado. The mate bonds suddenly pulled at my soul, and I gasped. I closed my eyes, sending them a thousand messages.

Laszlo gripped the back of my neck. "You will not speak to them. I cannot break the bonds just yet, but I forbid you to reach out to them. If you do, Michaela will pay the price."

My mind went silent even as I felt them shouting for me. But it was too late. I imagined a wall of steel around myself, cutting them off and keeping my mates out of my mind, my heart, my soul. Because I would choose her. They could survive without me, but I would never forgive myself for causing the death of another sister.

Laszlo smiled. "Good girl."

I whimpered, loving the praise he offered and desperate for more. My heart burned with fiery rage, but it was no use. The blood oath sealed my fate, my future. I was his.

I belonged to Laszlo Blackbyrn.

THE END

EPILOGUE
Michaela

I fought with everything I had against Samuel's influence, but he was so damn strong. My eyes darted to Seraphina, but she was whimpering beneath Laszlo's stupid oath. My wings brushed against the edges of the ash circle, and I hissed in pain. The magic keeping us in was powerful. But so was I.

"No." I ground out the word. "I will not be your captive again." I shoved away from the Kings.

Samuel's eyes widened, and he shouted at me. "How are you doing this?"

I could see Morax through the haze of power surrounding us. Phenex was lying on the ground before him. My mate's eyes snapped up and met mine. He roared in fury, his power seeking out my own. I had no clue what I was doing, but something in my blood came to life in that moment, and I used every ounce of my strength to blast a hole in the circle. The world rocked at the force of it, and the smallest opening appeared.

The oxygen was growing thin, and I could feel my body being pulled out of this world and into another, but I refused to go. I stuck my hand through the small opening, and Morax instantly clasped my hand in his. His voice called to me, laced with power and so much love my heart was about to burst.

Samuel was shouting at my back, and Belial roared his fury,

Resurrection

but it was too late. Morax ripped me out of their circle and we crashed to the earth. I turned back and screamed for my sister, but they were gone.

"No!" I shouted, scrambling to my feet. My heart broke in two.

Morax grabbed my waist, and I leaned against his chest. "Are you hurt?" His other hand brushed the tears from my face.

"No. But she's with them. I left her," I cried out, angry tears spilling down my face and making the world blurry.

Phenex groaned, and we turned to him. There was a bloody gash across his stomach, deep enough to kill a human, but he was already healing. His face mirrored my anguish, and he let out his rage to the sky.

The Princes dropped from that very sky moments later, shouting for Seraphina. I couldn't bear it, couldn't tell them she was gone.

"Where the fuck is she?" Ty snarled, his body shaking with fury and fear.

"She is gone. Belial took her to Caligo." Morax spoke softly, holding me close.

Andras snarled, showing more emotion than normal. "Can we go to them?"

Phenex groaned as he stood, holding his healing stomach. "Yes. And we will. Gather our people. Kill everyone else. If Belial wants a war, we shall bring an army."

ACKNOWLEDGEMENTS

MY READERS. MY BELOVED STREET TEAM. Where would I be without you?! The community of people in my corner while I write these books has grown so much since I began the series. I am so very grateful for the people I have met, and the ones who have continued to love my novels. Your support means the fucking world to me. Don't ever leave me. (Because I'll find you and bring you back).

Thank you to my family and friends who have also been supportive of my writing journey, even if the books aren't exactly your cup of tea. Just have a shot of whiskey and give it a read. Who knows, you might find some new kinks.

Milton Keynes UK
Ingram Content Group UK Ltd.
UKHW020915111124
451035UK00018B/1593